MURDERGRAM

Buy

for Melodrama

MURDERGRAM

NISA SANTIAGO

Murdergram. Copyright © 2014 by Melodrama Publishing. All rights reserved. Printed in the United States of America. No part of this book may be used or reproduced in any manner whatsoever without written permission except in the case of brief quotations embodied in critical articles or reviews. For information, address Melodrama Publishing, P.O. Box 522, Bellport, NY 11713.

www.melodramapublishing.com

Library of Congress Control Number: 2014943095
ISBN-13: 978-1620780428
ISBN-10: 1620780429
First Edition: January 2015
10 9 8 7 6 5 4 3 2 1

Interior Design: Candace K. Cottrell
Cover Design: Candace K. Cottrell

BOOKS BY NISA SANTIAGO

Cartier Cartel: Part 1
Return of the Cartier Cartel: Part 2
Cartier Cartel - South Beach Slaughter: Part 3
Bad Apple: The Baddest Chick Part 1
Coca Kola: The Baddest Chick Part 2
Checkmate: The Baddest Chick Part 3
Face Off: The Baddest Chick Part 4
South Beach Cartel
Guard the Throne
Dirty Money Honey
Killer Dolls Part 1
Killer Dolls Part 2
Killer Dolls Part 3
Murdergram
The House That Hustle Built

ONE

BACK THEN…

"Yo, pass the rock! Pass the fuckin' rock," the shirtless, sweaty ball player shouted to his partner on the basketball court.

He was posted up near the basketball rim, his arms outstretched and ready to take his opponent into the paint.

Four men were engaged in a pick-up basketball game in a Brooklyn park in East New York in the hot summer sun. They moved around the half court, dribbling, passing, and dunking on each other like young athletes ready for the NBA. The game was intense; the men were strong, skilled, and aggressive against their opponents. And they had a reason to play so intensely: one thousand dollars was up for grabs for the winner of the game.

The ball was passed to the player shouting out for it by the rim. He gripped the rock tightly and posted up near the paint with his back against his opponent as he dribbled the ball and threw his weight into the man behind him, almost pushing the rival off his feet. It seemed like he was toying with the man.

"Yo, take that shit to the hole, Pike. That nigga can't guard you!" his teammate shouted.

"I got this!" Pike shouted back.

Pike swiveled while bouncing the ball to face his opponent. He glared at the man, who was taller than him, but Pike had more bulk to his physique.

"Play D, nigga! What you got? You can't guard me, nigga. I'm like Jordan on this fuckin' court," Pike taunted, dribbling the ball between his legs and showboating for the crowd watching the game.

"Nigga, you wack," his rival shouted.

His rival stepped toward him to defend the basketball rim. Pike crouched lower to the concrete court, bouncing the ball rapidly and showing how skilled he was. His handle on the rock was on point. He was like Allen Iverson out there. He'd been a point guard once for a champion team, but that was long ago. Now, things done changed.

Pike smiled and pressed forward like lightning striking, riding the baseline to the basketball rim. His defendant ran into action to guard the basket to prevent the final point from being scored. Five hundred dollars was a lot of money to lose. Pike crossed over and leaped into the air, getting ready to make the layup and score the winning basket. But he was quickly fouled while airborne, which sent the ball flying out of his hands. When he landed back on his feet, he shouted, "Foul nigga! You a fuckin' butcher on this court!"

"Man, no blood, no foul, muthafucka!" his opponent returned at full volume.

"What? Nigga, you knew that was a foul. You practically took my head off!" Pike retorted as he jumped up in his rival's face.

"You lost the rock, nigga. I ain't fouled you. You just a scrub, nigga."

Pike was clearly upset. His fists were clenched. He was ready to take his respect and win this game. Things were heating up. A small crowd watched the game nearby, including Cristal and Tamar. They stood on the side gawking at the shirtless men playing basketball, but their attention was mostly on Pike. He was the one all the girls wanted to be with.

Pike stood six-three with a powerful physique glaring in the sun. His six-pack and strapping chest were eye candy to the ladies around watching the game, and his midnight complexion, swathed with a few tattoos, glistened with the sweat that covered his body. He was twenty-two years old and had finished high school with a C average—one of the few neighborhood kids to actually finish high school. Pike thought that he had a shot at the NBA. All through high school, he was always the star on the team, the point guard averaging twenty-five to thirty points per game. They said he would become better than Allen Iverson, maybe become the next Michael Jordan.

However, with his love for the game also came his love for the streets—the same old cliché with kids growing up in the hood: Michael Jordan and the obligatory neighborhood drug dealer becoming their conflicting role models. In school and on the courts, he was known as Lightning Pike because of his speed and control of the ball, but on the streets, he started to sell weed to earn some extra cash. Then, in his senior year, a bullet that ripped through his knee changed all of his dreams. In a botched weed deal that erupted in gunfire, everything went downhill for Pike from there.

Georgetown, North Carolina, Syracuse, Notre Dame, St. John's, and several other Division One schools were all looking at Pike closely and were willing to offer him a full scholarship if he would play for them. Once he couldn't play anymore and the media slandered his name, all the scouts dropped him like a bad habit. They just gave up on him, like his parents had when he was young. He became an angry man after that—angry that he wouldn't be playing college ball and then going on to the NBA to sign a multimillion-dollar deal. But he never gave up his day job: hustling weed to his peers. At first, it was low-level stuff where he didn't get his hands too dirty because he didn't want to jeopardize his NBA chances, still believing he could make it to the pros after everything that had transpired in his senior year.

However, as time moved on and he grew older, it all started to come clear to Pike that it was only a pipe dream and his chances of making it to the NBA would be as unlikely as a devout Muslim eating a pork sandwich. Now that those dreams were over, Pike expanded his small operation into hugging the block with cocaine and other drugs.

Cristal and Tamar waited patiently for the game to be over before they could run over and flirt with Pike. The small crowd surrounding the pick-up game knew Pike was going to win the cash. He hated losing. He was just too nice with his skills to lose on the courts. Even though he had been fouled and it was a close game, the crowd felt things were about to get very interesting.

Pike ate the foul and allowed the opposing team to take possession of the ball at the key. He scowled heavily at the man who had brutally fouled him. The look on his face revealed he was ready to take his revenge. The ball was passed and the man Pike was guarding took possession of the rock. He dribbled toward Pike, ready to blow past him and score. Pike was ready for him. Pike crouched low defensively with his arms spread, shielding the basket and timing that right moment to embarrass the man.

"Nigga, you ain't Kobe or LeBron, you just some washed-up, wannabe athlete with a blown knee who's about to lose this paper," his opponent mocked.

Pike remained quiet, choosing not to respond but staying focused. He was going to prove to everyone, like he always did, not to doubt him. He was always going to be the alpha on the basketball courts. Suddenly it became a one-on-one match as both players' teammates decided to stand aside and watch the match-up. The man dribbled with his right hand. Pike immediately spotted his weakness. When his opponent drove hard to the right side of the court like a locomotive toward the basketball hoop, Pike went into action. He was on his opponent like white on rice, and when he went to score, Pike leaped into the air like he was on a trampoline and smacked the ball out of his hands so hard that his opponent went crashing to the ground. Pike's teammate recovered the rock before it went out of bounds and threw a chest pass to Pike. Pike's opponent jumped to his feet and saw Pike charging his way to score the winning basket. He sprang into defense mode quickly. Pike charged with intensity and leaped toward the basketball hoop with grace, his opponent doing the same, jumping up with his arms outstretched to block the final score. Pike dunked on him so hard, the entire basketball hoop shook like it was caught in an earthquake, and his rival went crashing toward the ground a second time. Pike lingered on the hoop with a smirk at his rival.

Everyone cheered and screamed. The game was over. It was a dynamic ending. Pike had won. He had embarrassed the other team. He dropped down to the concrete, gazed at his opponent and shouted, "Nigga, I told you, I'm the fuckin' best out here, and don't ever go against the inevitable. I'm the fuckin' king on this court. And where's my fuckin' money at?"

Cristal and Tamar hurried over to Pike before the other thirsty bitches around could get up in his face. With five hundred dollars in his hands, Pike was ready to hit the club. He counted his half of the money out in the open, smiling—another hustle, another dollar.

"You gonna spend some of that on me tonight, right?" Cristal asked with a teasing smile.

Pike turned around and replied, "It depends. Are you worth it? Because you know what I like."

"What do you like?" Cristal asked, placing her hand against his chest, feeling his muscles flex.

Cristal and Tamar were dressed like two young, sultry whores: tight, coochie-cutting shorts and tight tops that accentuated their breasts. They were beautiful. However, Cristal was an extremely beautiful woman with long, shapely legs and long, raven-black hair. Her eyes were framed by long lashes and she was slim up top, but a little curvier on the bottom.

All the boys wanted her, but Pike was the man she wanted to sip on her milkshake.

Cristal threw a smile at Pike. "You lookin' good, Cristal, gaining that weight in all the right places," said Pike.

"And you can touch in all the right places," she flirted.

"Yeah, I know."

"Oh, you know, huh? And how you know?"

Pike smiled. "Cuz I always know."

"You so conceited, Pike," Cristal returned.

"What, y'all need a room or something?" Tamar asked with attitude.

"You want in on the action too, Tamar? Cuz you know it's gonna take more than one to handle a nigga like me."

"Like you can really handle us two," Tamar said.

"You know I got hands and skills not just on the courts."

The girls laughed. Pike was clearly arrogant and somewhat self-centered. He stood on the basketball court remaining shirtless and looking like a general that had just conquered a small kingdom. His winnings were still gripped in his hand, his accolades for the day.

"You know, you're better than half these players in the NBA, Pike," Cristal said. "And you have an ego like them too."

Pike nodded, knowing Cristal was right. He was built to play in the NBA. He was born to make millions of dollars and become somebody important in life. He felt it was his destiny, and he was going to get his, either through basketball or drug dealing.

Cristal peered across the park and noticed Lisa, Mona, and Sharon coming over to join in the conversation. Cristal and Tamar became somewhat annoyed seeing the three girls coming their way; it meant that there was more competition coming over. They didn't like competition, even amongst their own friends. It was already enough that the two of them were competing against each other.

"What y'all over here talkin' about?" Mona asked, popping the gum in her mouth and staring at Pike.

"Nothing, we were just congratulating Pike on his game," Cristal replied.

"Damn, we missed you playing, Pike." Mona sucked her teeth and continued with, "We came all late cuz you know we had to stop by and get some smokes. I need to get high tonight."

"What you got?" Pike asked.

"Some Kush. You know Brooklyn got that good oohwee shit out here," Mona joked.

"Nah luv, Harlem is where it's at, believe me," Pike argued mildly.

"Pike, the Jamaicans out here have some of the best quality weed that will have a muthafucka like 'Whoa.' Fuck Harlem. Brooklyn in the fuckin' house. Wait till you start smoking this Kush, it's gonna make you feel like Superman."

"I'm already the man of steel," he joked back, grabbing his dick.

"Whatever…"

Mona was always the party girl and heavy smoker in the crew. She had sarcasm and attitude like her peers. And she knew her weed like Einstein knew his $E=mc^2$. She was steadily ready for that next rush and yearned for that push into an exhilarating lifestyle, the one she always saw on TV and in the movies. She and her friends were all looking for the same come-up.

The girls' forte was boosting, either keeping the items they stole for themselves or fencing pricey goods to earn a living. They were good at what they did and made it into a criminal career.

Pike stood among the ladies, holding court like a pimp on the streets. He knew he could have any bitch he wanted. Being the heartthrob of the hood, and over the years he ran through dozens of women—sowing his royal oats, and surprisingly, having no kids. Bitches were trying to get pregnant by him, to no avail; Pike stayed with condoms or would always pull out. He had a street reputation that preceded him. He was fine, and word throughout was that he had a really big dick and knew how to use it. Like a diamond, he was a bitch's best friend. Pike's small operation on the block was picking up, and with his business partner, Rich, he had street dreams.

As the girls chatted and flirted with Pike, music blaring from a Honda Accord caught their attention. It was Pike's partner Rich. Jay Z and Drake's "Light It Up" played from his car. He stepped out nodding his head and rhyming to the track like he was a rapper himself. He was always affable despite being a drug dealer. His stout frame was clad in a black-and-white Nike velour sweat suit and his round head topped off with a gleaming bald scalp. He wasn't a very attractive man, and he wasn't an ugly man— mediocre in appearance, but his personality was magnetic.

He walked toward Pike with his genuine smile and hollered, "Ladies, ladies, why y'all crowding around my dude like some chickenheads? He can't get all of you pregnant at the same time. Share some for me too. I need loving, too."

"Fuck you, Rich. You just mad because ain't nobody crowding around you," Tamar barked out.

Rich rubbed his protruding stomach and replied, "Look at me, I'm crowded enough already. But I'll tell you what, Tamar, why don't you get on ya knees and suck some air out of me? I can lose some weight like that."

Laughter stirred up, but Tamar didn't find Rich funny. She frowned and gave him the middle finger.

"C'mon Tamar, ya lips around my dick, with you sucking it, I probably can lose more weight than being on Slimfast," he added.

There was more laughter.

Rich flicked his tongue at her, being the nasty and lecherous pervert that he was.

Tamar scowled. "Nigga, you don't have enough dick for me."

Tamar flipped him the bird again. Their witty insults back and forth were a common thing. Even though they cracked on each other, there was a mutual respect between them.

Rich was a drug dealer, but he always brought humor and fun around. He was a different type of hustler. Originally from the Bronx, he had made Brooklyn his new home several years earlier when he'd started betting heavily on basketball games and befriended Pike at a Brooklyn tournament. Pike threw a game for Rich once, and they came up on ten thousand dollars. Pike hated to lose on the courts, but he hated being broke even more.

"So where we gonna smoke at?" Mona asked.

"Back at my place," Pike suggested.

"Harlem? Why we can't stay in Brooklyn?" Lisa spoke out. She was the Aaliyah of the bunch, a sweet, slim, and pretty young girl. She was the only girl in the crew who came from a two-parent home. Her mother worked for the Board of Education, and her father was a conductor for the MTA. She grew up more privileged than the others. However, Lisa had her ways, too—always carrying a razor, following behind her friends, and ready to ride or die for those she loved.

"My apartment is small, but it's set up nice, and I just got the flat screen put in."

"But that's Harlem. Who wants to travel to Harlem?" Sharon protested.

"Y'all gonna be with me and Rich," Pike added, like they were Jay Z and Kanye West.

Sharon was the least pretty out of the girls, the darkest one with her tarlike complexion, round eyes almost like a bug, and natural hair in an afro. She was a slim girl also with a nice booty and ample tits, and like so many of her friends in Brooklyn, came from a broken home with both parents being on drugs.

"Y'all get to chill with me for the night. I'm telling y'all, y'all gonna love my crib."

While Pike boasted about his small apartment, Cristal gazed across the park and noticed something unusual: Tank. He was never in the park. His business wasn't long walks in the park or recreational activities with others, but only murder. When he was around, bad things happened. And today, on a sunny afternoon, he marched toward the basketball courts with an emotionless gaze, like he was on a mission.

Tank was a hit man for the Brooklyn 69 Bloods. He was feared like HIV—a ruthless muthafucka with a heart of ice and a passion for killing. Everyone kept away from him, knowing what he was capable of.

Cristal peered at Tank, fearfully, and wanted to yelp when she saw the .9mm in his hand. For some reason she was fixated on what he was about to do next—create a crime scene. It seemed like she was the only one who was seeing him. He kept the gun low, down to his side, and casually walked toward a group of men playing a three-on-three pick-up game.

Without provocation, Tank opened fire on the men.

Bak! Bak! Bak! Bak! Bak! Bak!

Panic quickly ensued on the basketball courts. Everyone in the park took desperate cover as shots rang out, a tidal wave of folks rushing toward the exit. Even Cristal's friends took off running, leaving her aghast at what she was witnessing. Four of the men were violently gunned down by Tank, their bodies and blood scattered across the hard blacktop.

When the gunshots stopped and the smoke cleared, two men lay dead and two seriously injured. Tank hurried toward an idling car parked nearby and escaped from the chaos he created. It was gangland horror.

Cristal stared at the massacre. It wasn't anything new to her—violence and murder were common in her hood, but it was amazing how a man could easily kill another man, especially out in public. Tank got his respect because he was a killer. He didn't even flinch when he pulled the trigger. An ambivalent feeling swept over Cristal. Murder, how cruel it was, but also how captivating and hypnotizing it was to her.

Sirens wailed from a distance. The Brooklyn park was once again stained with violence.

"Cristal," Tamar shouted from a distance. "What you doing?! C'mon!"

Cristal snapped herself out of her daze and hurried away from the bodies. For a minute, everything seemed so unreal and movielike. She finally pulled herself away from the violent incident and ran away. It felt like she was running on air as her sneakers rapidly pounded against the pavement. She felt guilty somehow. She'd watched them die like animals, but she didn't feel too sad about it. For some reason, she felt fortunate to see Tank in action. It was like always hearing about the boogeyman from other children, and then finally seeing the boogeyman in your own closet one night. It was scary, yes, but it was also exciting.

The girls decided to go to Harlem with Pike and Rich after all. East New York was too hot to be around.

TWO

●●●●●●●●●●●●●●●●●●●●●●●●●●●●●●●●●●●

"Yo, that shit was wild out there today. Tank is fuckin' crazy, my heart is still beating hard from that shit happening," Mona hollered. "How you gonna gun niggas down in broad daylight like that?"

"Cuz that's Brooklyn, that's how they do. Niggas don't give a fuck out there, especially Tank. He's a special kind of loco. But that's how you get ya respect out there, by being fearless and not giving a fuck," Tamar blurted out with animation in her tone.

"And I don't get my respect out here? What am I, a pussy?" Pike asked.

"You do, but not like Tank. He gets respect because he's feared. You're respected because you're admired," Tamar countered with some admiration for the killer.

"We too busy gettin' money out here." Rich stepped in and offered an explanation. "And murder brings around the feds and too much heat on the block."

"Nigga, please. Y'all ain't makin' that kind of money like Tank and the 69 Bloods are making." Tamar rolled her eyes. "And besides, I don't think y'all got the heart or balls to murder someone."

"Damn, the way you talkin' about the nigga like you ready to fuck him. What, Tamar, bullets flying got ya pussy wet?" Rich joked crudely.

"I just respect the gangsta in that nigga, that's all," she said.

"Yeah, I know what you respect," Rich replied sideways. "You love them type of niggas, don't you?"

"I love a man who's about his business and ain't scared to pop off when the time comes."

Rich chuckled. "Yeah, you want a twenty-five-to-life type of nigga, a death-row nigga. And you can become the jail bride."

"Fuck you, Rich. You just mad cuz you ain't the nigga I'm attracted to. And who is you to judge someone like you a saint, when you out there doin' dirt too?"

"Yeah, I'm doin' dirt, but I ain't puttin' niggas *in* the dirt. That type of business only brings bad karma."

"So how you gonna be a hustler and don't buss ya gun, or scared to buss ya gun," Tamar challenged.

"I'm the subtle type of hustler. I know my lane, and I plan on staying in it," Rich countered. "In ten years I'll still be around, running a legit empire from reinvested drug money."

"And what happens when niggas decide to come in your lane by cutting you off? What you gonna do then, be a bitch?" Tamar asked.

"I do what I gotta do then, but until that day comes, I'm just gonna do me right."

"That sounds like you ain't gonna do shit."

"You don't know me, Tamar. I ain't a killer unless I have to be."

Pike lit up the weed and took a strong pull as he listened to Tamar and Rich's conversation. His small kitchenette apartment that he was renting on 116th Street in Harlem was cozy. Hearing them talk about murder brought up some haunting memories for Pike. When he was young, his mother had been a severe alcoholic living in the projects, and she never encouraged his dreams. Several years ago, his sister Kim, had been killed by a stray bullet while she was walking to the corner store in Brooklyn. She was going to the bodega to steal their mother a can of beer. She was only fifteen years old. The tragedy was so damaging to Pike that he almost quit playing basketball and was about to fall into a deep depression. He always felt that it was his mother's fault for sending Kim to steal beer after-hours, and he vowed to never forgive her. The bullet that struck his sister in the head was meant for a lowlife stick-up kid named World, who was a menace to society since the day he was born. His sister's murder troubled him greatly. Why did his sister, who was an A student and was never into trouble a day in her life, have to die that night? It was a question he would never get the answer to. She was an angel, but she lived in hell.

Pike exhaled the weed smoke and decided to add his two cents into the discussion. "I'm with Rich on this. I may be a lot of things, but I'm no killer. Some coward took my sister's life by accident years ago, and I can never forgive that shit."

"I know, I heard about that and I'm so sorry for your loss, Pike. I lost my little sister too, a few years ago," Sharon interjected with sincerity.

For a moment, the two locked eyes in the apartment. They seemed to have some mutual understanding toward each other. Sharon smiled at Pike, her eyes displaying sincerity. Pike grinned back slightly and took another pull from the burning weed and shared it with the others.

"And Cristal, are you stupid or crazy? How you just gonna stand there lookin' dumbfounded like you bulletproof or sumthin'?" Tamar exclaimed at her best friend out of the blue.

"Please, he wasn't worried about me," Cristal returned loosely.

"Fuck that. What if he thinks you're a witness? Matter of fact, you are a witness, Cristal. You stood right there and watched it all go down," Mona mentioned.

"Tank is a paid killer for them 69 Bloods, believe me, he ain't worried about me snitchin'," Cristal defended.

"That's our point! He ain't gotta worry about you if you dead."

"I ain't scared of him like everybody else," Cristal said with assurance. "I ain't scared of dying."

"You say that now because ain't no threat out there coming your way," Tamar said.

"And if it was a threat coming my way, I'd handle it. It's them before me. That's how we grew up, right? Brooklyn, ride or die," she declared.

"Yeah, right," Lisa uttered.

"What, you don't think I'm capable of killing somebody?"

"No!" Lisa answered frankly.

"Then you don't know me, Lisa. I thought you did." Cristal exclaimed. "I hate when people say that they could never commit murder. Let someone run up in your house to do you or your fam harm and you got a pistol. You sayin' you wouldn't use it?"

"Yeah, I would use it, but that's different," Lisa answered.

"Keep telling yourself that. Murder is murder."

"Shit, it's survival out here in the hood, and I would kill somebody in a heartbeat, just give me a gun and I'll aim and fire," Tamar chided.

"That's because you a twisted bitch, Tamar," Rich said.

"Call me a bitch again and you'll be my first fuckin' victim," Tamar threatened.

Rich smirked.

Suddenly murder became the topic in the apartment. Killers from New York and all over either still alive or dead were brought up. Pappy Mason, Pistol Pete, Sammy the Bull, John Gotti, and others were talked about heavily as the weed was passed around.

"I wanna be rich, by any means necessary," Tamar stated.

"Even if it means losing your soul in the process?" asked Lisa.

"Hey, I want all my good will and fortune here on earth while I can enjoy it. You can't take it wit' you when you're dead, right? And I want my respect," Tamar replied.

"We do get our respect," Mona said.

"Yeah, but I want everybody to know not to fuck wit' me and my crew."

"They rarely fuck wit' us now, Tamar," Cristal said.

"They don't, because they fear us. And why they fear us? Because we gets it poppin' on the streets. We earned our respect out there by fighting and doin' whatever," Tamar exclaimed proudly.

"So, let me ask you a question. What is more important to you, to be feared or loved?" Pike asked.

"Loved!" Sharon blurted out without giving her answer a second thought.

"Why love?" Pike asked her.

"Because love is a beautiful thing. To be truly loved by someone is why we're put on earth. I want to feel love, give love, and be in love," Sharon declared. "But fear is a horrible feeling caused by someone or something that is dangerous. I mean, someone or something that is likely to cause pain, or a threat. And when people fear you, eventually, they're going to go against you. Then they'll want to hurt you, and I don't want anyone coming at me. I don't want to be a threat to anyone."

"Okay, Mother Teresa," Mona joked. "But you know love hurts, too."

"It do. Everything hurts, but how you deal with that hurt is what truly matters," Sharon stated.

Pike was smitten by her answer. He saw that she was intelligent and somewhat different from her peers. Her beauty wasn't up to par like the others, but her persona, her voice, and her speech was appealing.

He gazed at Sharon and said, "I respect that. You gotta respect love."

"Fuck that, I would rather be feared," Tamar continued.

"Me too," Cristal cosigned.

"Well, I would rather be loved, too," Pike said while staring at Sharon.

"Yeah, you loved this bitch and that bitch, and the next bitch, and I know you wanna love me too, right? Me love you long time." Tamar laughed. "You a male whore, Pike, face the fact. Bitches love you and you love them right back, for a whole five minutes."

"Whatever, Tamar," Pike replied, waving her off.

Tamar spread her legs sexually in his direction, gesturing her need for some dick and playing around for a laugh. "You want this pussy too, Pike? It's all yours. You know how tight it is."

"You tripping, Tamar."

"What? You turning down some pussy, Pike? Get the fuck outta here. That would be the first. It must be freezing in hell."

"Leave him alone, Tamar," Sharon interjected.

"What, you wanna fuck him too, Sharon?" Tamar continued to taunt.

"No!" Sharon blurted out with attitude.

"I mean, he passes out his dick like pamphlets and flyers in the hood," Tamar teased.

"That's enough, Tamar. Like you a saint," Sharon shouted out.

"Damn, let me find out someone is getting touchy and shit. I mean, you ain't fuckin' him and you acting like that. Shit, imagine if you were fuckin'."

"Tamar, chill out," Mona scolded.

"I swear, everybody in this room is too uptight. We smoking and having fun, right? So let's have fun," said Tamar.

"I'll have some fun wit' you Tamar. How do you want it?" Rich smiled.

"Come and eat my pussy then," she replied with a lecherous grin.

"Only if you return the favor . . . and ladies first," Rich replied.

"Yeah, right."

As Tamar and Rich joked around with each other and the other girls got high, Pike for some reason couldn't take his eyes off of Sharon. She smoked and smiled with her friends, but then she noticed Pike's eyes fixed on her. There was something radiant about her—something intriguing and maybe rousing. His lingering stare made her blush and turn away.

"I like your hair. I love natural hair on a black woman," Pike complimented with an engaging look.

"Thank you," Sharon returned with a humble gaze and smile.

Sharon found that she was somewhat flabbergasted by Pike's sudden attraction toward her. Everyone in the room was also shocked. What did Pike see in Sharon that he didn't see in them? She was the least attractive girl in the room.

"Let me find out you got a thang for my girl Sharon, Pike," Cristal announced.

"Please, that nigga just tryin' to fuck her. Sharon got a big booty and some nice tits, he wanna squeeze them goodies till juices come out," said Tamar.

"Tamar! Damn, why you gotta always be so ghetto and loud?" Sharon shouted heatedly.

"Cuz I am!" she spat back. "And best believe; don't get hype cuz the nigga lookin' at you special. He do that to all the bitches he wants some pussy from."

Rich laughed. He took a pull from the blunt and said, "Hey that sounds like hate to me, Tamar."

"Fuck you, Rich!" Tamar shouted, giving Rich the middle finger.

"Please do."

Sharon became uncomfortable all of a sudden about the subject being on her. She stood up, saying, "I need to pee," and left the room for the bathroom.

The weed continued to be passed around with a thick fog of it lingering inside the apartment. The girls continued talking loudly and being reckless with their words. They were a ghetto crew from Brooklyn that boosted from stores and shopping malls, along with jumping and cutting bitches with razors and knives, dabbling in drugs and doing whatever it took to earn a living or sustain their reputation. They were all looking for a come-up or a way out of the hood, and getting with a rich nigga was usually their formula.

"You really like my friend?" Lisa asked Pike.

"I think she's cute . . . different," he responded coolly.

"Cute? We all are cute in here, and no offense to my friend, but she can't hold a candle to any one of us, Pike," said Tamar callously.

"Tamar, just shut up!" Mona retorted.

"It's the truth. You know me, I always keep it real, no matter if you like it or not," Tamar returned sternly.

"Yeah, and that's the problem wit' you," Lisa said.

"Fuck all y'all," Tamar retorted.

"We love you too, bitch," Cristal joked.

The room stirred up with laughter while Rich started rolling up another blunt. With another blunt being smoked and passed around, Pike decided to lighten the mood and asked, "What y'all got planned for tomorrow night?"

"Why you asking?" Cristal asked with a raised brow.

Pike took another strong pull from the burning weed and said, "Have y'all ever heard of the name Easy P, or E.P. for short?"

"Yeah, we heard of him before, ain't he supposed to be somebody big-time? And he's really rich, right?" inquired Cristal.

"Yo, E.P. is big not just on the streets, but everywhere else. He's smart and shit. He's doing his thang and he got more money than train smoke, and the man has his hands in everything," Pike boasted.

"Okay and how do you know him? Or do he know you?" Mona asked, being facetious.

"I know everybody. I got connects," Pike bragged.

"Yeah, your mouth and lips must be really tired after all that sucking and ass-kissing," Tamar joked.

"Ha ha, you funny, Tamar. Just for that, you ain't invited," Pike said halfheartedly.

"Where my crew go, I go," Tamar snapped back.

"Yeah, too bad for them."

"Are we really invited to his party tomorrow night?" Cristal asked.

"Yes. He asked me to bring some beautiful and classy females to his joint. I guess we have to work or pray on the classy part for y'all, huh?" Pike remarked with a grin.

"Oh, you got jokes tonight, too, huh?" Mona responded.

"But anyway, E.P. is a big basketball fan. NBA, college and even high school—like Rich here, he'll bet on any game. We met several years ago through a mutual friend. He likes my game. We became cool friends," Pike boasted.

"I heard that E.P. is one of the biggest drug distributors on the East Coast. They say he's connected to the Mexican drug cartel," Mona revealed.

"Nah, I heard he's this high-profile lawyer that represents the Mafia, and he once helped John Gotti get off a murder charge," said Lisa.

"They say he's gay and runs an elite escort service with men and women," Tamar mentioned.

"Where the fuck do y'all hear these rumors from?" Pike asked. "Ain't any of them close to true."

"So since you're good friends with him, or claim to be, what do he do, huh? How does infamous E.P. make his millions?" Cristal asked.

Pike shrugged and returned, "I don't know."

"Exactly," Cristal said with some sarcasm.

"Listen, all I know is he told me to bring some fine ladies to his party tomorrow night, but they couldn't make it, so I thought about y'all. Second string is always good, and I know y'all can clean up well, right?" Pike asked, with his signature smirk toward them.

"Oh fuck you, Pike!" the girls exclaimed all together.

"In due time," he continued to joke around.

"So, y'all coming or not?" Rich asked.

"Hells yeah, we coming! We ain't tryin' to miss out on what could be the party of the year—an exclusive VIP party at that. We is up in there and we gonna be the finest bitches at his party," Tamar announced excitedly.

"And you know this, girl," Cristal shouted out, slapping fives with her best friend.

"Ooooh, I can't wait," Mona said.

Sharon exited the bathroom feeling much better. Once again, she and Pike exchanged pleasing glances at each other. She smiled. Pike smiled. Everyone in the room paid attention to their flirting.

"Damn, y'all want some privacy or sumthin'?" Tamar spat.

"Give it a rest, Tamar," Sharon tersely shot back.

"No jokes here, just tryin' to look out for my homegirl. And speaking of homegirls, how's Mesha, Pike?" Tamar asked, referring to his ex-girlfriend.

"I haven't spoken to that bitch in a minute," he replied coolly.

"Okay, cuz you know that bitch is drama."

"And you just a go-happy Disney character, right?" he returned matter-of-factly.

Rich laughed loudly.

The atmosphere in Pike's kitchenette apartment was lively with jokes, weed smoking and conversation about E.P.'s upcoming party. The girls were excited about it. They'd heard through the grapevine about the kind of parties E.P. hosted. He always had the elite attending his functions, and the venues were always breathtaking. They were expensive and, most of the time, extremely formal.

With each one smoking on their third blunt, music playing, and time passing by, it was getting late. Everyone was lying around and high. Tamar and Cristal had already talked about the special outfits they wanted to get for E.P.'s party and the store they planned on boosting them from. They had some special techniques they implemented in the stores to prevent getting caught and arrested. They were professionals at taking from others.

With midnight approaching, a loud knock at Pike's door caught everyone's attention. Cristal and her crew rose up and stared at Pike.

"Late-night booty call?" Mona asked flippantly.

"I don't know who that is," Pike responded, clueless.

He stood up and approached the door. He looked through the peephole and sighed heavily. "Damn," he uttered.

"Who's that?" Tamar asked.

The knocking at the door continued and was loud and obnoxious. "Pike, open the fuckin' door. I know ya home," a woman shouted out.

Pike looked at his company with a scowl and said, "I ain't know she was coming."

Pike relented and allowed her into his apartment, but surprisingly, she hadn't come alone. Mesha came through with her crew of girls and automatically started scowling and beefing with everyone.

Mesha, with her long weave, light skin, and nasty attitude, charged into Pike's place like she owned it. Two of her homegirls stood right behind her like bodyguards. Immediately, the tension in the room heightened. There had always been bad blood between Cristal's peoples and Mesha's crew. They were like oil and water—just weren't meant to mix around each other, and when they did, it took a while to clean up.

Mesha had always been insecure and overprotective of Pike. They had an on-again and off-again relationship. She wanted babies by him, but Pike didn't want to have any kids. She was always tired of his cheating ways, but she would always take him back when he came running and fucked him when he was horny—in other words, allowing Pike to have his cake and eat it too. She was in love with him, but he wasn't in love with her. Pike's true colors were exhibited daily: He was a womanizing, arrogant and self-centered drug dealer who wasn't changing his ways anytime soon. Knowing every woman wanted to be with him made Mesha a jealous, raving bitch who wanted to bite the heads off all of her competition.

"What the fuck are these bitches doin' in ya apartment, Pike?" Mesha exclaimed heatedly.

The drama was already starting.

Sharon, surprisingly, stood up before Tamar and Cristal. She scowled and shouted back, "Bitch? Who the fuck you callin' bitch?"

"You, bitch!" Mesha retorted.

"Damn, it's about to get real up in here," Rich said, amused.

But no one else thought he was funny. Tamar, Cristal, and all their crew stood up. Their high and the good times came to an abrupt end. Mesha stepped toward Sharon, sullen, with her lips twisted. Her crew was behind her. The only thing on her mind was hate and jealousy. She assumed one of the bitches in Pike's apartment was fucking him. Even though they were off again, she couldn't handle him being with anyone else. "Why you got these bitches in your place, Pike?!" Mesha screamed out.

"We ain't even together, Mesha. Why you trippin' like this?" Pike retorted.

"You know how I feel about you!" she exclaimed.

"Fuck that dumb bitch, Pike! Look at her, she's fuckin' wack, no wonder you came over to sumthin' better," Tamar shouted.

Mesha spun toward the comment coming from Tamar. "Bitch, who you think ya talkin' to like that?!"

"What you gonna do, bitch!"

"Bitch, you don't fuckin' know me!"

By now, everyone stood on high alert, scowling at one another. For some reason, Mesha pivoted in Sharon's direction again and screamed out, "And look at this dark-ass, wack bitch, lookin' like a house slave. Pike, I know you ain't tryin' to get wit' that bitch."

Before Tamar, Cristal or anyone could defend their friend, Sharon snapped like a rubber band upon hearing the harsh comment said about her. She was nice, but sometimes people underestimated her. Like lightning striking, she struck with vengeance, charging and swinging with her fists. Mesha caught two hard hits to her face and went stumbling backwards like the Leaning Tower of Pisa. Sharon was a strong, proud woman, and she wasn't about to take any disrespect from anyone.

A fight ensued in Pike's kitchenette apartment, leading to an all-out brawl amongst everyone else. Mesha's crew wasn't about to stand to the side while Sharon was getting the best of their friend. When they tried to jump in, Sharon's friends jumped in.

"I told you bitch, don't fuck with me!" Sharon screamed out heatedly as she sat on top of Mesha, bashing her face in with her fists.

Pike and Rich stood aghast at what they were witnessing. Weaves were being torn out, clothing ripped apart and his furniture toppling over. Tamar and Cristal tore into Mesha's friend Quinn like lions with a prey, while Lisa and Mona handled the other friend, Shay. They stomped her repeatedly with their sneakers in a nearby corner.

"Yo, y'all really need to chill the fuck out. Y'all fuckin' up my crib," Pike shouted.

But no one cared what he was saying. They were heated and belligerent toward each other. There were multiple fists swinging in every direction and some blood spewing. Sharon was ready to kill Mesha for the disrespect toward her, but she held back her anger somewhat, knowing too many blows to that bitch's head would get her locked up for murder.

"Yo, y'all need to take this shit outside! I'm 'bout to call the police on everyone," Pike shouted out in desperation.

Shit was getting broken in his place, and when they knocked over his flat screen TV, he started to see red and became highly upset. He pivoted toward Rich, who seemed aloof from the violence around him. He was smiling and enjoying the scenery of women fighting each other.

"Yo, you just gonna sit there and let them fuck up my place like this?" Pike cried out.

"Hey, man, this shit is better than Pay-Per-View."

The disturbance from Pike's apartment started to catch the attention of his neighbors. It brought some of the building residents out of their apartments and had them lingering in the hallway. Pike and Rich pulled Tamar and her friends off of their victims and the fighting started to dwindle down.

It was clear that Sharon won the fight, and Mesha and her friends got their asses beat down like they owed some pimps money. Pike and Rich dragged Mesha and her friends out of his apartment with them kicking and screaming. Sharon smirked, knowing who the better bitch was. She didn't even have a scratch on her. But the girls knew that with their win against Mesha, they would forever have to watch their backs. Mesha was a crazy bitch who always held grudges, also known to cut bitches in the face, and she was linked with the 69 Brooklyn Bloods. And this wasn't going to be the end of their beef. Mesha and her crew were going to retaliate—when and where, the girls didn't know, so they had to always be ready.

Today, the girls felt good about themselves—together, they felt unstoppable. Together, they were the shit. Always together, they were a force.

THREE

●●●

Roosevelt Field Mall on Long Island was always a gold mine for Tamar and Cristal. It was considered to be an ideal family place, offering many name-brand stores as well as a carousel for children. It was the name-brand stores that Tamar and Cristal took advantage of. They had some connects inside the stores to help them with their boosting, and with their subtle schemes to steal, they seemed impervious to getting caught. Having done it for so long, the girls knew the ins and outs of shoplifting.

Cristal and Tamar walked into one store after another, cleverly surveying the area and picking out what outfits and other items they wanted to steal for tonight's party. The clothing had to be classy and stand out. It had to be something to get people's attention. They were always considered ghetto and hood, but tonight, at E.P.'s exclusive party, things were about to change.

Along with having store employees helping them in their scam for a share of the profits, Cristal and Tamar were smart at stealing from any store and had an elite network going on. They had the right tools to bypass the security system. That day, both girls walked out of Nordstrom, Bloomingdale's, Burberry, and Bebe with several nice stolen dresses.

Tonight, they were going to look like goddesses. The girls walked toward the food court to grab a quick bite to eat.

"Girl, that shit was smooth," Tamar said.

She took a seat opposite Cristal at the table. Both shopping bags were placed underneath the table, containing pricey dresses in their sizes.

Cristal chuckled. "They don't know how we do."

"Right, we the best at this," Tamar replied, slapping a celebratory high-five across the table with her friend.

They lingered in the food court for a short while and left with a feeling of accomplishment. They made their way back into the East New York neighborhood. They couldn't stop talking about E.P.'s party. They felt special being invited. The only thing the girls could talk about was snatching up a baller to trick on them. They had the looks and the goodies to grab all the boys' attention, and with the dresses they'd stolen from the store, they were adamant it would be a sure thing.

They arrived in front of the towering project apartment Cristal resided in with her mother, Renee. It was a sweltering June summer evening. The minute they stepped on the block, a couple shopping bags in their hands and their beauty overflowing, all the boys were gawking and calling out at them. Tamar and Cristal didn't have time to play with boys in the hood; their attention was on greater things.

They took the pissy elevator up to Cristal's fifth-floor apartment. The city's heat wave made it almost unbearable to do anything that evening. It was 98 degrees, and the humidity was just as high. Air conditioners and fans were on full blast, and people walked around almost naked and sweaty.

With the smell of urine, trash, and sweat mixing around in the pocket-sized elevator, Cristal and Tamar screwed up their faces at the horrendous smell and felt like they were about to pass out and die.

"I can't wait to jump my ass in the shower," Cristal said.

"I feel you."

"Muthafuckas are so nasty in this building. I swear, I can't wait to move," Cristal said.

"If we meet the right people and make the right connects tonight, anything can happen."

"We gonna make it happen."

When the lift stopped at their floor and the metallic door slid back into the wall, Cristal and Tamar hurried out of the reeking elevator and walked down the narrow, graffiti-filled hallway. Walking into the apartment, Cristal saw her mother lounging on the couch, asleep with an expired cigarette in her hand. The place was silent but messy, with unwashed dishes piling up in the sink and a dirty, cigarette-stained carpet, with clothes and empty beer cans scattered everywhere.

How could anyone live like this? Cristal asked herself that every day.

Her mother was quiet, not a loudmouth, but she was very lazy. And she had other vices. She was forty years old and had given up on life a long time ago. She was an alcoholic, constantly downing beers and liquor from sunup to sundown. And when she wasn't drinking heavily, Renee was either smoking weed, playing cards, gambling, or playing her numbers. She held card games inside her apartment and took frequent trips with friends down to Atlantic City—playing blackjack and poker on an obsessive level. The funny thing about Cristal's mother was that she always carried a fresh deck of cards to play a quick game wherever she was at.

Surprisingly, she had a man in her life, Johnny, or Mr. Johnny, as Cristal called him. He was sixty-seven years old and still working as a janitor at a local public school. His paltry checks only paid his rent and allowed him to give Renee a few measly dollars for whatever.

Occasionally, when Renee needed some extra money, she would babysit the kids of the young girls in the building while they went out partying. She was always good with kids—maybe not with her own—but the young mothers in the projects loved her. She was always around and dependable for thirty dollars a night.

Cristal looked at her mother and frowned. The living room smelled. The fridge was empty, and it was always embarrassing to bring friends over. When Cristal's crew did come over, Renee allowed them to do whatever they wanted. They ran her apartment, with any parental authority being nonexistent.

"Damn, your moms is twisted again," Tamar said.

Cristal sucked her teeth and said, "You know she's always like that."

"Sad."

"Yeah, she is."

Renee remained comatose to the girls' criticism.

The girls went into Cristal's bedroom, a contrast from the rest of the untidy apartment. Her bedroom was neatly decorated with a stylish queen-size bed, wood dressing table, and a 55-inch flat screen with multiple DVDs scattered around. Most of the items were goods stolen for her own benefit. Cristal's bedroom looked like a dreamland while the rest of the apartment looked like hell.

The girls dumped all the stolen items onto the bed and beamed at their prompt come-up on some more pricey goods—further items added to their collection.

"Lisa, Mona, and Sharon should be on their way soon," said Cristal.

"Shit, let's take the good stuff now."

Cristal nodded.

Cristal opened her closet door and flipped on the lights. Inside were several stolen dresses and other clothing with the price tags still on. Her wardrobe was all hot. In real life, she couldn't afford any of the clothing she wore or what was concealed in her closet. The prices on the clothing ranged from one hundred to four grand.

Cristal and Tamar delicately shifted through their score, trying to pick out the right attire to wear for tonight's party. With the right dress had to come the perfect accessories. They wanted to look super sexy, but at the same time, classy. Pike and Rich always joked about how hood or ghetto they were. Tonight, it was their chance to prove them wrong, and also, to not embarrass themselves. They were mixing it up with a different kind of folks—the city's elite.

"I need to get high before we do anything," Tamar said.

Cristal agreed.

They called the weed man who proudly delivered, and then they ordered some Chinese food, and put on some hip-hop music to listen and dance to. They had plenty of time to get ready. The event started at 10pm. It was in Manhattan, just over the bridge and in Midtown. Pike and Rich were picking them up.

Tamar sat on Cristal's bed taking apart a cigar with a razor in her hand. There was a dime bag of some pink weed next to her. It was the most potent to smoke. Cristal took a few pulls from the cigarette and stripped down to her pink underwear. Her figure was magnificent. Even Tamar gazed at her friend's body with a tinge of jealousy in her eyes. Cristal seemed to be the picture of perfect with everything on her natural and curvy, from her juicy round booty to her succulent, protruding breasts and her long lashes.

Tamar knew it was inevitable that her friend would catch the attention of a fine, maybe rich man tonight. Tamar wasn't on the chopping block of prettiness either. She was cute too, and curvy, but wasn't as endowed in certain areas like her friend. Cristal was taller and shapelier. She was so pretty that even without makeup and dressed down she turned heads.

Cristal lingered by her bedroom window in her underwear and gazed outside, puffing on her cigarette and exhaling. The sun was gradually setting over the projects, transitioning day to night and creating a dark hue in the sky over Brooklyn. The Chinese food had satisfied her hunger, and her mind was on tonight.

"Are you nervous about tonight?" Cristal asked her friend.

"A little."

"We gonna be divas tonight. And niggas and bitches in there ain't gonna have a choice but to respect us." Cristal already had the perfect outfit picked out.

Tamar was still indecisive on what she wanted to wear. Cristal continued gazing out her fifth-floor window, smoking and waiting for Tamar to finish rolling up the blunt. She stuck her attention on two fiends walking briskly through the trashy courtyard, Marvin and Henry. They were life's worst—two bottom-feeders in society with nothing in their future but despair. Marvin was her older cousin, but she had no remorse or concern for him. If he wanted to smoke crack and ruin his life, then it was his choice. Henry was his close friend. They used to be bright, young men with promising futures; now, they were dirty, soulless fiends whose main purpose in life was to smoke crack.

Tamar precisely sprinkled and loaded the freshly ground pink weed into the cut-open blunt wrap. She noticed something had Cristal's attention.

"What you lookin' at?" Tamar asked as she rolled the blunt with her mouthpiece in her right hand and burned the other end in her left, rolling left to right.

"Lookin' at my stupid cousin trying to score crack," Cristal said.

"Crazy. I can't believe that's your cousin."

"He's distant, like third cousin or sumthin'."

"He slipped that far. Wasn't he smart and some scholar growing up?"

"Yup, he was."

Tamar tucked the bottom flap of the blunt under the top flap, using her thumbs and thumbnails. When it came to rolling up weed, she was the expert—she and Mona.

"How do people get like that?" Tamar asked rhetorically.

"Being stupid," Cristal replied indifferently.

"Well, we about to get this money. We got over two dozen items in your closet to sell off, not including what we kept for ourselves, so we gonna get paid regardless. And if things work out tonight, girl, we about to see the hood in our rearview mirror," Tamar proclaimed.

"I cosign on that," Cristal replied, walking over and giving her friend another celebratory high-five.

With the evening moving on, their friend Lisa opted not to attend the party tonight. She was having issues with her man, but Mona and Sharon were still going. The girls rendezvoused at Cristal's place, as usual, and they all got dressed in her bedroom. As always, weed smoke crammed the bedroom, ladies' clothing was scattered everywhere, and the music had gotten louder.

By 9pm, the girls were halfway ready. Makeup and hair still needed to be done, but their attire was well put together. Excitement was in the air about meeting E.P. at one of his parties. Some considered him a legitimate and shrewd businessman and some considered him a violent gangster, but whatever they said about him, he was highly respected by everyone.

"What time is Pike picking us up again?" Mona asked.

"He said around ten," answered Cristal.

"Shit, we need to hurry up then. I still need to do my hair," Mona said.

It was a mini party: four young girls confined in the small bedroom with big dreams and aspirations. Twenty minutes after 10pm, all four girls stepped out of the building looking stunning, from ghetto to classy. Rich and Pike gazed at them from the burgundy minivan they were about to pile into.

Cristal looked marvelous in a Herve Leger signature scoop dress and stilettos that made her smooth, defined legs stretch to the stars. Her makeup was flawless, her long black hair radiant, and her jewelry glimmering like diamonds. The price tag on the stolen dress was two grand.

Tamar wore a Chanel lace dress with her Jimmy Choos, and her long hair looked sensuous. She carried her chic clutch and was ready to do her tonight.

Mona sported a simply stunning Stella McCartney ruched dress and Sharon wore a sexy, silk, one-piece jumpsuit and Christian Louboutin stilettos. Her natural afro was wild and her Ruby Woo lipstick made her just as pretty as the others. The girls' transformation was unprecedented. Pike and Rich looked surprised from the front seat of the minivan.

When the girls piled into the back, Tamar commented, "Damn, y'all pickin' us up in a dusty minivan."

"Well, next time we'll take your Benz," Rich countered wittily.

It was always something from him or her.

Tonight, they were going to be like four princesses in the king's castle.

FOUR

The 5,000-square foot Royal Penthouse Suite in midtown Manhattan was breathtaking from wall to wall. The suite took up a quarter of the 36th floor, which was the top floor and had four great bedrooms, its own spa-treatment pod, and a striking spiral staircase. Minimalist and furnished with pieces by the likes of designers Antonia Citterio and B&B Italia, the suite featured a wide, picturesque view of Central Park. For real luxe, the helicopter transport above the suite was out of this world.

E.P.'s guests entered the suite via a private courtyard that continued up to a sky lounge with an outdoor bed. There was a 46-by-12-foot pool and terrace. Stone floors and concrete walls added to the natural feel, and a bench carved out of one of the outer concrete walls emphasized the oneness with the surrounding land. Out on the wide glass terrace, guests marveled at the constellation-filled night sky above.

E.P.'s party was classy and well attended. The cream of the crop guests were in attendance—from distinguished CEO's of Fortune 500 companies, music moguls, a sprinkle of celebrities and high-profile athletes, and some of the most beautiful, stunning women ever seen. Everyone was suited up stylishly, the men clad in tuxedos and bow ties and the ladies in lavish dresses and gowns.

Expensive champagne was being sipped from long-stemmed glasses with hors d'oeuvres being passed around, people mingling, and contributory talk filling the room. The music was low, Jill Scott, Alicia

Keys, Maxwell, and other platinum singers moderately playing in the room. Each invited guest had to give a password to enter—"Machiavelli."

E.P.'s party was also heavy with security, dressed formally in suits with holstered weapons concealed underneath their jackets, earpiece communication showing in their right ears, and their presence felt strongly as they moved around subtly.

Pike and Rich walked into the impressive suite in their dark suits with the girls following behind them like they were two pimps leading a stable. Instantly upon arrival, each girl felt out of their league—like fish out of water. They looked around; the atmosphere was entirely foreign to them, and the sophisticated folks around made them feel a touch of intimidation. These people were exceedingly educated with numerous degrees and top-ranking positions in the business world or were the best in their careers, from sports and singing to Wall Street or marketing. The majority of them spoke more than one language, had traveled the world, and were able to speak complete sentences, not including Ebonics.

Some of the partygoers interned at Global Grind, Sean John, and MTV, some were in law school or were A-list actors with major movie roles. Who were Cristal and her crew—a bunch of wannabes from rough neighborhoods with little education and violent pasts? Yes, they looked the part for the moment, but the way the snobbish bitches in the party stared at them disapprovingly it was already becoming an unsettling environment and it seemed like their cover was blown.

"I need a drink," said Cristal, leaving her crew and walking toward the open bar. The men she walked by gazed pleasantly at her.

Tamar followed behind her friend, and then the other two also got courage and moved in the direction of the bar. Pike and Rich were now following behind them. At the bar, Cristal ordered a Cîroc Peach and Sprite. She took a few sips and sighed. It was going to take some liquid courage to deal with these people.

"Shit is really nice," Mona said, looking around the suite with high regard. "Now this is how a bitch should be living."

"I feel you," Tamar agreed.

Immediately, the girls started to look around for E.P., the host of this extravagant affair, but he was nowhere to be found. And even though Cristal never met or saw the man before, she had a feeling that once she saw him, she would immediately recognize him. It would be easy; he would be the man with all the swag in the room.

Pike played Sharon closely at the party. He repeatedly complimented her on her outfit and how good she looked. She blushed and ate up his flattery with a silver spoon. It felt good to be wanted, especially by a man whom the ladies yearned to be with. But she wasn't a fool and couldn't be sure of his angle. Was it a game to try and get some pussy, or did he genuinely like her? She didn't want to be hurt.

After a few drinks, with that liquid courage mixing into their bloodstreams, the girls started to work the room and mingle with other guests. They took advantage of the hors d'oeuvres being served and being among some of the city's elite.

An hour passed and still, no E.P. It seemed like either he wasn't going to show or planned on making a grand entrance to his own party. However, Cristal and Tamar had the eyes of some of the wealthiest men in the room. They smiled and flirted, and enjoyed the undivided attention that they were receiving from such handsome business executives. It felt good. One was an investment banker, and the other was a stockbroker—both in their early forties.

"You're an angel, Cristal, and it's finally good to know what a piece of heaven feels like," the investment banker said with his weak game.

Cristal blushed. White boy had some game to him, and he wasn't bad-looking either. But he wasn't the grand prize. An hour later, before midnight struck, E.P. finally made his presence known. He walked through the double oak doors flanked by two beefy bouncers. Instantaneously, he had everyone's attention, including Cristal and Tamar's. Their eyes were fixed on him from afar with admiration in their stare. E.P. definitely had swag. Tom Ford was against his skin in the charcoal suit he wore, and he screamed masculinity. The man couldn't help but stand out amongst any crowd he engaged with. He had titan shoulders along with his burly physique, and his onyx-colored eyes exuded confidence.

Cristal felt excited just to be in the same room with him. Her attention was fixed on his every move. She watched him walk through the room greeting his numerous guests casually. He smiled and worked the room like a politician. And then just like that, E.P. went upstairs into an upper room of the suite flanked by a few of his business associates and held a private meeting.

Cristal hurried toward Pike and asked, "Are you goin' to introduce me to him?"

"In due time. Can't you see that he's a really busy man?"

"Yeah, but you're the one who boasted you knew him well. So I would like to get to know him well too."

Pike smiled. "I bet you would."

"It's business," she shot back.

"And what business is that?"

"None of your concern."

He laughed.

Unbeknownst to everyone, E.P. stood above the party watching everyone and everything cautiously. He knew almost every face at his party; it was his business to know the people in his surroundings. Every face he met in life, he remembered. He had a photographic memory. Some of the people at his high-end event he did business with, and a few were just personal in his life. He sipped champagne and smoked a Cuban cigar. The room he was in was filled with computers and high-tech surveillance equipment, including state-of-the-art facial recognition scanners. E.P. watched the room. He noticed Pike and the beautiful young lady he was with. She caught his attention. She was a new face to him, and so were the friends she'd come with.

With his attention fixed on Cristal and the phenomenal dress she was in, E.P. studied how she handled herself in the room. She stood out because of her cocksure demeanor. Cristal didn't appear posh like the other women at his party. She was able to mingle in with his astute guests and had Wayne Bronson, a prominent CFO at Mumma Industries, and a billionaire at that, laughing and eating out of the palm of her hand. E.P. knew Wayne Bronson was a hardass—an asshole, and it was hard to have his undivided attention. Many beautiful women had tried but failed to do so. But there she was, with his eyes upon her like she was the crown jewel. Interesting. What was she saying to him? It didn't take long for E.P. to deduce that this beautiful woman in her form-fitting dress was the head bitch in her crew. She seemed intriguing and also daring.

E.P. took a few pulls from his expensive cigar and felt it was time to make himself known again. He stepped out of the private room, walked down the spiral stairway, and slid back into his event. Pike, Cristal, and Wayne Bronson were on the other side of the main room, standing near the terrace entrance. E.P. navigated his way through the chatting crowd, turning down everyone that wanted a quick word with him. He moved their way smoothly like skates on ice.

When he didn't want to be bothered with, E.P. didn't bother with you. He was focused on getting to know this beautiful woman in the distance.

His steely glare was fixed on Cristal. Pike noticed E.P. approaching and his posture changed. His hands became clammy. He fidgeted a little. He would never admit it, but he always got nervous when he was around E.P. They were casual friends. However, this business tycoon was hardcore and shrewd, and was a mystery to everyone.

When Cristal saw E.P. coming their way, and a slight feeling of trepidation swooped through her. She tried not to stare, but she couldn't help it: The closer he came, the more handsome she noticed he was, with his thick goatee and dark skin. She breathed lightly, trying not to have a panic attack. Cristal was the type of bitch that never got nervous around any man, but with E.P., she found her heart beating rapidly and butterflies dancing in her belly.

"Wayne, I haven't seen you smile this hard since your company's merger with Global Media last year," E.P. said composedly, with his award-winning smile.

The man chuckled at E.P.'s rare humor.

"E.P., nice party, and nice scenery too," Wayne said, glancing at Cristal. She smiled.

"I'm glad you're enjoying yourself," said E.P.

"Which reminds me, E.P., before night's end, would it be any hassle to you if we could talk and go over the PSKG account?"

"I'll have my people come talk to you real soon," he said.

Wayne nodded. The two men shook hands, but E.P. seemed more interested in other things.

"It was nice conversing with you, Cristal. It's been my pleasure," said Wayne.

"Same here," Cristal returned pleasantly. E.P. turned to Pike and said, "Pike, I'm glad that you and your beautiful friend could make it to my party. Please, make the introduction."

"E.P., this is Cristal. She's a good friend of mine from around the way."

E.P. extended his bejeweled hand toward Cristal, gazed at her loveliness and said, "It's a pleasure meeting you, Cristal. You are an extremely beautiful woman."

"Thank you," Cristal said, blushing somewhat.

"Pike, where have you been hiding this beauty for so long?" he asked.

"Brooklyn," Cristal said.

"Well, I see I'm going to start making frequent trips into Brooklyn if they're breeding beautiful ladies such as you." E.P. was clearly flirting and his words were smooth, his demeanor confident.

Cristal gazed into his eyes and his firm stare was almost hypnotic. His stature was tall and alluring. Cristal had the urge to wrap herself in his arms and exhale like Angela Bassett. She was flattered to have this man's attention. Pike played the background while Cristal and E.P. were engaged in conversation.

"So tell me, what is your secret?" E.P. asked.

"My secret?" Cristal replied, looking slightly dumbfounded.

"How did you get a man like Wayne Bronson's attention? The man's a hardass; he makes Karl Marx look like Mickey Mouse."

"I told him he was ugly and poor in my book," she joked. "I'm just real like that."

E.P. chuckled. "Maybe I need to use some of your technique in some of my meetings; lighten the mood a little and squeeze more money out of my clients."

"It's fine wit' me, as long as I get my percentage."

"I'm a reasonable man."

"And I'm a real woman."

The two locked eyes while talking and feeling some chemistry mixing between them, but their private little conversation was curtailed when Tamar looked over and noticed Cristal had E.P.'s undivided attention. She and her friends marched over their way with a sense of urgency, with Tamar not wanting Cristal to have all his attention.

"I see you met my best friend," Tamar chided, and smiled widely in E.P.'s face.

Cristal cut her eyes at her friend, feeling Tamar was trying to cock block with her pussy.

"And you are?" E.P. asked Tamar nicely.

Pike stepped forward to make the introduction. "E.P., this Tamar, Mona, and Sharon; also friends from the area."

"It's a pleasure meeting all of you. I hope y'all are having a great time at my party."

"We are. This joint is nice, E.P.," Mona said with an impressed expression.

"Thank you. I paid a pretty penny for it," E.P. revealed.

"How many pennies?" Mona asked daringly.

"Mona!" Cristal exclaimed, being embarrassed that Mona would ask him such a personal question. "You don't ask the man his business like that."

"It's okay," E.P. said, chuckling slightly.

"But she shouldn't be asking you those types of questions."

"It's a free country, and I can ask any questions I want," Mona spat back.

"It's called manners," replied Cristal sharply.

"Ladies, please, no arguments because of me. We are all here to have a good time tonight, right?"

"Right," they replied.

E.P. looked around for one of his well-dressed waiters in black moving about the classy crowd carrying a tray of champagne, and he snapped his fingers. The waiter hurried over and E.P. put a glass of expensive champagne in everyone's hand.

He smiled and then raised his glass in the air. Everyone else followed his motion. Getting ready to propose a toast, E.P. stared at Cristal, then at the others and proclaimed, "Life is good, and let it continue to be that way."

They all toasted, clinging their glasses together and then downed the bubbly like it was water. The girls felt privileged to be drinking champagne with the infamous E.P. in one of the most luxurious penthouse suites in the city. It was like a dream come true. They were surrounded by money, power, and respect. Though Midtown was only a few miles away from Brooklyn, it was a world away from their homes. It was a world they had always craved to become a part of. Pookie, Tank, Hitch, and the other Brooklyn thugs who sold drugs in the hood and got money on the block couldn't even compare to the power and wealth these men had. Compared with E.P. and his associates, drug dealers in Brooklyn didn't know what making real money was. Wall Street, banking, computers, real estate—these men made money and tons of it.

For the duration of the night, E.P. continued to show Cristal so much attention. It was obvious who E.P. was interested in, making Tamar feel somewhat jealous that Cristal was able to snatch up the main catch. With Pike's interest on Sharon and Mona chatting up a cute ballplayer, Tamar felt left out in the cold.

Around 3am, the party started to wind down. With the guests dwindling from the penthouse suite, E.P. got some time alone with Cristal outside on his towering terrace. The sprawling view of Central Park from above was a first-time experience for Cristal. She gazed at the greenery below with astonishment. She stood underneath a blanket of black with a sprinkling of white stars showing above her head, even with the glare of lights coming from the city.

"This is so beautiful," she said.

"It is," E.P. agreed.

The view from the top floor above was different. Being on top the world, even if it was temporary, was an exhilarating feeling for Cristal. She wanted to nestle in E.P.'s arms and feel wanted and secure. She wanted this life.

E.P. asked her to stay the night with him, and she happily accepted. She was down for whatever. Tamar and the others looked reluctant to leave without their friend, but E.P. assured everyone that she was in good hands. Tamar remarked, "Cristal, we came together so we should leave together."

Cristal wasn't ready to leave together. She stated she was staying with her newfound friend. Tamar showed some jealousy and when she said, "Cristal, you don't even know this man." She clearly was upset that she wasn't the one who had E.P.'s undivided attention. Tamar was leaving alone with no perks or benefits. She huffed and frowned, ready to become the bad apple out of the bunch. Cristal was adamant in her decision. She was staying. It had been a really fun night for her so far, and she wanted to continue on with the fun.

With the crowd gone, the two had their privacy. The suite was quiet. E.P. didn't waste any time making his move on Cristal. Seeing her alone and admiring her backside in the dress she wore, he slid behind her like the wind blowing and wrapped his arms around this beautiful creature.

"You're so beautiful," he whispered in her ear.

She smiled.

He nestled her into his arms and squeezed her gently.

"I love it out here," she said.

"I do too."

E.P. kissed the back of her neck lightly, his lips feeling so good against her skin. Cristal's thoughts and fantasies began to fill with the need to be with him—to feel him inside of her, to become one with each other.

He moved his hand up her thigh and underneath her dress. She longed to feel his mouth on every part of her. She desired to be covered with his sweet kisses as she felt his body pressed into her. He pushed aside her panties and slipped his fingers into her honey-sweet nectar and targeted her clit, making Cristal squirm from the overwhelming sensation.

Cristal cooed, needing to feel his lips exploring every curve, every crevice of her caramel-colored frame. She wasn't ready for the slow and gentle lovemaking with candles burning and Teddy Pendergrass playing in the background. Cristal was ready for a hardcore fuck. She wanted that million- or billion-dollar dick to be rammed inside her pussy so hard and fast she wanted to spit out cum. E.P. needed to understand that her body was a gift to him. She loved getting fucked. The way he touched her, fondling her body like he was molding clay, made her pussy quiver like a small earthquake.

Under the cool summer night air, E.P. pulled her dress up and snatched her panties down. He started to unbuckle his pants. Removing his thick, piece of hard flesh, E.P. stroked his pulsating tool near her goodies.

"You got a condom?" Cristal asked, ready to practice safe sex.

"Yeah, I do."

Removing a Magnum condom from his pocket, he was becoming so incredibly aroused that he was driven to a fit of lust. He played with her hard nipples until she was burning with passion. She was ready to spread her legs and invite him inside of her to explore her erotic folds of femininity and tease her aroused clit gently and softly, ensuring that she whimpered and pleaded for release. E.P. fondled her below like he created the pussy, making love to her with his hand, feeling her slippery wetness.

"I wanna fuck you so hard and deep," he growled into her ear.

"Mmmm," she moaned, feeling his fingers penetrating her smoothly.

E.P. sat Cristal on the terrace railing, her legs spread, and her panties ripped off. E.P. rolled the Magnum condom onto his hard, throbbing steel piece of flesh. His manhood was very impressive.

At first, he penetrated her slow and deliberately, deep and hard. They both suddenly found themselves wrapped in a sexual frenzy. E.P. thrust inside of her tight pussy as Cristal jerked forward, gripping the railing. He cupped her tits and squeezed her ass. She wanted to feel every hot, hard, throbbing inch of him inside of her.

He fucked her.

She was dripping with desires from everywhere as their bodies collided in unison and ecstasy. He fucked her for a long moment, the summer swirling them up. Her pussy swallowed up his hard, pounding flesh as he gazed into her lovely face. He tasted the softness of her lips and his tongue explored further. Their tongues danced together. It was a rhythmic dance; it was kissing as an art form. E.P. palmed her fleshy backside and cupped her tits again. Her body was a masterpiece. He could feel the underside of his tongue gently grazing her bottom teeth. He inhaled her breath as his own. E.P. couldn't stop kissing her.

Cristal was like a sensual fruit he wanted to devour. He was savoring every inch of her with his mouth, his lips, and his tongue. He kissed her body fervently. He peeled away the expensive black dress from her curvy frame, absorbed by her nudity.

Once again, he uttered the words, "You're beautiful."

Cristal was his main course. She had never fucked a millionaire before, and it was everything she dreamed of. E.P. pulled her into his arms and positioned his beauty of the night on her back against a table on the terrace. She opened her legs for him and he was ready to slam himself between her meaty thighs. He was consumed by lust.

The freaky action transitioned from the terrace to inside the suite, and then into the plush bedroom. E.P. pulled his naked beauty close to him again and she fell on the bed next to him. Fucking her throughout the suite like rabbits, he still didn't need a minute to calm down.

Sprawled butt-naked on the king-size bed, E.P.'s stomach rippled with abs. His arms defined with cuts and his chiseled features indicated he worked out on a regular basis.

Cristal straddled him and slammed her pussy down on his hard shaft. Her pussy fit like a glove.

"Fuck me!" she cried out.

She rode him. There was something about her pussy that made him moan loudly, the way she ground her body into him, wrinkling the silk sheets underneath them. Cristal was a woman on a mission. Placing her feet on the bed and her hands on his chest, she rode E.P. like a champion. She made eye contact with him and used her muscles to milk him. E.P. fidgeted with pleasure underneath her. He reached up to play with her nipples as her juices coated him.

"I'm coming!" he hollered.

"I'm going to cum all over you," she hollered subsequently.

Panting and breathing with juicy and squishing sex like they'd both run the NYC marathon, they both were at the point of no return. Cristal couldn't hold back any longer. As she came, she screamed as E.P. gripped her hips and delivered his essence into the condom as they both exploded together in the wee hours of the next day.

She rolled over on her back and breathed. E.P. did the same. In her mind, this was one of her dreams come true. She put that pussy on his ass and now she was ready to sleep for hours.

FIVE

●●

The morning sun percolating into the luxurious suite indicated that it was going to be another beautiful, summer day. The radiant light seeping through the floor-to-ceiling windows made Cristal stir awake and she found herself naked and alone in the bed. E.P. wasn't by her side. She'd slept like a baby for seven hours straight. The king-size bed she lay in was so comfortable it felt like she had slept on clouds, and the white silk sheets beneath her seemed to be massaging her skin. The room was quiet. Cristal propped herself up against the headboard and gazed at the décor of the bedroom. It looked completely different in the daylight. Maybe it was because she was too busy taking dick the night before. The décor of the room was tastefully done up in various cultures— European art and sculptures displayed on the walls and shelves. There was a sixteenth-century ivory mask from Benin, and a twelfth-century Yoruba bronze head sculpture from Nigeria, with long spears and uncanny shields from villainous African warriors and what looked like a picture of Shaka Zulu over his bed. Then there were the customized steel samurai swords hanging on the walls of the room and a life-size samurai warrior in full armor poised for battle near the bedroom door. E.P. seemed to have a taste for weaponry and warriors.

It was kind of interesting, but also creepy.

Where was E.P.? Cristal asked herself. She removed herself from the bed and walked toward the window naked. She stepped out onto the terrace and gazed out at Central Park in the sunlight, hearing the city alive with movement. Manhattan was bustling below. She took a deep breath and felt wonderful. Last night with E.P. had been so magical. Having had a millionaire fuck her vigorously—how could she go back to the average muthafucka in Brooklyn?

A few moments passed and E.P. joined her out on the terrace. He was clad in a long, blue terry cloth robe and had made them some coffee. He handed Cristal her cup and she took a few sips.

"Good morning," he said.

"Good morning." Cristal smiled with last night still lingering in her head.

"How did you sleep?"

"I slept fine."

"Good."

"I could get so used to this," said Cristal, turning and gazing at the picturesque view for the umpteenth time since she arrived last night. She took another sip of coffee. She wasn't a coffee drinker, but it felt great to do something different in her life. It was strong and black, just how she would describe herself, and it went down her throat like hot water. She stood naked in front of E.P. like it was natural. He gazed at her body with an emotionless stare. The fire that he had in his eyes last night had dissipated. Now he seemed aloof, almost a different person.

Was he bored with her already?

Cristal hoped he wasn't going to be an asshole and just toss her out after he'd gotten what he wanted. If so, she wasn't afraid to give him a few choice words.

"Maybe I should put something on," she said.

"No need to," he said.

"You wanna fuck again?" Cristal asked nonchalantly.

E.P. ignored the question. He looked at her, not with desire, but as if he were studying her—sizing her up. His rapt gaze made Cristal somewhat uncomfortable. Knowing that he was a man who could have anything he wanted on this planet, she thought, why her? She saw the pictures on his wall: E.P. had been with A-list actors, supermodels, and women much more classy and elegant than her. He could get pussy from anyone he wanted. He was extremely handsome with a masculine physique. What was his true interest in her?

E.P. walked into the bedroom. Cristal followed behind him. Why didn't he answer her question? she thought. She wasn't in any rush to get dressed. She now wanted some condom-less dick. Hey, maybe she could hit the jackpot and become pregnant by him. It was farfetched thinking, but a girl could dream—even if it was super crazy, Cristal thought like a chickenhead. She didn't have her high-school diploma, she had no real trade, and she'd come up rough while living in Brooklyn. A rich baby daddy, and then maybe all of her worries would be solved.

E.P. went toward the small bar in his room. He substituted the hot coffee for some red wine. He took a few sips and looked at Cristal. She sat on the bed naked and kept quiet. EP walked closer to her. He took a few sips of wine and out of the blue asked, "Are you a get-money type of bitch?"

"Excuse me?" Cristal returned, looking taken aback by his question.

"How do you get paid?" he asked so calmly.

Cristal was still speechless for a moment. What made him ask that? She wondered. And what could she tell him? This man was on top of his game. He had everything in life and some. She didn't have an education. It was embarrassing to tell E.P. that she had to mooch off her mother's welfare checks. Or that she was a criminal, selling drugs, being a drug mule for a local dealer, and boosting with her friends. Or that she fucked random niggas in Brooklyn—all to keep Giuseppe heels on her feet and designer fabric around her skin.

"I'm in school at the moment, and I work in the mall," she lied.

"College, huh? What is your major?"

"Business," she replied.

"Business, huh," he replied dubiously. "You don't look like a business major."

His incredulous stare already told Cristal that he didn't believe her lie. Cristal fidgeted around uneasily on his bed. His hard look burned into her. It felt like he could see right through her as if she were transparent. Unexpectedly, he said to her, "I want you to come and work for my organization."

Dumbfounded by his proposition, she uttered, "Me?" She didn't know anything about his organization.

"Why not? What else is there for you out there?" he replied indifferently.

She looked at him and purred, "Like what, a nine-to-five sucking your dick or something? Being your sex slave? Some twenty-four-hour pussy on call?"

"Is that all you're good at? Do you think that low of yourself?"

The response from him made Cristal think for a second. It made her feel small suddenly. It felt like she was shrinking in the room. In Brooklyn, she was that bitch, but in the city, she was just some random jump off. But no matter what, no man had the right to talk to her in such a belittling tone.

She stood up with her face shaping into a frown.

"Look, I keep it real. If I can't keep it one hundred wit' me then I can't expect no one else too," she announced while slamming her hand against her chest to prove her point.

Suddenly, she didn't feel natural or comfortable anymore around him. She was offended by his statement. She was from the hood, but that didn't make him better than her.

E.P. didn't care if he offended her or not. They were in his domain, and he was calling the shots.

"So you like to keep it real? Then keep it real, Cristal," he said in a stern tone, his look fixed on her nudity. "What are you good at?"

"What you think I'm good at," she replied sleazily.

"Sell yourself; not your pussy." It was a cold response.

Cristal didn't see that one coming. She pulled the sheet from off the bed and covered her nakedness with it, suddenly feeling vulnerable around him. She wanted to get dressed. But her dress was nowhere in the room.

"I was good at math, until I dropped out of high school," she revealed.

"You can't put 'high-school dropout' on your résumé. Try again. Sell yourself. Sell me a skill, make me believe in you," he said harshly.

"I can cook coke," she said meekly.

"Okay, give me something that's not a cliché. What else?" he continued to press on.

Cristal didn't know what to tell this man. Why was he unexpectedly giving her the third degree? What was his angle? He didn't want to fuck anymore; now it was Q&A in his suite, like it was a job interview.

"Umm, I think I got mad boosting skills. I can walk into any high-end store with security and cameras and walk out wit' tens of thousands of dollars' worth of merchandise. Me and my homegirl, we been boosting since we were ten years old, and we rarely get caught. Only twice, when we were, like, fourteen," she boasted.

"You walk out yourself with the merchandise?"

"Sometimes. But most times I have one of the little shorties walk out holding the bag of merchandise. See, we got this scheme we do call bag-switching, and we be robbing these stores blind," she said proudly.

E.P. wasn't impressed.

"What other skills do you have? And think before you answer. You only have two more skills to tell me about before I make my decision. So it will behoove you to make these count," he said.

Behoove me? Cristal didn't even know what the word meant. She had really no idea what to say to him. She was suddenly thrust into this interrogation like she had committed some crime. If she only knew what job she was applying for then it would probably help tremendously with her answers.

"Well, on a real job interview I would know what to write or say because I would be applying for it," she revealed.

"Do you truly believe that?" E.P. returned.

She nodded.

"So would you lie depending on what position you were applying for?"

"Hell yeah," Cristal quickly answered.

"Okay, so that's skill number two . . . being manipulative," he said. "Next."

"Wait, I didn't mean it like that," Cristal said with some panic in her voice. "You can't use that."

"So, you're indecisive?"

"Huh?"

He sighed.

"I was asking you a question, and how can you say that, just tell me where all this is goin'," she exclaimed. "Do I really need to answer you?"

"Sweetheart, let's get one thing straight. I'm the boss, so I can do whatever I want. Do you understand me?" he returned in a stern but cool voice. His eyes pierced into her while she was still wrapped with a bedroom sheet.

Cristal nodded submissively.

"Now, what is your last skill? Do you have any more? And Cristal, before you speak, I want to let you know it will get no realer than this job. You might want to keep that in the forefront of your mind," E.P. said.

While Cristal thought long and hard about her next answer, E.P. picked up the room phone and dialed a number. Someone picked up and

E.P. said into the phone, "Yes, deliver me my usual today . . . over easy, and grilled."

E.P. glanced at Cristal while she was still mulling over the right answer to give him and asked, "Are you hungry?"

She shook her head, no. E.P. ordered a few more things and hung up.

The minute he was off the phone, Cristal blurted out, "I get really busy wit' my hands. I have been known not only to beat bitches down, but I'm nice wit' a razor and knives. I don't get fucked wit'. I get mad respect in the hood."

That was all she had to give him. She exhaled, almost defeated. E.P. just nodded. He reached into his robe pulling out a few wad of bills and tossed the cash at Cristal. She caught it, confused, and then she watched him dismissively excuse himself from the room. He needed to take a shower before his room service arrived.

Cristal stared at the money in her hand. Five hundred dollars he'd given her. She felt like a prostitute—such a slut. And then she started to question herself. She felt so stupid to think that she had some marketable skills for a job, especially when it came to working for a man like E.P. Ghetto and stupid was how she felt. The skills she'd told him about weren't anything but average or subpar, things she could never put on any résumé, even if she were applying for a job at McDonald's. She didn't know anything about computers—advanced Excel, spreadsheets or how to put together a PowerPoint presentation. She had no real trade. The realization sunk into her: She was a hood bitch and there wasn't any way she could ever work for someone like E.P. and his corporation.

Cristal started to think about the females she saw at his party last night—classy women with eloquence and style who had mountains of degrees and spoke numerous languages. They were educated and intelligent. Cristal knew she wasn't. She couldn't hold a candle to these bitches. If they were on the streets, then it would have been a different story. These bitches would have been food to her. However, how could she have been roped in so easily by E.P.? All he wanted was an easy fuck and she lived up to it—gave him what he wanted.

While E.P. was in the shower, Cristal removed the sheet from around her and walked around his suite naked, gathering her things. It was time to leave. She felt played and had overstayed her welcome. She slid back into her stolen dress which had been left on the terrace overnight, grabbed her shoes, and looked around for her panties and clutch.

In the bedroom, she glanced down at the money he left for her on the ruffled comforter and soiled sheets. She wrestled with the decision of whether to take the money or not. She needed the extra cash.

While E.P. was still in the shower, she searched frantically for her purse and panties. She didn't want to leave anything behind. She found her Victoria's Secret underwear and Chanel clutch wedged in between the sofa and pillows.

Cristal knew this wasn't her level. These people were so far out there, it hurt when she tried to breathe. She felt way in over her head. It had been fun while it lasted, but now the high she felt from last night came crashing down on her.

With her things in her hand, she made a beeline for the door, but before she could make her exit, his voice boomed out. "Stop walking!"

Cristal froze by the door. Her breath hitched. She turned around slowly to see E.P. standing behind her with a white towel draped around his waist and five hundred dollars clutched in his hand.

"What do you want from me?" Cristal cried out. "I'm tired of the questions and these games."

"If you want the job, then you have to learn not to get too emotional. I gave you this money because I wanted you to have it. It's yours," he said coolly.

"There isn't any job, is there?"

E.P. chuckled. "You're going to need more work than I thought. Drop your things, take a shower, have breakfast with me, and I'll explain everything."

Cristal was reluctant. She was filled with questioning and apprehension. Could she trust him? And what was hidden behind his layers? These were the hardest questions of her life.

E.P. approached her slowly. Cristal stood still, not knowing what to do with herself. Their eyes locked; the room was still and brightly lit with the morning sun. Cristal couldn't run from him. He reached for her things, taking her clutch bag from her hand and tossing it on the sofa as if to say, "Stay put!" He took her hand in his, pulled her forward, gently kissed her on the cheek and softly said, "Trust me. What I have to say will benefit you greatly."

Cristal felt she didn't have a choice. She had the job whether she wanted it or not.

SIX

●●●●●●●●●●●●●●●●●●●●●●●●●●●●●●●●●●●●●

Sharon just couldn't turn her head away as she watched Pike walk around his apartment shirtless. He oozed sexiness. He was in the kitchen getting himself a beer from the fridge. Sharon was seated on the couch feeling ambivalent about being in Pike's apartment alone. Why had she agreed to spend the night with him? She didn't want to regret it. She really liked him, but men only wanted one thing—sex. And Pike was the epitome of a male dog. She wasn't about to be some booty call. With her friends and Rich not around talking, smoking weed, and joking, Pike's apartment felt a little more intimate than it had on her previous visits.

Sharon decided to come back to his place after they left E.P.'s party because it was something to do. Her own home was in shambles and dysfunctional. Being at Pike's place gave her some temporary peace of mind from her cracked-out mother and her mom's perverted boyfriend.

Pike had dropped her friends off in Brooklyn, and then Rich. Afterwards, the two went to get something to eat at a twenty-four-hour diner in the city, and then it was back to Harlem during the wee hours of the morning.

She wasn't tired at all. She wanted to sit and talk.

Talk. Pike was never the one to talk when he had a woman over. There wasn't one woman who didn't surrender to his lust and desires—after a half-hour or less in his place, girls had their clothes and panties off, and took his dick whichever way he threw it inside of them.

He had Sharon in his sight for next.

Pike emerged from the kitchen taking a swig from the beer in his hand. He eyed Sharon seated on his cushy couch with her thick legs crossed. She appeared to be comfortable around him and was quiet. Pike's abs rippled with sexiness and his smile was inviting. The basketball shorts he wore caught Sharon's attention because his big, fat dick was bulging out from underneath, indicating he wasn't wearing any underwear.

"You good?" Pike asked.

"I'm okay."

"You sure you don't want anything to drink?"

"Pike, I had enough to drink at the party," she said.

Pike took another mouthful of beer. He burped loudly, which was followed up by a quick, "Excuse me. Where are my manners?"

Sharon smiled. "It's natural."

"Yeah, just like you," Pike said with a lustful grin aimed at her.

He decided to take a seat next to her. He was ready to make his move. Sharon's thick thighs and balloon tits covered up snugly in the jumpsuit she wore were driving him crazy. He undressed her with his eyes and he instantly knew she had that good, chocolate berry pussy. He was ready to sink his dick into her like an anchor and fuck the shit out of her. Pike nestled himself next to Sharon and placed his arm around her. The TV was on, and he thanked God it wasn't broken during the fight between Mesha, and Cristal's crew.

"You know, you're beautiful, Sharon," he said, smiling pleasantly.

"Thank you."

"Why is it that you don't have a man in your life yet?" he asked.

"I'm still waiting on the right one," she responded.

"What's your type of guy then?" he asked.

It was a simple question to answer. Smiling with innocence, she said, "Someone who's smart, ambitious, caring, and sexy."

"I can be that guy and more."

"You can, huh?"

He nodded. He locked eyes with her and yearned to have Sharon twisted in every freaky position he could think of. He wanted to kiss her. Her lips were so full and pouty. Pike wanted to slip his tongue into her mouth and taste her breath.

Leaning forward, he kissed the side of her neck gently and slowly. She laughed and smiled. "That tickles," she uttered.

"It do?"

"Yes."

"So, what else is ticklish on you?" said Pike, placing his hand on her thigh and moving it upwards slowly.

He was ready to palm some of her goodies. He neared his touch near her pussy, but Sharon wasn't having any part of it. Not tonight, not now. She gripped his wrist and pulled away his touch. Her strength was impressive.

"What's wrong?" he asked, looking perturbed that she interrupted his quest for her glory.

"I didn't come here for that," she revealed.

"So what did you come here for?" Pike spat.

"I came to talk and get to know you better."

He chuckled, and then said, "This is how we get to know each other better."

Pike pressed forward, placing his hand against her thigh once more, yearning to fondle her goodies below and caress her breasts like a masseur. He tried to kiss her, but Sharon quickly pushed him away and stood up like she had been ejected from the seat. She straightened her ruffled jumpsuit.

"C'mon! What the fuck, Sharon? I want you," he hollered.

Pike was enticing, Sharon had to admit that to herself, but he was spoiled. He was always the high-school and neighborhood star and the girls always gave in to him. The word "no" was a different language to him, but Sharon wanted to be different. He wasn't going to have his way with her—this wasn't Burger King. Yeah, her pussy throbbed and tingled for some dick, because it had been a long while since she'd had some, but she was able to resist the temptation. She wanted to be respected as a woman.

"I'm not ready," she said.

"You a virgin?"

"No!" she replied tersely.

"So what is it?"

"I'm just not fuckin' you tonight," she said with conviction.

Pike looked aghast that this bitch had the audacity to turn him down. He glared at her. He had finer and better women than Sharon in his apartment, and they weren't hard like she was.

"You serious?"

She nodded.

Pike pulled down his basketball shorts and revealed the long, black and thick fleshy machine that hung between his legs. It was pulsating to be thrust inside of her. He palmed his dick and started stroking himself gently in front of Sharon. He had no shame in his game. He figured if Sharon wanted to be difficult then showing his big, black dick would definitely change her mind.

Sharon was impressed by it, it looked so healthy and strong, but she still wasn't changing her mind. She didn't budge from her decision.

"You know not wanting to fuck me quickly isn't going to make me like you more," said Pike with his arrogant thinking.

"Sex can wait," Sharon replied.

"Wow, you really not trying to let me fuck tonight," he said, feeling defeated. "Are you fuckin' serious?!"

"Just sit with me and let's talk. I really like you, Pike. And honestly, I had this crush on you for a very long time, and I don't want to be one of those girls feeling used by you. I want to be different," she said wholeheartedly.

"Different..." he laughed while pulling up his basketball shorts.

"Yes."

"You know what, if you ain't giving up the fuckin' pussy, then you need to get the fuck out my crib. You ain't nothin' but a cock tease!" Pike barked angrily. "Fo' real bitch, you know who the fuck I am, I always get what I want...and bitch, you ain't no different."

Pike snatched her purse off the couch and then gripped her arm, and he started to drag Sharon to the front door, trying to expedite her departure.

She yanked her arm away from his grip. She was upset.

"Pike, I have no money to get back home. I thought you were going to drive me. And it's late," she told him.

"I don't give a fuck...walk home then, cuz if you ain't fuckin' me then you ain't staying."

The transformation within him was abrupt. He was a different man suddenly. He was selfish and self-centered. Sharon was taken aback by his harsh outburst and his rudeness. She was truly hurt by his belligerent and callous action.

It was 4am and it was going to be impossible to make it back to Brooklyn from Harlem with no cash and limited public transportation.

Sharon stood in the center of his apartment becoming adamant. A few tears trickled down her cheeks. She glared at Pike and exclaimed, "Are you really goin' to throw me out like this, Pike? Because I'm not fuckin' you! I thought I was your friend and that you really liked me. Everything you said the other night, it was all a con for some pussy—a temporary pleasure. Then you know what? You gonna keep having temporary bitches in your life! I thought for once, maybe you might want something real in your life; a real fuckin' woman like me. Ain't you tired of all the bullshit with these bitches? You keep thinkin' with your dick and you know what? You gonna miss out on the best thing in your life and end up alone, and if you lucky, maybe you won't catch some STD. Cuz you know what, Pike? Karma is a bitch!"

Sharon had said enough. She was seething and Pike seemed speechless. He stood near his front door with this surprised look. It was the first time any woman had stood up to him and been so frank. In high school, ladies kissed his ass and spoiled him because they knew he was going to make it to the NBA and they wanted a piece of that dream. After high school, they still wanted a piece of the dream. But Sharon, she treated him like a regular nigga. Yeah, she had a crush on him, but she wasn't hyped to fall victim to his desires like every other bitch before her.

With nonchalance in his voice, he said, "Only for one night, you can sleep on the couch, but in the morning, you better be gone."

He saw her hurt and decided to change his mind. Sharon sighed heavily, that sexual demon inside Pike was something vicious—it was another side of him that was definitely hard to deal with. But she fought it and it was the first time Pike ever relinquished his desires.

Sharon couldn't sleep. She sat on the couch wide awake and had some things on her mind. Dawn was coming. She looked around Pike's untidy apartment and shook her head. It was a mess, clothes everywhere, dishes piling up in the sink—the trash needed taking out and he had empty beer bottles all over.

Damn, he was a slob, she thought.

Being the woman that she was, she decided to do something about it. With morning approaching, her womanly instinct took over and the first task she decided to tackle was the sink. She washed every item in the sink thoroughly, hand-dried everything, and put things away like she was in her own kitchen. Next, she took out the trash, tossing a lumpy and smelly bag down the hallway chute. After that, it was the living room, where she picked up his scattered clothes and folded everything neatly. The ones that were really dirty she tossed in the clothes hamper, and if she'd had time, then she would have done his laundry.

She cleaned Pike's apartment in the early morning while he was sleeping in his bed like she was his paid maid—Florence Jefferson herself.

Why was she doing this after Pike had been so rude and disrespectful to her? She wanted to show him how a real and thorough woman got down. She needed to demonstrate to Pike what a good woman was and the things she did—even when the man didn't deserve it. A chickenhead, regular bitch would have thought she was crazy, and broke and smashed things in his place just to prove a point. Sharon refused to be that bitter. And though she was hurt, she wasn't going to give Pike that pleasure of angering her. She was determined to be the better woman in this situation. And the better woman held her own and was patient.

Exhausted, Sharon folded herself across his couch like paper and closed her eyes. Sleep caught up to her and she passed out on the couch in his now-cleaned apartment.

Several hours had gone by when Sharon opened her eyes to the late morning sun flooding through the living-room window. She sat up and glanced at the time and saw that it was almost 10am. She was never the one to sleep long, and this morning wasn't any different. Pike wasn't up yet—he was a heavy and late sleeper, and with it being the weekend, he didn't need to be in any rush to get out of bed before noon.

Sharon decided to do him one last kindness. She went into the kitchen and cooked him a hearty breakfast—pancakes, eggs and bacon—then walked to serve him breakfast in bed.

Pike was sleeping on his back butt-naked, dick out and flaccid with no shame in his game. Sharon gazed at him for a short moment and then nudged him awake. Pike opened his eyes to see Sharon standing over him with some hot breakfast in her hand, smoke still steaming from the plate.

"I made you breakfast," was all she said to him.

She set his breakfast on the nightstand near him and quickly left, leaving behind a confused Pike. He was speechless. He removed himself from bed, still naked, and found his place spotless. In fact, he'd never seen his place so clean. He was astonished.

Pike walked to his bed and stared at the breakfast she made. His stomach was growling. Hungry, he devoured Sharon's home-cooked meal like a starving slave. He never had any cooking better. But what shocked him more was the note Sharon left behind:

"Thank you for last night, it was fun!"

There was a smiley face next to the word "fun," and her cell phone number.

Fun? He was befuddled. He had been nothing but rude and mean to her. How could she have had fun and done something totally nice for him? He didn't understand it.

Of the dozens of women he'd been with, he never came across a woman like Sharon. She was definitely different in his eyes.

Pike walked to the window in his living room and gazed outside. It was another beautiful day. He then took a seat on the edge of his bed and read Sharon's note again, and stared at her cell phone number. He sighed heavily with Sharon on his mind.

SEVEN

Clad in a white terry-cloth robe matching E.P.'s, Cristal sat cross-legged on the large bed eating her breakfast, an egg omelet and crab cakes, two of her favorites. E.P. was posted by the window, talking on his cell phone. It was business. He took a few pulls from his cigarette and then paced around the bedroom. Cristal overheard bits and pieces of his conversation. She really wasn't paying him any attention. Her focus was on food and BET. He was discussing another multimillion-dollar business merger and something about unions and 401(k)s; it was foreign talk to her.

A deck of playing cards was scattered on the table nearby; numerous cigarette butts filled the ashtray on the table, along with their food order from a city café and a half-empty bottle of red wine with two empty glasses. Her clothes were on the floor. Cristal was a little more comfortable in E.P.'s presence. It was another glorious morning in his luxurious suite—however, there were more questions for E.P. about some job she had no details or clue about.

The only thing she knew about this elite position was that it paid well and came with a few perks, including some paid traveling expenses. But this job was more of a mystery than Big Foot. And also, it wasn't anything sexual.

Cristal wasn't concerned about going home anytime soon. She was having a wonderful time experiencing the good life and had not once thought about calling her friends or home. She knew her mom wasn't missing her; the woman barely knew she existed when she was around. But her friends, Sharon, Mona, Lisa, and Tamar, were a different story. Not a day usually went by without them hearing from each other—or there was some concern.

Cristal finished off her meal and downed a bottled water. Her pussy was still throbbing from this morning's early sexual rendezvous. E.P. fucked her six ways from Sunday—position after position; he tore into her good pussy like he was devouring a good meal, and she was sexually drained and satisfied.

E.P. curtailed his business call. He took a few pulls from the burning cigarette between his fingers and once again focused his attention on Cristal seated on his bed looking like a woman enjoying a slice of Paradise.

He exhaled some smoke and said to her, "I have another question for you."

Cristal fretted a little. More questions. He pretty much had gotten to know everything about her in the past two days—sex, family, friends, et cetera. E.P. didn't want any secrets kept from him, yet he was the biggest secret of all.

"Ask away," she said, coyly.

"Did you ever get arrested?" he asked.

Cristal swore he asked this same question before, but in a different form. She answered willingly, like she did with all of his questions.

"Yeah, for petty shit, though," she answered.

"Felonious?"

Cristal rolled her eyes at E.P.'s use of big words. She got it, he was educated and smart. "Felonious?" she repeated with a puzzled gaze.

"It means criminal," he explained dryly. "Any felonies on your record?"

She smirked. "Nah, not me," she replied.

"Were you ever fingerprinted?" he asked.

"Nope, not really. Each time I was a minor," she told him.

"Did you ever learn anything?"

Cristal felt the question was irrelevant. She blurted out, "That's a stupid question!"

Suddenly, E.P.'s mood changed. His monotone voice became gruff and he barked, "What did you learn?!"

His question made Cristal shift uncomfortably on his bed, unable to take her eyes off of him. She felt a tinge of trepidation.

"Well, it wasn't pleasure if that's what you wanted to know," she replied with some sarcasm in her response.

"Wrong response!" E.P.'s voice deepened and he stared intently at Cristal. "One last time. What did you learn?" he demanded.

"To never get arrested ever again?" she replied with some apprehension.

E.P. smiled slightly. "Smart girl."

She felt relieved that she got something right. "I have my moments."

E.P. took one last pull from his cigarette and dowsed it into the ashtray on the table. He went on with his next question. "What would you do for money?"

"Anything," Cristal replied honestly.

E.P. smiled widely. "I knew I saw something in you that I liked."

It was good to hear. She exhaled. For some reason, Cristal really wanted to be down with his clique or organization. There was this sense that dealing with E.P. would place her on top of the food chain called life, and she would become someone of importance. The bottom was no longer a place for her.

Cristal shifted on his bed again. This impromptu interview was becoming tiresome and eccentric. But Cristal stuck with it. "Is there a job interview I have to go to?"

He grinned. "We just had it."

Cristal was befuddled. "Huh? Those questions were my job interview?

But how does that make sense?"

E.P. was ready to make sense of it all to her.

"You said you know how to cook cocaine, which means you know how to learn and follow directions. Someone had to teach you to cook coke into crack, and obviously you graduated. You also stated that you're a professional shoplifter. A skill like that means risk-taking and knowing how to be subtle and stealthy. And it also tells me that you're good at deception. And you have to be good at putting on an act to walk into high-end stores, especially a heavily guarded and secured area where they keep those expensive dresses."

He pointed toward her Herve Leger dress on the floor, and continued with, "And steal from under their noses. I'm familiar with that type of dress, and they keep merchandise like that not only with a Sensomatic, but also with a security chain. Am I correct?"

She nodded. "I boosted the master key to the lockbox in Nordstrom's. I can unlock all their shit."

E.P. was somewhat impressed. But he remained cool.

"My point exactly. And key or no key, you can't walk in there looking like a project chick and expect to be in that place for more than a minute without the entire store being on you like white on rice. So again, in order for you to get away with this illicit act, you would have to be good at deception . . . creating an illusion, a role," he explained.

"Is that helpful?"

"More than you'll ever know right now," he said.

E.P. walked over to where breakfast was displayed on the table. He had ordered the same egg omelet as Cristal, with some fruit and toast. He took a large gulp from his freshly squeezed, overpriced orange juice, before continuing, "And to throw in that you're a liar, and that you're also a fighter pulls you into the front of the line. But what makes you stand out in my mind, Cristal, is your skill with handling a razor and your war stories. To me, it shows that you can be heartless and can defend yourself when the time comes. When it comes to confrontation, you can fight with the best of them…your beauty can be crippling to most, but the fire I see in your eyes tells me never to underestimate you. And when you find yourself in a vulnerable situation, your survival skills will kick in and you'll do anything to win. And we only want winners on our team."

Cristal couldn't take the anticipation any longer. He was talking in code and she was ready to hear the truth about this job she seemed to be interviewing or auditioning for, for the past forty-eight hours.

Finally, she asked, "I need to know, E.P., what does your organization do? And why do you want me to be a part of it?"

He gazed at Cristal for a moment, after that he took another gulp of orange juice. After that, he removed a cigarette from the dwindling pack and lit it. He seemed to be taking his time answering Cristal's question. E.P. took a long drag from the cancer stick, exhaled, then gazed at Cristal like he was about to tell her the meaning of life with his voice cavalier. "Murder. We do murder."

EIGHT

••

Sharon was floating on cloud nine when she walked out of her project building on Vermont Street. She couldn't stop thinking about Pike for some reason. Despite being treated rudely by him, she still liked him and wanted to see him again. What was it about the bad boys that attracted good woman like herself to them? It was the age-old question. Leaving her cell phone number on the nightstand, hoping he would call—she didn't see it as desperation, but an invitation into her life. He was going to call; she felt that she'd left a good impression on him. She could only be herself and she wasn't changing for anybody.

With the sun shining brightly and the weather feeling like the Bahamas, Sharon decided to walk to meet with her friends in the park near the projects on Linden Boulevard. She passed Smokey and his crazy crew loitering and rolling dice on Cozine Avenue, and saw New York's Finest jacking up a few brothers with police harassment on Flatlands Avenue. It was another typical summer day in the hood.

Looking comfortable in her white shorts and white Nikes, and sporting a Beyoncé Live in Concert T-shirt, Sharon felt different. She strutted across the football field toward the playground and handball courts where her friends lingered on the rotten wood benches on the regular, smoking cigarettes, eyeing the shirtless cuties on the basketball courts nearby and talking shit to each other. Tamar was the one holding court near the playground—the loudest one in the bunch, telling her friends some crazy story about some nigga she fucked with like she usually did.

Mona was boldly rolling up a blunt in public, knowing police had a routine of patrolling the area either by foot or squad car. She didn't care. Her weed was always more important than worrying about being arrested. And Lisa was her casual self like normal. The stigma of the bloodshed that happened a few days ago because of Tank still lingered in the park like a bad taste. The ball players that were brutally murdered in the park, blood still stained the concrete courts. Some felt unsafe in the Brooklyn park.

Despite what happened there—shootings, police harassment, fights and murders, it didn't deter the girls from hanging out there and having a good time. It was summer, and there weren't many places for them to hang out. The park was one of their favorite spots where they were known.

Sharon walked toward her crew with a smile more gigantic than the Titanic. She was weird like that with the persona of trying to always be optimistic—and though the other night with Pike didn't go too well, she always kept a positive attitude about things.

"So this bitch-ass nigga gonna come up to me like he some pimp, wit' his run-down, Harriet Tubman lookin' boots and gumbo haircut and gonna try an' play me and have the audacity to disrespect me," Sharon heard Tamar say to Lisa and Mona from a distance. "So I slapped the nigga like the bitch he was . . . damn sure did, slapped the dog breath outta that nigga's mouth."

"Damn Tamar, you hit him like that?" Lisa asked.

"Fuck yeah, I ain't scared of no nigga, and I dared the nigga to put his hands on me. I got niggas that will fuck him up," Tamar exclaimed.

Sharon looked around and noticed there was one missing, Cristal. She walked into the middle of Tamar telling her crazy story. Tamar had everyone laughing. The girls greeted each other with love, always excited to see each other.

"Where's Cristal?" Sharon asked.

"We haven't seen her since we left the party. She's probably still with E.P. gettin' her brains fucked out, cuz I know E.P. is slingin' some good-ass dick inside of her," Mona said lightheartedly.

The girls laughed.

"He is one fine-ass muthafucka, I would love to be a squirrel so I could climb that tree, ya feel me?" Tamar shouted humorously.

"Girl, you and me both," Mona agreed. "Lisa, you shoulda came, E.P.'s party was off the fuckin' hook."

"I cosign on that," replied Sharon.

"Damn, it's been two days too, the bitch better come back pregnant by the nigga, so the bitch can eat and live," Tamar said uncouthly.

"Tamar, you too much," said Lisa.

"I'm just sayin'…fuckin' wit' a nigga like E.P. is an opportunity of a lifetime. And if I was Cristal, hells yeah I would be tryin' to take advantage of the situation and get paid! I would have a nigga pop a baby in me… child support!" Tamar stated excitedly.

"And yeah, you ain't too worried about getting an STD, huh," Sharon chided.

Mona and Lisa laughed.

"Whatever bitch!" Tamar spat, flipping her friend the middle finger.

"Tamar, you know I just care about y'all," Sharon replied.

"Anyway, what's the dirt on you and Pike? Damn, that nigga was on you like Ike on Tina," Tamar laughed. "I know you went back to his apartment after the party and spread your legs like wings to a 747. Shit, you talkin' about STDs, I hope you ain't fuck that nigga raw," said Tamar.

"We didn't fuck," she revealed.

"What? You were at Pike's place and y'all ain't do shit! I don't believe you. Pike had you alone in his dungeon and he ain't show you the dragon?" Tamar continued.

"Dragon, cute," Sharon replied lightheartedly.

"He was really feelin' you, Sharon," said Mona.

"He came on to me—showed me his dick and everything. But I didn't want to fuck him, not that night anyway. I want it to be special between him and me," Sharon said.

"Special?" the girls laughed.

"Bitch, you stupid. I heard Pike got a mean sex game and that dick is good, and you turned that down. Shit, you tryin' to marry the nigga?" Tamar hollered.

"Damn, Sharon, you fucked that up," Mona chided.

"Yes, she did," Tamar agreed.

"If Sharon wanted her night to be special, then I commend her for that. Pike's a dog anyway, ain't no telling what type of diseases that nigga has," Lisa said.

"That is why they have condoms for sale," Tamar countered.

"Y'all crazy," Sharon said.

"No, you crazy…out here lookin' for love instead of some good dick. Pike ain't the loving type of nigga, Sharon."

"He damn sure ain't," Mona cosigned on that, and slapping Tamar a high-five.

"See me, I'm the type of bitch that need some of that good dick in her life, cuz you know if Pike was comin' on to me like that, I woulda fucked his brains out and got me some money for it. True indeed," Tamar proclaimed proudly. "Cuz I gots to get me some good sex and have some paper in my pockets."

"Okay!" Mona shouted with accord to Tamar's speech.

"Well anyway, we got into it because I wouldn't give him any ass, and he threatened to kick me out at four in the morning," Sharon revealed.

"What? I told you he was a jerk," Tamar uttered.

"Oh, but you was just ready to fuck him a moment ago," Lisa scolded.

"We ain't all the Virgin Mary like you, bitch," Tamar countered.

Mona laughed.

Sharon wanted to finish telling her story.

"I didn't leave, though. I told him about himself, said he was a selfish, self-centered asshole that was going to grow old and die alone, and that I was the realest bitch he was going to ever know," Sharon proclaimed.

"And he let you stay after that?"

"He told me I could sleep on the couch but I had to leave early in the morning."

"How charitable of him," said Tamar.

"So what he do? Got up and kicked ya ass out early in the morning?" Mona asked.

Sharon decided to tell them everything that happened, even if they were going to judge and clown her for it.

"Not exactly," she started. "I couldn't sleep, so I cleaned up his apartment and cooked him breakfast before I left."

"What?!" the girls exclaimed simultaneously, not believing what they just heard.

"Sharon, I know you ain't just cleaned this nigga's place and cooked this nigga a good meal after he disrespected you like that. Are you stupid?" Tamar spat.

"It was a mess, and I figured he would be hungry."

"See, that's what the fuck is wrong wit' you. You too damn dumb!"

"I just felt it was the right thing to do."

"The right thing to do? Sharon, you think a nigga like him gonna appreciate that?" Mona asked rhetorically.

"Nigga, how you gonna play housewife to a dog like that, especially after he came clear that the only thing he wanted from you was some pussy! And you cleaned this nigga crib, cooked him breakfast? Damn, where they make bitches like you at?" Tamar exclaimed bluntly. "Stupidville?"

"I rather get some dick from a nigga than become his housemaid, real talk!" Mona said.

"What, you on that 'kill 'em nicely wit' kindness'?" Tamar blurted. "You think being nice to a nigga like that gonna cause him to have a change of heart?"

"I definitely need to smoke after hearing this shit," Mona said, lighting up the blunt in the park without any regard for anyone else around—kids, parents, the cops.

Lisa was quiet. She didn't actually agree with Sharon's actions. She wasn't too open with her thinking, but the way she looked at her friend, it was clear that she also disagreed with treating Pike with that kind of hospitality.

"Damn girl, you make us look bad," Tamar said.

"Do I?" Sharon retorted. "Because instead of fuckin' a nigga, having a one night stand, giving my pussy out, and chancing in either getting pregnant or an STD from the nigga, I decided to cook and clean up for him. And by doing that, I make y'all look bad? Bitch, please!"

"We just sayin' Sharon," Mona returned in a more amiable tone.

"What are you sayin', Mona?" Sharon asked gruffly.

Mona didn't want to finish her sentence. She decided to leave it alone. She took a strong pull from the weed in her hand and then shared it with Tamar. They felt the tension growing between them and Sharon, so weed was going to be the peace treaty between them.

"Bitch, you know we love you," Tamar spoke out. "We just don't want to see our girl get hurt and played by a nigga like that. Yeah, he's fine and all, got a big dick, but c'mon, you deserve better than that, Sharon. And besides, we don't want you to have wishful thinking wit' him."

Sharon understood.

"I didn't mean to get loud wit' y'all," she apologized.

"Bitch, we still cool," Mona said.

The girls daringly got high in the park in broad daylight while gathered around the bench. They relived E.P.'s party and joked around with each other. While they did so, Sharon's cell phone rang. She looked; it was an unknown number. She decided to take it. When she heard his voice on the other end, Sharon was surprised. It was Pike.

"Hey," she greeted with a smile.

"Hey, you busy?" he asked.

"No, not really," she responded.

"Can you come over today? I wanna see you," Pike said cordially.

"After everything that happened the other night?" she reminded him. "I don't know."

"I know. I'm sorry for the way I acted. We've been cool for too long to let this get in the way. But I need to see you."

"Okay."

Tamar, Mona and Lisa stopped what they were doing and became focused on their friend's phone conversation.

"Sharon, who's that?" Tamar asked, assertively.

They already had a speculation who she was talking to.

"I'll see you soon," Sharon said, and ended her call, triumphantly.

"Sharon, who was that? Pike?" Tamar asked again.

Sharon couldn't help but to grin from ear to ear. She nodded.

"He asked you to come over again?" Mona asked.

"Yes."

"Yo, I know you ain't goin' back over there," Tamar said.

"Sharon, if you go back over there, you only gonna be playin' yourself," Mona warned her.

"How you gonna hop back on the train to Harlem to see this nigga after he kicked you out and disrespected you?" Tamar added.

"Because I want to," Sharon returned.

Both girls sighed with frustration for their friend. But Sharon was adamant to see Pike again. They went on to tell her she was a dumb ass if she was to travel back uptown.

•••

Sharon knocked on Pike's door with some nervousness. Why had she come back? What if her friends were right? Could this be a mistake? She thought about the note she left him. Had it changed his heart? Was it desperation instead of an invitation? Maybe she had faith in him—faith that he could change. She could change him. Sharon stood in the hallway of his building and took a deep breath. Clad in her white shorts and T-shirt, she fidgeted with her natural afro and waited for him to answer his door.

The apartment door opened and Pike stood in front of her, clad in a wifebeater and jeans this time. He smiled and invited her inside.

Sharon looked at him; he seemed to be in a more delightful mood. The apartment was still clean, which was a good thing. Pike stood next to her. He scratched his head, looked around his apartment, and sighed.

"I need your help with something," he said.

"With what?" she asked.

Soon, Sharon noticed a couple of ounces of weed and an ounce of cocaine on the kitchen table. It would have been Mona's nirvana. Her friend wouldn't hesitate to try and smoke it all in one day. The cocaine was new to her. She knew Pike sold weed, but it seemed that he'd upgraded to pushing the white powder.

Pike walked into the kitchen. He seemed to have been busy bagging up his product alone when Sharon came knocking.

"What do you need my help with?"

"I need you to make some runs for me," he had the audacity to ask her.

"What?" Sharon was shocked. "Are you crazy? Is this the only fuckin' reason why you called me over?!"

"Listen, you're the only one I can trust right now. I'm in trouble here, and if I don't get this money up by tonight, then some serious people are going to come looking for me," Pike said. "I gotta stay behind and bag this shit up, and I can't do two things at one time."

"Where's Rich?"

"He got business of his own to handle."

Sharon sighed. She knew she was being used, but for some strange reason, she couldn't bring herself not to help him. Despite his flaws, Pike was still her friend, and she didn't want to see anything bad happen to him.

Halfheartedly, she agreed to do him this service, one time.

"I love you for this," Pike said.

"I want you to love me regardless of what I do or don't do," she returned.

Pike smiled and gave her a strong hug which was followed by a heated kiss which she didn't resist. Sharon wanted to melt in his arms, the way he held her and slipped his tongue into her mouth. He felt so good. And he smelled good, too. She looked up at him, not wanting him to let her go. But it was a daydream at the moment. Pike went into the kitchen and placed three ounces of weed and an ounce of cocaine into a black bag and handed it to Sharon. She took it with little skepticism.

"This is my life you're holding in your hands," he told her. "Protect this with yours."

"I won't let anything happen to you, Pike," she assured him.

He smiled.

Sharon placed the drugs into her purse, slung the bag over her shoulder and took a deep breath. Before she was to leave, Pike handed her a .380. She took the gun reluctantly. She wasn't familiar with guns. It wasn't her world, in spite of her being from the projects. Sharon stared at the gun and thought, what was she getting herself into?

She walked out of his apartment with a strong feeling of apprehension. With three ounces of marijuana and cocaine in her bag and a loaded pistol, there was no telling what might happen. Cristal and Tamar were built for shit like this, not her. She was about to make various stops to dangerous drug dealers and supposedly pick up cash. Pike had to be truly desperate or stupid to trust Sharon with this great responsibility.

Sharon's first stop was Washington Heights. She went up a four-story tenement and delivered the cocaine first. Some fledging Hispanics mixed up with Pike needed the product. When they saw Sharon in the hallway, they couldn't believe he sent a woman to do some grown-man business.

One of the Hispanics in the apartment, clad in a tank top, jewelry and dark beard with a cigarette in his hand, smiled at Sharon, uttering, "*Mira este*...he sent you?"

"He sent me," Sharon replied with a hardhearted tone.

He took a pull, exhaled. "Anyway, what you got for us?"

Sharon took a deep breath and felt uncertain about walking into the apartment. From where she stood in the hallway, she could see about four guys inside. She stepped inside the place regardless, praying niggas didn't kill or rob her. She noticed how they were staring at her, and some anger toward Pike started to set in. If anything happened to her, then how could she forgive him?

The deal with the Hispanics went through without any incident, thank God. She collected the payment and hurried to her next drop-off, in Harlem.

Surprisingly, all the drop-offs went smoothly, and she collected four grand for Pike. When she returned, he was pleased. To celebrate, he ordered Chinese food and gave Sharon one hundred dollars for her services. One hundred dollars, it was a joke—cheap bastard.

But she wanted to enjoy his company and not think about how she allowed him to put her life at risk, sending her out to distribute drugs to dangerous men in dangerous neighborhoods. Instead, the two sat nestled on his couch eating Chinese food together and playing PlayStation games for a while, drinking beer and smoking weed. Sharon wanted to spend another night with Pike—an intimate and romantic night, but it appeared that once more, Pike had different plans in mind.

Once again, he was horny and infatuated by Sharon, and gave her the choice; if she wasn't fucking then she wasn't staying. He had some nerve, after what she did for him. He sent Sharon on her way before it got too late for her to make any excuses this time. She thought they were having a good time and she was getting to him, but she was wrong. Again, the muthafucka became a jerk!

NINE

●●●●●●●●●●●●●●●●●●●●●●●●●●●●●●●●●●●●●●●

Cristal stepped out of the shower feeling fresher than mountain spring water. E.P.'s showerhead gave her an exhilarating feeling. It left her feeling invigorated and stripped clean of any stress. She toweled off in front of the large mirror and looked intently at her reflection. What gazed back was a new her.

She thought about E.P.'s proposal of becoming some assassin for hire. Was he for real? And if so, why her? With his wealth and power, he had to be for real, though. When he spoke about murder, he seemed cool—stoic. Killing was just business for him, it seemed. Big business.

Cristal took a deep breath and continued to gaze at herself in the mirror. Could she really kill someone? She remembered talking all that shit in Pike's apartment after she witnessed Tank gun down several people in the park. Niggas like him made it look so easy. Could she ever make it look so easy, too?

She stood, pensive.

The difference between Tank and E.P.'s organization was that Tank was reckless and stupid; E.P. was highly orchestrated and funded by some very influential people. How could she go wrong dealing with him?

It was late in the evening, and three days had passed since Cristal had spoken to any of her friends or gone home. Her cell phone vibrated on the marble counter top in the bathroom. It was Tamar calling once again. Cristal decided to ignore her call and let it go to voicemail for the umpteenth time since she'd been with E.P. She knew her friends would be worried and upset about her absence, but this was important to her and she didn't want to deal with any interruptions from anyone. She needed to think and she needed to get to know E.P. better, in ways other than him between her legs. His conversation was very intriguing, and his occupation was even more intriguing. And staying at his place was paradise. Why would she rush to go back to Brooklyn?

But nothing came for free; there was a price for everything. E.P. looked like a man you didn't want to cross or betray. And there had to be a reason why he'd picked Cristal out of the crowd.

Murder? Could she really become some killer, or was E.P. setting her up to become a pawn for some elaborate conspiracy—maybe to kill the president or some important figure? How cool it would be to become some government assassin?

She chuckled at the thought. Maybe she was watching too many spy and conspiracy movies.

Cristal wrapped the towel around her glistening body and walked into the next room only to see they had company in E.P.'s suite. She was startled by the tall, lanky, well-dressed Caucasian man with a comb-over, pencil-thin goatee and eyes as blue as the ocean. He sported a diamond pinky ring and diamond earrings in both ears. He was clean and stylish.

Cristal noticed the buffet of dresses, shoes, and pocketbooks spread out everywhere in the room. She was shocked to see such high-end and pricey clothing all in the same room—Chanel, Gucci, Fendi, Donna Karan, Versace, and more all under the same roof and for her to choose from. Christmas came early this year.

"Hello, Cristal. I'm Vinny, E.P.'s stylist, and it's a pleasure meeting you," the man greeted in a effeminate tone.

He greeted Cristal with a handshake and seemed animated.

It was obvious that he was gay. But he was extremely handsome.

"As you can see, Cristal, compliments of E.P., we have nothing but the best outfits for you to choose from for tonight. And might I say, you are beautiful, girl," Vinny declared.

She smiled.

"My client is a lucky man. I wish I had your figure, honey, I bet you drive all the boys crazy," Vinny said with his girlish hand gestures.

Cristal chuckled.

E.P. was in the background talking business on his cell phone. His stylist from Saks Fifth Avenue was the best. He worked with notable and elite clients like Kelly Rowland, Mary J. Blige, Kim Kardashian, Alani "La La" Anthony, Beyoncé, and more.

Cristal was taken aback by everything E.P. was doing for her. The stylish clothing presented in front of her was costly. The price tags were still on the dresses and bags, and one of the price tags on a dress was twelve thousand dollars.

Whoa!

Cristal really wouldn't have minded washing her panties out in the sink and putting on her same dress. It's what she knew and where she came from, but she was being seduced by the royal treatment. And who could say no to such eye-catching goodies?

"Girl, I know the perfect dress for you. I figure you to be a size four or six, and you're going to look marvelous when I'm done with you," Vinny said elatedly.

"I hope so." Cristal looked over at E.P., but he wasn't paying her any attention. He was doing his usual business call.

"Girl, he can't do anything for you. You're mine to dress up for the night. And believe me, girl, when I'm done with you, I'm going to have you looking more marvelous than Beyoncé," he proclaimed with conviction. "Like, fabulous!" Vinny snapped his fingers excitedly.

Cristal smiled and chuckled.

She couldn't wait.

Cristal went up to the chic clothing and lavish items that she would see in the extravagant stores display windows on Park and Fifth Avenue, and it was definitely difficult for her to choose. Everything was on point.

"Girl, with your lovely complexion and hair, might I suggest you try on this." Vinny picked up an electric-pink, sexy silk dress with spaghetti straps, low open back, and gold chain details. The designer was Versace, and the cost of the dress was eight thousand dollars.

Cristal couldn't wait to try it on. It was beautiful and sleek. She never wore anything so expensive in her life. Vinny picked out two more dresses for her to try on. Tonight, E.P. was taking her out to eat at a five-star restaurant in the city. She went into the bedroom and came back out ten minutes later with the dress hugging her curvy body perfectly.

Vinny smiled and said, "Girl, like I said, you look 'fabulous' in that dress." He emphasized the word *fabulous* and snapped his fingers wholeheartedly to stress his statement. "Cristal, you cannot go wrong tonight."

"You think?" She beamed with joy.

"I know. And the shoes, they go perfectly."

Cristal had on three-thousand-dollar black, YSL heels. Her feet had never felt better. E.P. walked over with his attention fixed on her from head to toe. The look in his eyes showed he loved the attire. He nodded, giving his approval.

"See girl, even he likes it, and it's hard for me to get him to like anything because he's so picky, but you are so gorgeous," Vinny stated with enthusiasm. "You are an A-plus-plus on a calculus exam."

Cristal chuckled. She really liked Vinny. He was so lively and funny. She had never hung around anyone like him before—so gay and animated like a Looney Tunes cartoon. And the clothes she wore were far from her normal reach. She definitely could get used to this.

"Okay, Cristal, you ready for some more?" Vinny asked with his huge and bubbly smile.

"You're going to spoil me, Vinny."

"Girl, as fine and fresh as you are, spoiled shouldn't even be in your vocabulary. You're honey, Cristal and you know honey never spoils, and I love me some honey," he said amusingly.

Cristal laughed. Vinny was just too much.

She couldn't wait to go out to eat tonight. She was starving and ready to eat a horse, hooves and all.

●●●

The five-star restaurant on Barrow Street in the West Village was lovely, charming and romantic. E.P. and Cristal were met with a remarkably warm ambience. To their left was a grand piano being put to great use. The two were escorted up the stairs to a cached-away corner of the restaurant. The tables were all candlelit and the lighting dimmed. The colors, the classic detailing; it all lent itself to a wonderful sense of romance.

It was all new to Cristal. She felt like a princess. The ambience alone was overwhelming. Her beautiful figure in the dress turned heads. They were seated and instantly received service; the waiter suggested a few tasty appetizers to start off with. Cristal was unfamiliar with the selections on the menu. It might as well have been written in Spanish. Duck terrine, Branzino fish, brie cheese, brioche, and chutney—what kind of food was that?

"I suggest you try the duck terrine for start. You'll like it," E.P. recommended.

Cristal was ready to try whatever he recommended. E.P. ordered the same thing. The duck terrine, served with a pear chutney, brioche toast, and mixed greens, tasted better than she expected. The terrine had great flavor and was excellent.

The two conversed while enjoying their appetizers. He started explaining to Cristal how the process worked. She listened intently.

"If you get hired, you'll receive an anonymous telegram—"

Cristal interjected, "Oh, like a kite?"

E.P. looked at her. *Kite?* She needed some work. "You're not locked down in a penitentiary, Cristal," he said dryly. "Out in the unconfined world we call it a telegram."

She raised her eyes, leaned closer across the table and whispered, "A telegram sounds positive. And if what ya telling me is true, then we gonna be deading muthafuckas like crazy."

Deading muthafuckas? E.P. looked around and returned, "As I was saying, you're receiving a telegram—"

"Murdergram," Cristal said with a sly grin on her face.

E.P. couldn't help but grin back. He relented. "You'll receive a murdergram from the Commission."

"Commission?"

"Yes, the Commission. These are people who sit on the board and make decisions if someone lives or dies."

"So they playin' God," she interrupted.

He ignored her last comment.

"These are people that you'll never meet, under any circumstances. Are you clear on that?"

She nodded.

"And there's one golden rule, Cristal. You never cross the Commission. Do you understand that?" he asked with a stern tone and inhospitable stare buried into her.

Cristal gulped and nodded.

"No, I want to hear you say it. Do you understand that you will never betray us?"

"I understand. I will never betray the Commission."

"And you need to be ready at all times. And when you receive these murdergrams, there will be a name and location of the intended target. You take out the target, no questions asked within the reasonable time frame of my client's request. I stress again, if it's not done within a certain time frame, there will be repercussions."

Cristal wasn't a fool. She understood "repercussions" meant she would be murdered. She was dealing with dangerous people, but knowing this still didn't deter her from wanting to work with E.P. It was something different in her life—something exciting.

E.P. went on to warn her, "You may never question why this target was chosen or plead on behalf of the target. It would behoove you to follow these instructions closely."

They hadn't even put a gun in her hand yet, and already they were controlling her life.

The waiter came by with his welcoming smile to take their orders. E.P. remained normal. He glanced at the man and sized him up. It was his job—in his blood to read people and determine if someone was a threat to him or not. In his line of work, you couldn't trust anyone and had to be careful. In twenty years in his line of business, murder for hire, he'd made some powerful enemies—men and women who would go to any length to see him dead.

Cristal ordered an apple martini.

"Try again!" he uttered sharply.

She was confused, and so was the waiter. What did she do wrong?

"Order champagne," he told her.

She paused for a moment, being slightly taken aback. Was he still testing her?

During dinner, without looking at the wine menu, she ordered a glass of Moët. He cut his eyes toward her sharply. Cristal appeared nervous. E.P. told the waiter to bring them a bottle of Cristal. She thought she figured out the puzzle.

"You ordered Cristal champagne because it's a nod to me? Because that's how I spell my name."

He smirked. "I ordered Cristal champagne because it's the best. Remember that. What we're doing here tonight isn't about you. It's about business."

Cristal nodded.

For the main course, they ordered the Branzino fish, which was served with a pesto risotto and an herb salad with raspberry dressing. The fish was perfectly prepared and was fresh and flavorful. Cristal had never had fish like that before, and she truly enjoyed it. For dessert, they had the superb milk chocolate fondant cake, classically accompanied with sorbet.

After an experience like this, it was going to be hard to return to the projects and rekindle her ghetto ways with her crew. For the past three days, she had felt like a whole new woman. Spending fabulous nights in his lavish suite, the clothes, the great sex, Vinny the stylist, and dinner in a five-star restaurant—yes it all came with a price—eventually; she would have to kill for it. She would have to sell her soul.

E.P. locked eyes with Cristal and said, "This lifestyle can be all yours if you do the right thing, Cristal. I give the best and I want nothing but the best."

She nodded.

"So are you ready to give me your best?" he asked.

"I wanna continue this type of living by any means necessary," said Cristal with assertiveness. "I can't go back to being that same ghetto chick scraping the bottom. I really want this."

E.P. smiled.

His job was done.

"You're hired."

TEN

●●

"Bitches be fuckin' selfish!" Tamar spat to herself. Cristal had been absent from her life for more than three days now without answering or returning her phone calls.

Cristal got with E.P. and forgot about friends and family. Tamar couldn't help but be furious at her friend. It seemed like the bitch's true colors were coming out.

The weekend was coming around, and Tamar wanted to go boosting at the mall again to get some fly shit and earn some extra money. But she couldn't do that without her best friend. Cristal was her right hand, and it had gotten cut off when they went to that fancy party and her friend became smitten by E.P.

Tamar smoked her Newport alone in the pissy, narrow stairway of her building. She was also upset at Sharon for running around the hood bragging about being with Pike and the measly hundred dollars he'd given her. She heard about Sharon running drugs around town for Pike. *Dumb bitch,* she thought. Sharon was a friend, but the bitch was just stupid sometimes—maybe too desperate to find love and risking everything for a dog like Pike.

Her friends were losing their minds over some dick.

But she was dealing with her own problems at home. Her dysfunctional family was a hot mess. She needed to get away from her moms, her young siblings, and hating-ass bitches in her life. Tamar couldn't help but to worry about Cristal's disappearing act. Where was she and why wasn't she calling?

It was becoming a miserable day for Tamar. She'd just had a serious and heated argument with her mother, whom everyone called Black Earth. It had almost come to blows between the two of them earlier, in front of her sisters and brother. Tamar was tired of her mother's dumb, selfish ways and outlandish antics. With Black Earth, it was always something. This time Tamar was highly upset with her mother for selling the EPT food-stamp card for cash again, and spending the money on herself. There were mouths to feed and barely enough food in the apartment to feed her and her siblings. Tamar was also extremely tired and frustrated that her mother kept stealing her clothes out of her closet. The big bitch couldn't fit any of her shit, so she knew Black Earth was selling the things Tamar had worked so hard to steal.

Tamar's three siblings were eleven-year-old Jada, nine-year-old Jayson, and six-year-old Lena. They all had different fathers who weren't in their lives at all, and they rarely had a mother either. Black Earth had babies only to collect a check. She gave birth and changed some shitty diapers once in a while, but she wasn't a mother. She'd chain-smoked around her children since they were born, she cursed like a sailor around her kids, and she constantly brought different men home to please her sexual desires. Also, she was always out in the streets getting high or in the clubs partying until the sun came up, most times leaving her kids unattended.

Tamar grew up raising herself. She learned about life through various trials and tribulations that she had to get through on her own. Her only family was Cristal, Mona, Lisa and slow-ass Sharon, and her young siblings. They cared about each other a lot, and would do anything for each other.

Tamar puffed on her cigarette and exhaled. She didn't care who saw her seated in the stairway clad in boy shorts and wifebeater with no bra underneath. She just ran out the apartment quickly and escaped into the stairway. She wanted to punch her mother so badly, her temples throbbed just thinking about it.

It was early afternoon, and Tamar could hear the loud Jamaican music blasting from Sinbad's apartment. She could smell Ms. Gene's chitterlings cooking strongly next door. She always hated that smell; the unpleasant odor was sickening to her, but Ms. Gene was Southern old-school and one of the best cooks in the neighborhood, and when Tamar and her siblings went hungry, there was always Ms. Gene coming around to feed them some of her home-cooked meals. Tamar hated the smell of her chitterlings cooking, but she respected Ms. Gene, sometimes wishing the elderly woman were her mother.

She puffed and collected her thoughts. She fumed, thinking about the two-hundred-dollar dress and Chanel purse that had been taken out of her closet. It was clear that Black Earth had taken her shit and violated her bedroom. And then her mother had the audacity to lie about it.

The argument in the apartment got heated. Black Earth was a big woman, almost six feet tall and 240 pounds, and she was known to be a really crazy and violent bitch. But Tamar wasn't scared of her mother. She could be just as violent too.

Mona and Lisa were on their way over. Tamar hoped they hurried over soon. She needed her friends at the moment. And she needed Cristal even more. She felt empowered by her crew.

She exhaled and heard people coming up the stairway. She heard male voices. They loomed closer. She looked up and saw another neighborhood menace, Derrick; he was with Tank. Seeing Tank was a shock. His killing of those men in the park the other day played in her head like a movie. However, she kept her cool. Seeing Tank standing over her in passing on the stairway made her feel somewhat ambivalent—uneasy and excited. Unknown to her friends, she had a secret crush on Tank. Rich was right:

She loved gangster niggas who knew how to handle themselves on the block.

She'd always wanted to feel protected, especially after growing up in an abusive household—remembering how, when she was young, it was either her mother or one of her boyfriends physically abusing her. She had always had to fight, and for once, she wished she had someone who could do the fighting for her.

A nigga like Tank was her picture-perfect man.

"Hey, Tamar, you good? What you doin' on the steps?" Derrick asked.

"Had a fight wit' my moms again."

"Y'all be trippin'."

"She be trippin'," Tamar replied. "I hate that fat bitch."

"Well, she's a big woman and that's a lot to hate," Derrick joked.

She didn't find his humor funny.

Tank stood quietly behind his friend, looking emotionless. He was mean and aloof. He didn't give a fuck about anything. He didn't even acknowledge Tamar at first. But he saw that she had something he wanted.

"Shorty, you got another cigarette?" Tank asked in his raspy voice.

"Nah, last one."

"Too bad," he said.

There was a quick look exchanged between the two. She wanted to say more to the man, but he was a dangerous stranger, and Tamar had problems of her own.

"Just keep ya head up, Tamar," said Derrick.

She nodded.

They walked by her, leaving Tamar seated on the stairs smoking her cigarette. Seeing Tank so close and having him speak to her—in her twisted mind it was like meeting a celebrity. His name rang out in the hood like Sunday bells, and she had nothing but respect for a killer like him.

Tamar finished off her cigarette, stubbing it out against the stairs. She stood up and went back into her apartment still seething from the argument with her mother. She thought smoking a cigarette would calm her down, but it didn't. She felt worse.

She walked into the apartment. Her brother and sisters were in the bedroom watching TV, and Black Earth was in the living room, on the couch, smoking and watching a program on BET. The big, black bitch pivoted in her seat and glared at Tamar entering.

Both ladies scowled heavily. The tension in the apartment was thick. Seeing her mother on the couch stirred up that violent anger inside of Tamar. The dress Black Earth had stolen from out her closet was one of her favorites, one she wanted to keep. And her Chanel purse—there wasn't any replacing it.

Like a rubber band, Tamar just snapped. "I'm sick and tired of you fuckin' disrespecting me and taking shit out my fuckin' closet! Keep the fuck out my room, Ma!"

"Bitch, who the fuck you screamin' at?!" Black Earth shouted. She stood up to display her full height and size, and heatedly continued with, "I told you to stop fuckin' stealing shit in the first place, you dumb bitch, and if you bring it here, in my fuckin' home, then you the stupid bitch, cuz your shit gonna get got."

Black Earth's heated response was shattering, running rampant like wildfire.

Tamar stormed forward, retorting, "I fuckin' hate you, you lazy, fatass bitch! You a fuckin' bum, bitch! Take care of ya fuckin' kids!"

"Don't tell me how to raise my fuckin' kids, bitch! You ain't gotta live here."

"I don't!"

"Get the fuck out my house!" Black Earth screamed.

Their loud, heated argument echoed from the apartment and into the hallway, allowing their neighbors to overhear them once again. It was so common to hear Tamar argue with her mother daily that people could set their watches to it.

"I hope you die, bitch!" Tamar screamed into her mother's face. "You is a fuckin' loser! You ain't shit, you disgusting bitch. Take anything out of my closet one more time, and I swear I'll kill you."

The threat came through Tamar's clenched teeth, and her words were chilling toward her mother. Tamar's eyes burned intently into her mother, her own flesh-and-blood, wishing she could melt Black Earth with her angry stare. However, it was Black Earth who swung first, and a violent fistfight ensued between them.

The hit caught Tamar off guard. Black Earth was heavy-handed and strong like an ox. She went charging at her daughter like a bull seeing red. Tamar went flying over the chair, and her mother came barreling down on her daughter like heavy rain.

"Bitch, I don't care how old you are, you gonna fuckin' respect me in my fuckin' house," Black Earth shouted, beating on Tamar.

The fight brought the kids running out of the bedroom. They watched in horror as Black Earth pinned one of her children to the floor, attacking Tamar like she was a complete stranger.

They cried out in disbelief.

"Mommy, stop it! Stop it, Mommy, get off her!" Jada shouted with tears streaming down her face.

"Mommy, you gonna hurt Tamar," Jayson yelled.

"I don't give a fuck about this bitch!" Black Earth screamed heatedly with her fists pounding into Tamar's petite frame.

Black Earth didn't care who witnessed her violent actions. Even in front of her small children, she became a reckless animal. The fight caused six-year-old Lena to run away into the hallway crying hysterically. She hated when her mother and sister fought.

Tamar wasn't any punk, though. She swung and hit back, but it felt like a car was on top of her. Black Earth's blows were almost crushing.

"Get the fuck off me!" Tamar shrieked.

"I'ma kill this disrespectful bitch," her mother retorted.

The fight seemed like an eternity in the children's eyes. Fear and panic had set in. It felt like World War III had erupted in the ghetto-size apartment. When Jayson tried to pull his mother off of his big sister, Black Earth wasn't having any part of it. She belligerently pushed her son away from her and he went toppling into the TV.

Six-year-old Lena came running back into the apartment with help. Lisa and Mona came flying inside like a bolt of lightning striking to aid their friend. Mona snatched up a lamp and smashed it across Black Earth's head, and then Lisa started swinging on the bitch from behind. The two girls jumped in and wailed on the woman like she was some bitch on the street instead of Tamar's mother.

With the three of them attacking Black Earth at once, they had the advantage. They punched, kicked, and stomped Black Earth into a corner. Tamar, Lisa, and Mona were like hyenas in the wild. The fight was scaring her siblings and causing attention on the floor.

"Fuck wit' me, bitch!" Tamar shouted. "Don't ever touch my shit again."

Tamar kicked her mother in her ribs and punched her repeatedly.

Leaving her mother bleeding and lying in the corner severely beaten, the girls retreated to the bedroom thinking it was all over. But before Lisa and Mona could ask what happened, Black Earth came charging into the bedroom with a serrated blade in her hand.

"I'ma kill y'all fuckin' bitches!" she screamed madly.

The girls saw the knife and started screaming. Black Earth had rage and murder in her eyes. She swung the knife wildly in the girls' direction. They scurried out of her way as she barely missed cutting or stabbing them. Tamar tried to escape the bedroom, running for the door, but she tripped over the clothes and junk in her room. Black Earth stormed her way. She thrust the blade downward, scraping a line in Tamar's skin from her right shoulder blade down to her left butt cheek. One inch closer and her mother would have done some real damage. But it was enough to break her skin and hurt her like a son of a bitch.

Tamar screamed. Her shirt became saturated with blood from her flesh wound. Black Earth seemed unstoppable. She was ready to spill her daughter's blood in front of everyone. It was a whirlwind of chaos spinning in a frenzy in the room. Children screaming and a knife-swinging mother going at her daughter.

"Mommy, stop!" Tamar screamed out like she was a five-year-old girl. Her eyes were wide with fear and her body felt paralyzed to the floor.

In the middle of the chaos, no one realized Cristal had finally returned, and seeing her friend Tamar in danger, she reacted. Without any hesitation, she picked up a vacuum cleaner and bashed Black Earth in the head with it. The bitch went crashing down to the floor, and that's when all four girls went for broke and viciously beat her down. Tamar, injured and bleeding, went ham; hard as a muthafucka on her mother—now the shoe was on the other foot. It took police rushing into the bedroom to pull Tamar off of her mother. The neighbors had called the cops and the chaos was defused—temporarily.

Black Earth became so angry and volatile, she shouted crazily, "I'ma kill all of them fuckin' bitches! I'ma kill 'em!" She tried to attack the cops that were in between her and her daughter. A quick tussle ensued. The towering woman was hard to restrain, but eventually, Black Earth was forced to the floor and subdued, and then she was arrested.

The woman continued to scream and holler heatedly, cursing up a storm, difficult to handle even when she was in handcuffs.

"Calm down, ma'am! You need to calm down!" an officer shouted.

"Don't tell me to fuckin' calm down! Them bitches attacked me. You should be arresting them!" Black Earth shouted.

"Ma'am, be quiet!"

There was no calming Black Earth. "Fuck you!" she retorted. Her blood was boiling and her fists were clenched with her arms contorted behind her back, the hardy woman threw her mighty weight into the cop closet to her and sent him crashing to the ground.

The hectic scene unfolded and it went on in front of her children—each of them gazing, aghast with tears in their eyes at their mother's violent outburst.

"Mommy, no!" Little Lena cried out.

Mommy was out of control.

It took four cops to restrain their mother. She had to be brought under control by brute force; a cop threw her into a tight chokehold, and several officers roughly dragged her out of her own apartment. Neighbors were watching, and people were talking. But all in all, the neighbors were highly entertained by the fiasco.

Cristal, Lisa, and Mona accompanied Tamar in the ambulance. She was going to need stitches. Tamar looked at Cristal, surprised her friend had come back. "Damn, bitch, it takes your best friend getting cut up to bring ya ass back around," Tamar said.

"Good thing, too. I see I just saved your ass," Cristal replied.

Tamar sucked her teeth. "We had it under control."

"Uh-huh, I bet you did."

"Anyway, where you been at, bitch? Playing house wit' E.P.? Cuz you done forgot about your peoples. It must have been some good-ass dick for a bitch to get amnesia," said Tamar with sarcasm.

"It was different."

"Different? Bitch, after I get treated in this muthafuckin' hospital, we need to fuckin' talk, fo' real," Tamar said seriously.

Cristal smirked.

"I missed you too, bitch," Cristal said.

But yes, they needed to talk. Cristal had a lot to tell her friend, even having a job offer for her too.

At the hospital, Tamar received over a hundred stitches in her back. She was highly upset. "I hate my fuckin' moms, that crazy fuckin' bitch. Damn; this shit is going to scar."

"You'll be a'ight," Lisa said.

"Bitch, let you have this cut across ya back and see how you fuckin' like it," Tamar griped.

Cristal definitely didn't miss this kind of drama.

ELEVEN

●●●●●●●●●●●●●●●●●●●●●●●●●●●●●●●●●●●●●●●

Cristal hugged her Grandma Hattie tightly with so much love and was so happy to see her. Grandma Hattie was her heart. Her grandmother was everything that her mother wasn't—loving, ambitious with life, spiritual, a great cook, and a great mother to her own kids. Cristal wished her own mother was the same way. Her mother Renee had the same blood, but they didn't have the same traits. Grandma Hattie was a beautiful senior citizen in her early seventies and looked no older than fifty years old, with shoulder-length, gray-streaked black hair and brown skin that was wrinkle-free because of her great genes. Her bright brown eyes were always sparkling with life and the corners of her mouth were always turned up into a warm smile.

Grandma Hattie's two-bedroom apartment in the low-income area of Flatbush, Brooklyn was always home to Cristal and everyone else. If someone came knocking with their hat in hand and crying for help, she couldn't turn them away. And when things got rough for Cristal in East New York, she always made that escape over to where her grandmother was—always giving her kind and encouraging words and lifting up her spirits.

Her uncle Hardy was in the bedroom, apparently watching baseball. Right now, he was the only one staying with Grandma, but there were times when Hattie's place swarmed with family members living with her until they got back on their own two feet.

Cristal could smell dinner cooking in the kitchen—collard greens, pork chops, and macaroni and cheese. It was Hattie's favorite place to be, in the kitchen. It was where the soul of a home was always at—the kitchen, something her grandmother always preached to the family. Great cooking in the kitchen will always bring a family together. And when things got rough in the family, Grandma Hattie's cooking was always the foundation to healing.

Cristal sat at the kitchen table near the window cutting up onions and watching her grandmother prepare her famous pork chops. Hattie was in her housecoat and apron, slaving over the stove with a genuine smile and gospel music playing.

"Everything's okay with you, Cristal?" she asked, smiling at her granddaughter.

"I'm doin' great, Grandma," Cristal replied. "I just came by to see how you were doin'. I missed you."

"I missed you too, Cristal. You don't come by like you used to anymore. Something must have gotten your attention—or is it not cool anymore to hang around with a little old lady like me?"

"Nah, Grandma, I love comin' by to see you. I just been really busy lately."

"I hope busy doing the right thing."

"Yes, I'm doin' the right thing," she lied.

"That's good to hear. And I see you glowing over there. You must have met a man," she said.

She *had* met someone. She felt he was special, and she had a job. Cristal knew the job she was planning to do was something her grandmother would be totally against. Murder for hire was a definite sin. But the family needed the money. She needed the money.

"I have met someone, Grandma, and I think he's a great guy," Cristal said with a warm smile.

"So, give me the details. What is his name? What does he do?"

"Well, he's a really nice, smart and educated man. And he's well off, Grandma," Cristal revealed.

"That's good to hear, but you know money isn't everything. A rich guy isn't always the best guy for you."

"I know. But I know he really cares for me. He's hookin' me up wit' a job."

Grandma Hattie was checking in on her pork chops when she heard her granddaughter was about to be employed. It made her beam. "A job, that's great, Cristal. So that means you and your friend will stop this shoplifting nonsense in these stores and dealing drugs, and fly straight."

Cristal looked taken aback by her grandmother's words. She didn't think Hattie knew about her grind in the streets. She tried her best to keep it from her family, especially Grandma Hattie.

Hattie continued, "Don't look surprised, Cristal. Yes, I already knew about it, and I always worried about you. Stealing is wrong, young lady, and I'm not going to even preach to you about these drugs… you are so much better than that."

"I just did what I had to do, Grandma."

"Not by stealing, selling drugs, and acting a fool on these streets. That type of lifestyle will only take you one place, and that's no place where I want my beautiful granddaughter to be. Your mother may not have made anything out of her life, but I know you can, Cristal. You're still so young and have so much going for you. Just stay out of trouble and have faith in yourself, chile," her grandmother stressed.

Cristal listened and nodded, but despite what her grandmother preached to her, her mind was already made up. She was going to work for E.P. killing people. She was tired of living poor and just surviving. Cristal didn't even want the word "poor" in her vocabulary anymore. It was ready to be eradicated by employment with some heavy hitters.

She looked around her grandmother's kitchen. Everything was old and so used, the Salvation Army probably would've turned it away. She then gazed into the living room and shook her head at her grandmother's worn and tattered furniture. She was in need of an upgrade in style and technology. Hattie still had an eight-track in her outdated apartment along with a record player, and the shelves were filled with vinyl records dating back to the sixties. As far as she could remember, her family's life always had been subpar and so poor, they couldn't even dream rich.

It was the main reason why Cristal and Tamar had started stealing and hustling: to wear the things that they couldn't afford. They couldn't be popular and stand out in their neighborhoods with hand-me-downs and last year's clothing, and not having a penny to their name. The two always felt they were too good to live like that. Both of them had dreams of grandeur and yearned to live in prosperity.

"I do have faith in myself, Grandma, and I know I'm gonna be somebody in life. Watch me," Cristal said convincingly.

"You keep thinking like that, Cristal. You were always smart and had a strong will to you. Go back to school and get your degree, and never think that life owes you something, because it doesn't. You have to go out there and earn it, if you really want to keep it," Grandma Hattie advised.

Cristal was listening, but she wasn't trying to hear what her grandmother had to say right now. Those three days she spent with E.P. had opened her eyes, and now she could see what the finer things in life were—she had been missing out on so much for so long that there was a lot of catching up to do. She had a taste for the lifestyle of the rich and famous. Her mouth was drooling for the lap of luxury.

"And when I get it, I'm gonna keep it, Grandma, and give some to you," Cristal said.

Her grandmother laughed.

It was moments like this that Cristal adored and always looked forward to. Being in the kitchen talking to her grandmother about anything and while she was cooking and taking a whiff of that sweet aroma, it made Cristal never want to leave.

"I tell you this, Cristal, when you live wrong and are out there doing unspeakable things, sometimes it doesn't just come back on you, but it can also blow back on your family...the ones you love," Hattie said.

"I understand."

"Make sure you do. I love you too much to see anything thing happen to you."

Grandma Hattie was finishing up her wonderful meal in the kitchen when Uncle Hardy came walking into the fresh-smelling room clad only in his boxer shorts and stained wifebeater. It appeared he had just woken up from his long nap and was ready to eat.

He scratched his belly and asked, "Ma, what you got to eat in here?"

"Dinner will be ready in a few, Hardy," Hattie said.

"I'm starving like Marvin," he joked.

"You don't say hello to your niece?" Grandma Hattie uttered.

"Oh, hey, Cristal. I ain't see you sitting there," he said.

"Damn, am I that transparent?" she replied.

"Loan me twenty dollars," he asked Cristal out of the blue.

Cristal frowned and sucked her teeth. Uncle Hardy was always asking someone for money, no matter who they were. But he was asking the wrong one.

"I ain't got it," she responded sharply.

"Cristal, I know you holding sumthin' on you. I'll pay you back."

"How and when? You don't even have a job," said Cristal.

"Like you do. All that stealing and hustling you and your friend be doin' out there, and you broke," her uncle Hardy spat.

"Why you all in my business for?" Cristal exclaimed. "Get a job."

"You first!" Uncle Hardy shot back, smirking at his niece.

Cristal sometimes despised her uncle and his ways. He was always begging and always annoying. It was a shame that he was family.

"You a bum, Uncle Hardy," Cristal said with dislike.

"The two of you, cut it out. Y'all are family and we're always supposed to stick together," Grandma Hattie chided.

"Well, tell my niece she ain't better than anyone."

"I ain't got time for this, I'm leaving, Grandma. It's always good seeing you," Cristal said, standing up and ready to leave.

Uncle Hardy left the room first, though. When he was gone, Cristal saw the opportunity to do something nice for her grandmother. Hattie had never had much in life, so Cristal reached into her pocket and pulled out a small wad of twenties and tens. It was some of the money given to her by E.P. She peeled off a hundred dollars in twenties and handed it to her grandmother. Like common, Hattie refused to take it.

"Cristal, I can't take this," she protested.

"Why not, Grandma? I know you need it more than me."

"Because, it's yours and I'm doing fine," she returned.

Cristal knew that was a lie. She saw the bills piling up on the coffee table in the living room. The light bill was overdue, her rent was late, and the refrigerator was running low on food. Who wanted to live like that?

"Grandma, just take it," Cristal pleaded. "I told you, I have a job now and I'm gonna start helping out more around here. Ya always helping everyone else, so this time allow someone to help you."

Grandma Hattie smiled at her granddaughter, most times; she had the heart of gold and was so giving. It was hard to see Cristal doing any wrong on the streets. Hattie sighed and took the cash. "If it's going to make my granddaughter feel better, I'll pay the light bill with it."

Cristal smiled. "I promise you, Grandma, there's goin' to be plenty more where that came from."

"As long as it's coming from somewhere decent and hardworking, and not anywhere corrupt, then I'll be happy to allow you to help out around here, Cristal," Grandma Hattie said with civil tone.

Some guilt surged through Cristal's body. The money she was going to make was going to be blood money, but someone in the family had to do something and step up somehow. She wasn't going tell her grandmother the truth anyway; she was comfortable with telling her grandma a bold-faced lie, as long as she was helping out the family. It was the way she justified going to work for E.P.: to take care of herself and her family, because God knows, there wasn't anyone else doing it.

TWELVE

With the cat away, the mice began to play. Black Earth was being detained on Riker's Island for numerous charges, including assaulting a police officer and aggravated assault on her daughter. Also, she had a prior warrant out for her arrest. At her arraignment, the judge set her bail at fifteen thousand dollars. She didn't have that kind of money, so she sat in jail until her trial date came.

She was going to have to do six months in Riker's Island because of the warrant on her, and now with these new pending charges, Black Earth was fucked. Her kids were taken into custody by Administration for Children's Services. Even though Tamar was eighteen, and could be considered their legal guardian, she wasn't in any condition to raise three kids and she didn't want to anyway. She refused to take them out of the state's custody. Her life was too busy and hectic for her to take in her sisters and brother.

Lisa frowned at Tamar's choice.

"That's your family, Tamar, and you just gonna let ACS snatch them away like that?" Lisa had argued.

"I didn't have 'em, they ain't my kids, and they better off there in the first fuckin' place. I'm barely taking care of my fuckin' self, and you wanna add more fuckin' stress to my life. If you want my sisters and brother out so badly, then you go get them and have them live wit' you. Shit, you the one living at home wit' both fuckin' parents, Lisa!" Tamar had heatedly replied. She was upset that Lisa was all in her business.

Tamar didn't want to hear anything else about her siblings and her fight with her mother.

Plus, Tamar was still healing from the vicious wound down her back. It was ugly to look at, and Tamar hated it. She felt disfigured, and her pride was more hurt than anything. The doctors said it would take some minor plastic surgery to restore the side of her back to normal. Even though Tamar was still a pretty girl, she felt scarred and unattractive, and she wouldn't be able to wear open-back dresses for a long time.

Like clockwork, Mona started to roll up a blunt with the urge to get high. Music blared throughout the apartment. The girls had cleaned up the mess left during the fight, and now it was time to talk, smoke weed, drink, and grill Cristal about her whereabouts with E.P. They acted like the incident with Black Earth hadn't happened at all.

Cristal left the apartment and went out onto the roof to smoke her cigarette, and to peer out at Brooklyn from up above and think about some things. She needed some alone time, too. E.P. was heavily on her mind. She missed him already. He had to fly to L.A. on business and promised to be back in town before her departure.

She realized that E.P. wasn't the head of the organization, but more like the Human Resources director. E.P. only did the recruiting, and he did his job very well, and she imagined that he got paid handsomely for his part.

There was a Commission she had to impress. Who was this Commission? She didn't know. But now she had to focus on getting her crew on board with the job. They wanted a team of women, and Cristal felt her crew was right for this favorable opportunity. How was she going to pitch it to them?

Cristal took a few pulls from the cancer stick between her lips and gazed out at Brooklyn. From where she stood on the gravel rooftop, twelve stories up, Brooklyn was a metropolitan beauty. She could hear the life of Brooklyn below, but on the rooftop, it felt like she was a world above everything.

Cristal heard the steel door open from behind her, disturbing her solitude. She heard shoes crunching against the graveled ground and voices. She turned to see Lisa, Mona, Sharon and Tamar coming outside to join their friend under the canopy of a falling day and rising evening.

"Damn bitch, you tryin' to leave us? Don't jump!" Mona shouted jokingly, laughing.

"I was just up here thinking," Cristal said.

"Who you thinkin' about? E.P.?" Tamar asked. "So tell us, what was it like to live like Cinderella for three days?"

"It was fun . . . really fun," Cristal replied with joy in her tone.

"I bet it was, cuz you was too busy to answer my damn calls or call a bitch back," Tamar said.

"Damn, he must have eaten that pussy up like it was dessert," Mona interjected.

Enough jokes, Tamar wanted to hear details. Cristal didn't mind giving her friends a play-by-play rundown of what went on in E.P.'s private suite. She told them about the sex they had from the balcony to the bedroom. She told them how big his dick was and how he worked that piece of hard steel inside of her. She told them about the breakfast she had every morning and dining in a five-star restaurant. She told them about the designer clothes and Vinny, the gay stylist, and the money he had. Her friends listened intently, and each one of them wished it was them who'd had that type of experience, especially Tamar.

"Bitch, you get pregnant by him yet?" Tamar joked around.

"It ain't even that type of party, Tamar," replied Cristal.

"It would be my type of party. Get that nigga to put a baby inside of me—shit, twins if you're lucky—and I would be paid for life," Tamar said.

"Well, I might have another way for us all to get paid for life," Cristal commented.

She took another pull from the Newport and puffed out smoke. Her friends were lingering on her last statement.

"What you mean, Cristal?" Sharon asked.

"I was given the opportunity to be a part of something really big," she said.

"And what is this?" Lisa asked.

Cristal didn't want to tell them what it was. She was told to keep everything a secret—only to just recruit a few of her friends to come along and jump on the smoking train that was headed to success. She was giving them a chance to have gainful employment and make some serious cash— probably more cash than they had ever seen in their lives. But the jobs weren't guaranteed, though. She had already vouched for them with E.P. and had done the initial interview. But overall, there were steps to be taken and three interviews in total for each woman to endure, and once they all got the job—hypothetically, they would work in groups. It was the way the Commission wanted it.

The Commission. Cristal felt like they were the Illuminati—too secretive and too powerful. Nevertheless, she wanted a piece of that power for herself. It was enticing and exhilarating to know something like that was within her reach.

Her crew had so many questions.

"How much we gonna get paid?" Tamar asked.

"What kind of job is it?" Mona asked.

"Where is it?" Lisa asked.

The only person who didn't show any interest in the employment was Sharon. She seemed standoffish about everything Cristal was saying to them while everyone else seemed like they were ready to sell their soul to the devil.

The only thing Cristal was allowed to speak on were the prerequisites for the job—how they couldn't have ever gotten their fingerprints taken, especially recently. None of them had any current arrests. Their only arrests happened when they all were minors and now, being young adults, they all had their criminal records sealed. Each girl had a clean slate with the law.

Cristal went on to say to them that they had to be able to leave town for ninety days for training without anyone reporting them missing or asking too many questions. They couldn't have any children and they couldn't have a significant other, like a husband, or be in any type of long-term relationship.

"What is it, fuckin' boot camp?" Tamar blurted out.

"So many rules," Lisa pointed out.

"But it will be worth it," Cristal stated.

She then went on to tell everyone that they would be paid handsomely for their ninety days of training, whether they got the job or not.

"Sounds like good news to me," Mona uttered.

"This is all too good to be true," Sharon said. "I'm not leaving for something I didn't apply for. We don't even know what job this is."

"First off, we don't have the job yet. And second, what else do we have goin' for us, Sharon? Huh? Look at us, barely making it out here, getting by, by the skin of our teeth. I'm sick and tired of living like this," Cristal exclaimed. "And besides, we have to leave. I already told E.P. about y'all, and the meeting is mandatory."

"Last time I checked, we were living in a free country, and I don't have to do shit but stay black and die," Sharon spat back with a fierce attitude.

"Why are you being so damn stubborn, Sharon?" Cristal hollered.

"Because, this all sounds suspect! You stay away with E.P. for days at a time and now you come back wanting us to work for him, no questions asked? Unbelievable," she uttered. "And I'm not leaving Pike."

"Pike? Are you fuckin' serious, Sharon?" Cristal exclaimed.

"Yes, I'm serious, Cristal. You seem to have found the man of your dreams, so can't the rest of us find him too?"

"Sharon, I swear, you's a stupid-ass bitch," Tamar reprimanded.

"Fuck you, Tamar!" Sharon cursed heatedly.

"No, fuck you!" Tamar shouted.

"Okay, enough!" Cristal screamed out. "I came to y'all for a good reason, not for us to fight and bicker on this roof."

"You really ready to stay for a dog like Pike, Sharon?" Mona asked.

Sharon nodded.

"Stupid," Tamar muttered.

Sharon cut her eyes at Tamar, and if she called her stupid one more time, she was ready to throw her friend off the roof. She was far from stupid, and she felt her friends were the stupid ones, in particular for leaving ninety days for a job that was a mystery. And furthermore, Sharon had waited too long for Pike. Even though she wasn't his woman yet, she wasn't going to jeopardize things by leaving him for ninety days, allowing Mesha to easily come back into his life. Pike may have been many things, including a horny asshole and jerk, but Sharon saw something sweet inside of him. She felt they were meant to be.

"Sharon, you gonna be a broke-ass bitch chasing behind a wack-ass nigga," Tamar continued with her insult.

"I remember not too long ago you was chasing behind the same wack nigga, Tamar," Sharon countered.

"And you know what, this bitch woke up and realized he ain't even worth my time," Tamar replied. "I'm ready to get paid."

Sharon sighed.

Regardless of receiving an earful for being so stupid, she wasn't going, and her mind was made up. Brooklyn was always going to be her home, no matter what.

"Listen, what I'm offering y'all is a major opportunity, and either we wit' it or not," Cristal interjected.

"Cristal, you know I'm wit' it," Tamar said.

"And you, Mona?" Cristal asked.

"Fuck it, I'm down," Mona said.

Cristal and the others stared at Lisa, who seemed somewhat uncertain about leaving for the job in a few days. "How about you Lisa, you in or are you out?"

Lisa stood quietly for a moment. It was a difficult decision to make, especially with vague information told about their unexpected employment. She looked at each of her friends with this ambivalent feeling, and then she gazed at Sharon for a moment. Lisa was the supporter of the group, wherever Cristal or Tamar went or whatever they did, she was right behind them. It was always hard to let her friends down.

Faintly, she answered, "I'm down."

Cristal smiled. She then looked at Sharon again for a change in her answer, but Sharon wasn't having any parts of it. She was alone in her defiance.

"I'm not going," Sharon reiterated sternly.

"It's your choice, but when we come back from training, making that serious paper and pushing our nice whips, don't come crying to us for help then, Sharon," said Cristal.

"I won't. I'm cool with my decision. I feel it is y'all that is making the mistake," she retorted.

"Whatever," uttered Tamar.

"I'm goin' back inside. It's getting chilly out here, and I need to get high," Mona said.

Lisa and Sharon followed behind her, but Cristal and Tamar lingered on the rooftop. When the girls were out of sight, Tamar pivoted toward her friend and asked, "Now that they're gone, let's you and I talk."

"About what?" Cristal asked.

"This job opportunity. I know you weren't wit' E.P. for half a week and you only come back with half the information. So what gives?"

"I can't speak on that at the moment, Tamar."

"And why not? We've been best friends since grade school, and we always shared everything. We never kept anything from each other, Cristal," Tamar replied with emotion.

"I know, but this is different."

"What's different about it?"

"It's just different, Tamar," Cristal repeated.

"I see. You get wit' E.P. and all of a sudden you wanna act CIA and shit, right?"

From Cristal's understanding, it seemed like they were about to get into some CIA shit. The Commission, the secrets, the killings; yeah, Cristal felt she was about to be thrust into a James Bond movie. Cristal was well-versed: E.P. had steadfastly instructed her that information would be released in stages while they were in training camp, and that she must not, under any circumstances, reveal to anyone that the real employment was to carry out the murders of people so high up that the Commission didn't want to get their hands dirty. The targets would range from Wall Street players, investment bankers, husbands who were cheating and wanted their wives out of the way once and for all, employees with grudges against their bosses, and good old-fashioned drug dealers who wanted to wipe out the competition without drawing any heat toward themselves.

The Commission's client list was broad and limitless.

Tamar was persistent. "I'm goin' in this thing blind, Cristal, because I trust you wit' my life and wit' secrets. You don't trust me? You let this nigga E.P. come in between us and separate us after our years of friendship," Tamar stated with conviction. "I told you things about myself that I never told anyone else. I feel I should get the same respect."

Cristal sighed heavily.

The two best friends locked eyes. Tamar's yearning to know the real truth started to bother Cristal. She hated lying to her friend.

Cristal lit another cigarette and took a long drag. Tamar was waiting to hear something. Cristal gazed out at Brooklyn for a moment, and then pivoted toward her friend, taking a deep breath. She fixed her eyes at Tamar without reserve and confessed, "We gonna kill people."

"Huh?" Tamar was befuddled.

"It's this powerful organization that does murders for hire, and they're willing to train us and pay us as long as we do what they say and stay loyal to them," Cristal informed.

It was weighty news to hear, but Tamar remained emotionless. "Whoa," Tamar muttered. "That's some heavy shit."

"I know," Cristal nodded her head in agreement. "But I promise it'll be worth it."

"We could get killed."

"True."

"We could get knocked."

"That's true too."

"Did you ever stop to think about all of this while you were gettin' dicked down? Did you stop to think about the proposition you were bringing to ya homegirls? Fuck it, I mean to your sisters?!"

"I have, Tamar, and I swear I can't do this without you. If you think this is a bad deal just say the word and I'll walk away. I'm only going if you down. Without you there is no me." Cristal didn't mean a word she'd just said. She was going regardless, but she realized that Tamar wanted to be begged and have her ass kissed a little.

Tamar took a couple moments to reply. "Fuck it, I'm down."

Cristal smiled. She knew her best friend would be.

PART TWO

DAY ONE

●●●

I t felt like a new day for the four girls on their way to Ronkonkoma, Long Island via the Long Island Rail Road. It was early in the morning when the girls took the subway to Jamaica station in Queens, and then transferred to the LIRR. When they stepped out of the subway and walked toward the LIRR, dawn was just about breaking in the sky.

It was a chilly summer morning, and rush hour was an hour away. The girls had an hour-long ride ahead of them into Ronkonkoma, Long Island, where they were to follow further instructions once they arrived.

The four friends packed light, overnight as Cristal advised them to do. They all were dressed in jeans, sneakers, and long-sleeved shirts, with hair styled into ponytails—looking like plain Janes.

The next train leaving for their destination was at 6am. The girls had about an hour wait. Their stomachs growled from hunger. They decided to get something to eat at a local diner around the corner. Over pancakes, scrambled eggs, and bacon, Cristal guaranteed to her friends once again that they were making the right choice. Their lives couldn't keep passing by like a plane in the sky without them getting a piece of the pie.

"Y'all ready for this?" Cristal asked.

"I'm down, Cristal. I ain't got nuthin' else to lose. My life's been fucked up for a long time now and if this is my chance to make it better, than I'm goin' for it," Mona declared.

"You don't even have to ask me," Tamar blurted out.

"We trust you, Cristal," Mona added.

Lisa sat at the table quietly. She ate away at her breakfast meal bit by bit and felt somewhat apprehensive about the entire plan. Cristal noticed her friend's distance from the table conversation and wondered what was bothering her. She assumed Lisa was having second thoughts about leaving.

"You okay, Lisa?" Cristal asked.

"I'm fine," Lisa replied.

"You sure?" responded Cristal.

Lisa nodded.

Cristal knew her friend wasn't fine. The look in Lisa's eyes showed uncertainty. And she and her friends had come too far for anyone to turn back now. It was the old saying, *Now or never*. Cristal didn't have the time or patience to deal with the never. She looked at the uncertainty in Lisa's eyes and coolly said to her, "We're in this thing together, Lisa, right?"

Lisa faintly nodded.

Cristal continued with, "Lisa, you trust me?"

"I do, Cristal," she responded.

"No, do you really trust me, and believe that I would never let anything happen to you? You're my friend and I love you like a sister. We came up together and we gonna succeed together, and we either go into this thing together and wholeheartedly, or we don't do this at all," Cristal asserted heartily.

Lisa smiled. "I'm in this thing wit' you, Cristal. I'm ready, too. I want something different in my life."

"What did you tell your parents?" Cristal asked.

"That I'm moving in wit' my new boyfriend and he live in the Bronx," she replied.

Cristal chuckled.

"Yeah, they nearly had a heart attack. We got into a heated argument, so I packed my things and just left. It explains my absence for ninety days," Lisa said.

"So we gonna do this and do it right."

"It would definitely feel better if Sharon was here," Mona said.

"Fuck her!" Tamar cursed. "She made her fuckin' choice and so did we."

Cristal agreed.

The girls finished off their breakfast and left the diner feeling a lot better. They had fifteen minutes until their train departed for Ronkonkoma. In their eyes, they might as well been leaving for Germany. They didn't know shit about Long Island or anywhere else. Brooklyn and Harlem were the only two places they had ever known in life.

The ride on the LIRR to Ronkonkoma was relaxing and stress-free. The seats were comfortable, and the ever-changing scenery as they passed through town after town was soothing. Finally, their destination was almost the last stop on the line. When they stepped out of the major railroad station on Lakeland Street, it felt like they were in Mayberry and were waiting to see Andy Griffith come greet them.

Ronkonkoma was a hamlet near the tip of Long Island, in the town of Islip, Suffolk County, New York. White people were everywhere, smiling, looking jolly like Santa Claus and hurrying to their purpose of the day. The four girls felt like fish out of water; everything was strange and new to them. The instructions given to Cristal once they arrived in town were to go to a Baptist Church located five miles away from the railroad station. There wasn't any pick-up service for them. They had to find their own way to the church.

The girls were fortunate to hail a local cab. They threw what little luggage they had into the trunk and climbed into the backseat. They finally made it to the white-steepled Baptist church on John Avenue in the quiet suburban area with the picket fences, tree-lined streets, and sprawling green lawns. It was ironic that they were meeting inside a church when their intentions were wicked. When Lisa and Mona saw the church, they were shocked.

"We meeting here?" Lisa asked, being to some extent stunned.

"I guess so. This is the right address," Cristal told them.

"What are we, applying to be priests and pastors now?" Mona joked.

It was early. Cristal walked up the concrete stairway to pull open the doors, but to her surprise, the church was locked down tight.

"What the fuck," Cristal muttered. She sighed and looked around. She checked the instructions once again and it was definitely the right place. Maybe they had come too early, but E.P. advised her to arrive early, warning her that the people he worked for didn't tolerate tardiness at all.

"What's goin' on, Cristal? We in the right place, or what?" Tamar asked.

"I think so."

"What do you mean you think so?"

Cristal looked around, confused. Something had to give. The cab driver was still parked on the street, car idling, waiting for further directions from the girls. There weren't any further instructions; they'd only been told to meet at the church before 8am. It was 8am and there wasn't a soul around. Cristal got nervous. Had she fucked up somehow? Did she screw up the instructions E.P. had given her? She hoped not. She'd made sure to follow everything he told her to do, to a T. The only mistake she made was telling Tamar the truth about the job. Had E.P. found out somehow? she wondered. The man had his resources and spies everywhere.

"The church is locked?" Mona asked.

"It is."

"What now?"

Cristal didn't know what now. "I don't know," she admitted.

"Don't tell me we came way out here for no reason at all. Does this job really exist, Cristal?" Mona asked.

"It does."

They all sighed. Cristal stood around looking dumbfounded. The last thing she wanted to do was panic or get angry. She kept her cool and walked toward the cab. The Caucasian driver didn't seem too pushy for his fee. He nonchalantly sat behind the wheel of his cab watching the girls pace around the area trying to come up with some solution. They were at the edge of nowhere, and home was many miles away.

"Do you have a name or a phone number?" Lisa asked.

"No," Cristal answered.

"Why not?" Lisa asked.

"Because I don't," Cristal replied sharply.

Cristal sighed again. Her crew trusted her to come out to Long Island; now she felt stupid in front of them. She'd guaranteed them a promising gig and payment; now it was hard to wipe the egg off her face.

"Cristal, what's goin' on?" Tamar asked with concern.

"We didn't leave Brooklyn for this," Mona uttered.

Cristal was ready to snap at them. "No, we didn't leave Brooklyn for this. I just need to think. Something's gotta give here, cuz I'm gonna make it right," Cristal said with assurance in her voice.

The cab driver gazed at Cristal and asked, "Is there a problem here, ladies?"

"Nah, no problem," Cristal returned unworriedly, focusing on the driver.

"You sure there's no problem here?" the driver reiterated coolly.

"Look, we pay you to drive us around, not to be in our fuckin' business," she scolded.

The driver laughed. He lit a cigarette and fixed his attention on the girls, and suddenly transformed into the foremost figure in their eyes, no longer looking like the humble cab driver who'd picked them up from the train station.

"You girls need help, I see," the man said.

"We don't need help," Cristal spat.

"You sure about that, Cristal?" he countered.

"How did you know my name?" Cristal exclaimed.

He puffed on his cigarette and breathed out smoke. He looked into the eyes of all four girls and had a steady calm about him. He wasn't in any rush to answer her question. She wasn't important to him. Like E.P., he had a job to do. He was paid by the Commission to subtly observe the girls' behavior upon their arrival in Ronkonkoma and give a vital report on them. They were potential recruits, and once recruits arrived into the town, they were watched like a hawk. The people watching could be anybody—the cab driver, a sanitation worker, a cop, the conductor, a housewife, a teenage girl; it didn't matter. The Commission employed people of all ethnicities, creeds, and occupations.

Cristal was stunned that the cabbie knew her name. She asked sternly again, "How did you know my name?"

"Because I was paid to know about you," the man replied nonchalantly.

It suddenly dawned on Cristal; he was part of the Commission or hired by them. Her heart jumped, her fiery attitude changed suddenly and she apologized to him for her behavior.

"I'm so sorry. We came to this place as instructed and the doors are locked," she told him.

"It's because we're not ready to start the process."

"Process? What process?" Mona inquired.

"The minute you stepped onto that train, we have been watching, and testing you," the man said. "We are everywhere."

"Oh, really?" Mona uttered.

"So what now?" Cristal asked.

"What now? This is what now," the man replied, motioning his hand toward the church door. It suddenly opened up.

The man continued. "One can never be too careful. Inside, we have a lot of work to do."

The girls entered the Baptist church. Inside were about thirty other people, mostly young and eager looking—supposedly new recruits from all over, vying for the elite job of working for the Commission. They were of all nationalities: black, white, Hispanic, and more. Everyone in the room stood around until they were told to find a seat in the pews. Each person looked lost and out of place. Out of the thirty people in attendance, only six were women, four of them from Cristal's crew.

It was about to become a very interesting day for everyone inside. An hour after entering the church, while conversations went on, and strangers tried to become familiar with each other, a well-dressed but hard-looking white man with a faded teardrop tattoo under his right eye and a strong German accent came out to greet them. The tattoo looked like he was in the process of having it laser removed—trying to erase evidence from his past.

"*Willkommen jeder!*" the man said loudly to the crowd in German, which meant "Welcome everyone!"

He had their undivided attention.

"*Sie haben einen langen Weg von zu hause gereist . . . fur diese große chance . . .*" he continued.

The man gazed heavily into the small gathering of people before him. He stood on the church platform with his strong presence speaking volumes. Not a soul in the room understood what he had just said in German. Their faces were baffled; some didn't even know he had just spoken in German.

"And in case you do not speak German, I just said 'Welcome everyone. You have all traveled a long way for this great opportunity.' There are many of you, but not all of you will be chosen. This is a grueling and challenging program, and we accept nothing but the best. As you know, discretion is one of our major rules. From here on, you will have no outside contract with family, friends, coworkers, or anyone else. From here on in, you belong to us," the German announced.

Cristal and her friends looked on in silence. They all were intimidated by him and his ominous looking cohorts that surrounded him. Cristal remained emotionless and focused. She slyly looked to see if E.P. was around, but there wasn't any sign of him.

The towering German continued, "My name is not of any importance to any of you. You shall refer to me as Mr. X."

He watched the room for a short moment, evaluating the recruits.

"In this program, we train you on everything, and within three months, we will have you speaking multiple languages, as well as being skilled in other areas. The people that recruited you are no longer of any concern to you and you will not see them during training, nor ever again. They have already performed their tasks; now it's time for the chosen ones to perform theirs. Your only concern these next ninety days is surviving this arduous training session. And I reiterate, not all of you will be chosen," Mr. X stated hardheartedly.

Cristal gulped hard. Lisa looked petrified, and Mona was concerned, but Tamar kept cool.

The German continued, "Now I know most of you will have questions, but questions, we do not answer here. We ask you the questions. You all came at your own risk. This is not boot camp, people. We make boot camp look like Disney World here, do you all understand that?" It was a rhetorical question.

Lisa looked at Cristal and whispered to her, "What have you gotten us into?"

"Relax. Everything's gonna be okay," Cristal assured her.

Lisa didn't look too appeased by her friend's answer.

Mr. X spoke for another ten minutes, and afterwards, each person in the room was handed an application that was thirty-five pages long, and it needed to be filled out ASAP. Some recruits started to moan and complained when they were handed the paperwork. The look in Mr. X's face showed he didn't like the griping. He stepped toward the crowd and exclaimed, "If there is any disapproval of filling out these forms, I will come deal with you personally."

He glared into the recruits' eyes, revealing his anger, and the griping stopped. No one said a word. Already, everyone was afraid of him, and he saw it in their eyes. He would walk up to certain recruits and scowl heavily at them. Most would shy away and avert their attention elsewhere, afraid to make eye contact with him.

Mr. X said, "I see fear in most of your eyes. I do not like it. Fear is a flaw, a weakness, and it will not be tolerated during this training session. Our people, we do not believe in fear. Does everyone understand this?"

"Yes!" the recruits shouted.

Mr. X walked away.

The first pages of the application were standard—name, address, date of birth, social security number, previous jobs held if any, and so on. Page two was about their health, allergies, illness, recent HIV/AIDS testing, or any other STDs, any asthma, and so on. The next page inquired about hobbies, favorite places, past vacation spots, best friends, worst enemies, bank account information, et cetera. The other pages inquired about family, siblings, any arrests, any troubles, and asked about political affiliation: Republican, Democratic, or Independent. They asked if you had voted for President Obama, and if so, why and if not, why. They wanted to know what shows you liked to watch, favorite movies, sports and more.

Page fifteen asked, "If you had a million dollars, how would you spend it?" Page thirty-one asked, "Would you kill a friend for million dollars?" Page thirty-two asked, "Would you kill your parents for ten million dollars?" Page thirty-five asked, "Could you kill a stranger for any amount of money?"

The questionnaire was long and tedious. It almost took two hours for everyone to fill the entire thing out. It was a dreary process, but it needed to be done.

After the questionnaires were filled out, everyone was led downstairs to the church basement in single file. They were given a number and escorted into a different area. It seemed like they were in some Nazi training camp. Everyone had their headshots taken, and then they were told to take off their street clothes and each issued a white jumpsuit and sneakers. The changing room was coed. Men and women stripped down almost naked in front of each other. For many, it felt embarrassing, but the staff didn't care. It was routine.

The girls kept close and stripped down to their underwear. Lisa covered her tits and private area, feeling like someone had violated her human rights. It felt like everyone was watching her. She felt like some animal in a cage and felt so humiliated. She truly started to regret coming along with Cristal and wished she had stayed behind with Sharon.

The recruits were watched closely as they peeled away their clothing and tossed everything to the floor. *What kind of job interview is this?* the girls thought. Everything had to go; no jewelry, and tattoos were thoroughly checked for any gang insignia or outrageous symbols. Tamar and Cristal went along with the program easily. Mona and Lisa, not so easily.

After the recruits were clad in their white jumpsuits and sneakers, they were handed another questionnaire. This time, it was only three pages long, and asked for their shoe size, sneaker size, waist measurement, and dress size. Then they had their fingerprints taken. The initial procedures in the church lasted a full day and night, and when late evening came, everyone was given a folder with their information. A white hood was thrown over each of their heads and then they were shuffled outside like cattle and placed on an idling bus parked in back of the church. They moved quickly and discreetly. They weren't allowed to see where they were being taken.

Several armed guards were on the buses with the recruits, to make sure no one cheated and took a look to where they were being driven to. Ironically, classical music was being played on the bus, befuddling the passengers, and no one was allowed to sit next to someone they knew. Four buses were in use; Tamar and Cristal were on the first bus, but they were separated from each other. Cristal sat in the front in a window seat, while Tamar rode in the back. Mona was on the third bus, and Lisa was riding on the fourth bus. She felt alone and scared. She had the urge to cry, but she held back her tears and said a silent prayer.

No one was allowed to talk.

They sat like statues in their seats.

The ride was over four hours long and most recruits assumed they were either in Connecticut, Pennsylvania, or New Jersey. But in truth, they never left the state of New York. They were in Syracuse—in some rural area where the nearest town was over twenty miles away. The Commission called this place "The Farm," because like a farm, they were to harvest the best and produce crops of killers in secret. It was a fortress resting on several large acres of land, nestled in the dense woods of upstate New York and as heavily guarded as the White House. The Farm was the breeding ground for some of the country's best assassins.

DAY TWO

●●●

The group arrived at the training camp in the wee hours of the morning, which was a warehouse in a rural area of upstate New York. It was clean and high-tech with the latest amenities. Cameras watched every area of the complex, and towering, electric fences kept out any unwanted company.

One by one, the recruits piled off the bus and stood in one line. The hoods were still in place over their heads until every person was off the bus and escorted into the sprawling facility. The brisk morning air nipped at their white jumpsuits like a towel whipping. Even though it was early summer, the cold upstate air was nothing to play with. The men and women could hear the voices of those in charge. They were loud, rough, and intimidating. It felt like they were convicted felons being led into jail. The shouting, the harsh demands; some of the recruits had never experienced such treatment.

Cristal felt like she couldn't breathe under the hood. Her fingers and toes were cold. She was hungry and hadn't slept in almost twenty-four hours. She wondered about her friends. She hadn't seen them since they left the church. Immediately, the group was split up. Cristal couldn't share a unit with Tamar, Lisa, or Mona.

The first procedure at the Farm was medical. One by one, each candidate went through a rigorous examination. Blood was taken from them several times, and they were issued shots from long syringes in both arms. The doctors checked their health methodically—eye exams, hearing, dental and mental health—asking the candidates various questions on topics from colors to violence. X-rays were taken, and their diet was examined.

After the lengthy medical procedure, Cristal was blindfolded and the white hood was thrown over her head again, and she was pushed into the warehouse and then thrown into a dark, nondescript room and told to be silent. She couldn't see. Everything was still, and the room felt dark and cold. She wasn't sure if she was alone or amongst dozens of other people. Cristal leaned against the concrete wall, trying to remain strong, trying not to feel fear. She slid down the wall and sat on the floor, breathing sparsely.

Several hours passed before any activity happened. She had nodded off. Sleep was becoming her best friend, and the cemetery silence in the room became to some extent comforting. But then ice-cold water was thrown onto her and she hollered loudly.

"Wake up!" someone hollered.

"*Wir schlafen nicht!*" another male exclaimed in German.

More cold water was thrown on her, and Cristal hollered like she was being tortured. The hood remained on and she shivered uncontrollably. A third bucket of ice-cold water was thrown on Cristal. Her clothes became drenched and an arctic chill swept throughout her body. Unexpectedly, she heard a door slam. Once again, she was alone, wet, and cold. The dark and pain was engulfing her.

"Stay strong. Just stay strong," she said to herself.

It was the next morning, but for Cristal, she didn't know it was morning; there was no sunlight or any kind of light seeping into the ordinary room. She shivered. She had dried off a bit. Her stomach was growling loudly. She hadn't eaten in two days.

Day three came, and it was the same. Cristal felt like she was about to pass out from starvation. She was ready to eat anything—rodents, insects, maybe chew on her own arm, and snack on her fingers. She had never been this hungry before.

Why were they doing this to her? Why were they treating her like she was some animal or some prisoner of war? It didn't make sense to her. She was supposed to be trained, not tortured. What part of the training was this? And what was she supposed to learn from being isolated, blinded, alone, and tortured with ice-cold water repeatedly thrown on her? She thought about her friends and wondered if they were going through the same harsh treatment as she was.

On day four, she felt paralyzed to the cold, hard ground. Her stomach growling was the only thing she could hear. It was roaring like a chainsaw going off. It felt like madness wanted to inhabit her mind. She heard the door open, followed by voices, people near her and suddenly the white hood and blindfold were snatched off her head, and her clouded vision came back slowly. Cristal could barely move. She looked up and saw a woman standing over her. She was dressed nicely, clad in Fendi, and had long, auburn hair, blue eyes, and olive skin—she was extremely beautiful.

"You're strong. I like that," the woman spoke in a thick, foreign accent.

Cristal could barely speak.

The woman gazed at her, her look impassive. Cristal had lost track of time and reality. She wanted to eat. She needed a shower. She needed a change of clothes. She was dirty, stinking, and almost hallucinating.

"My friends, where are they?" Cristal asked.

The woman gawked at Cristal with her unsettling eyes and said, "Four days in the program, and already ten are gone. You should be proud of yourself. You've no need to worry about friends here. Your life has changed. Your friends have changed. And you, you will no longer be the same. Understand?"

Cristal nodded.

"This is a test of endurance, psychology, and pain. Isolation is a form of punishment to many, but it can become a comfort to the right sort of mind. And you can have that right mind, Cristal; a strong mind," the woman said to her evenly.

Cristal was listening.

This woman, in her stylish heels and name-brand attire, radiated authority and strength in her demeanor. She also looked like she could become a cold-hearted bitch in a heartbeat. Her eyes were icy and tone chilling. Was she a killer or just an employee working for the Commission?

"Take her into the next room and have her cleaned up," the woman instructed the two men in the room with her.

They nodded. They went to help Cristal off the ground; she pushed them away, refusing their help. "I can get up by myself," she spat.

The woman smiled.

Cristal stood up and could barely move, but she willed herself forward and wondered what they had planned for her next. Her legs felt like jelly and she felt useless, but her spirit was far from broken.

Cristal washed herself thoroughly in the spacious bathroom. She was among others that had made it through the grueling first four days— mostly men, everyone hungry, dirty, and feeling boggled. It was her and another woman among the naked males showering in the washroom— there were big dicks and small dicks, fat dicks and skinny dicks, and she wasn't the least turned on. Sex was so far from her mind, it almost seemed unfamiliar to her. She looked around for her friends, but she didn't see them.

After showering and cleaning, the group had a hearty breakfast. The food going down her throat felt so nourishing and tasty, she had the urge to eat the plate, too. Afterwards, it was back to training.

DAY TWELVE

Cristal sat through class after class, day after day like it was high school again. Math, science, history, English, plus she had to learn two languages within a two-month period—German and Spanish. What did they think she was, a genius? The instructors were hard and brutal on their students. There were days where she went with less than four hours of sleep and no meals. It was like military boot camp: up before the sun, a three-mile run, an hour of calisthenics afterwards, and then maybe breakfast. In training, they were teaching the recruits the fundamentals first before they went on to anything advanced—endurance, survival, strength, stamina, and everything from books to explosives were covered the first weeks of training.

Day twelve was tedious and painstaking. When she'd been in high school, it wasn't this demanding. It also was a lot to take in: books to read, films to watch, and things to learn and study. Cristal felt like she was in a shadowy government agency somewhere unknown. It no longer felt like she had a choice; performance was expected of her.

On the twentieth day, the remaining recruits learned about computers—software, hardware, and viruses. They were expected to pass numerous psychometric, psychoanalytical, aptitude, and polygraph tests. And then the instructors taught the candidates the skills of espionage, covert operation protocols, and intelligence-gathering techniques. The candidates were trained in surveillance exercises.

On the thirtieth day, the candidates underwent training which involved basic combat training, infantry advanced individual training, and specialized infantry training. They did weapon training, learning to differentiate different gun calibers from the .9mm to assault rifles and grenades.

The Commission's agenda was to take the ghetto, the menace to society, and the unknown, and transform them from degenerate, subpar human beings into trained killers. And Cristal was expected to become a femme fatale—which meant *fatal woman* in French.

THIRTEEN

●●●●●●●●●●●●●●●●●●●●●●●●●●●●●●●●●●●●●

Sharon had Pike's kitchen smelling delicious with her home cooking. She had a chocolate cake baking in the oven and spare ribs, mashed potatoes, string beans, and yams cooking. It was a welcoming smell for Pike as he stepped out of the bathroom wrapped in a white towel. Sharon fixed her eyes on Pike's glistening body and smiled. He was strong eye candy from head to toe. They hadn't had sex yet, but every day she spent with Pike it became harder for her to resist the temptation. She continued to kill the man with her kindness; cleaning, cooking, ironing his clothes, and being his drug mule.

Since her homegirls were away, Sharon started spending more time over at Pike's place. It felt lonely in Brooklyn without her crew. Word on the streets was that Mesha was out for blood, holding a bitter grudge against Sharon and her crew. So she had to watch her back and keep a low profile, knowing Mesha didn't make idle threats.

Sharon checked her cake baking in the oven. It was coming out perfectly. She smiled. She couldn't wait until Pike tasted her infamous chocolate dessert. Her friends loved her cooking, and when it came to baking, there was not a soul who could resist it—every bit of it was finger-licking good.

"Who taught you how to cook like this?" Pike walked into the kitchen clad in only a towel. The aroma made his mouth water.

"My grandmother," Sharon responded. "With my parents fucked up on drugs and shit, I spent a lot of time over at her place, and she loved to cook. She loved the kitchen. She taught me all of her recipes. And I enjoyed every bit of time I had with her until she died two years ago," Sharon said, looking nostalgic for a moment.

Pike walked over to the stove and sampled some of her cooking, popped one piece of it into his mouth and he got hard. "Damn, this shit is good," he praised her heavily. "You can definitely burn, Sharon. I give you that."

Sharon beamed.

Her grandmother had always told her that the way to a man's heart was through his stomach. And she felt that her grandmother wasn't lying about that old folk tale.

"So, when can I eat?" Pike asked.

"When I'm done," Sharon said.

"How soon is that?"

"Soon."

He nodded.

Pike exited the kitchen and opened his closet in the living room. He pulled out a Nike shoebox and placed it on the table. Inside were several ounces of marijuana and two ounces of cocaine, along with some cash in the thousands. Sharon saw the contents and minded her business. She continued to busy herself in his kitchen while Pike went through his product. He counted his cash, and then looked Sharon's way and said, "Yo, you did ya thang the other day making them deliveries for me. I thank you for that. I owe you."

"I always got your back, Pike," Sharon returned.

"I see that."

She smiled at him.

"Yo, where's ya crew at? I haven't seen them around the way lately. They just, like, up and disappeared. I know they ain't hiding out from Mesha," said Pike.

Sharon had no real idea where her friends had gone off to.

"Nah, believe me, ain't nobody scared of that bitch. But they left town for a minute," she informed him.

"Left town? To where?" he asked.

"I don't know. Cristal was talking something about some job they were looking into, and they went chasing after it."

"Job? What them bitches know but shoplifting and hustling . . . and Brooklyn or Harlem?"

"It was something E.P. supposedly was hooking them up with," she mentioned.

The mention of E.P.'s name made Pike go quiet.

Sharon went on to say, "I don't trust it, and for some reason, I don't trust him." Even though she never met the man, she felt she had the good sense to understand when something seemed too good to be true, then it was.

"Did Cristal mention what kind of job it was?" Pike asked.

"Nah, she kept it a secret. And that was another thing that bothered me. She want us to go train for something and we don't have a clue what it's about? You cool with E.P., Pike. What is it that he does?"

Pike shrugged. "I don't even know."

"Anyway, just because the man is rich doesn't mean he is to be trusted," Sharon stated.

"You're a wise and smart girl," said Pike with admiration in his voice.

"My grandmother didn't raise me to be anyone's fool. Yes, I might humble myself and be kind to people, but I don't want anyone to play me for some fool and take advantage of me all the time," she proclaimed.

Pike chose to keep quiet about her last statement.

"But wherever they're at, I just pray and hope that they're safe and watchin' each other's back," Sharon added.

"They're good," Pike assured her.

"I just hope so."

"Y'all really close, I see that."

"We are . . . like sisters. You and Rich aren't close like that?"

"We cool, but I mean, it's mostly business wit' us, and most times he ain't around. He's always out of town doin' his thing, and I don't knock a nigga for that. He do him, and I do me," Pike said to her.

"I like Rich. He's cool. He's funny."

"Oh, and I don't make you laugh?" Pike asked, looking somewhat offended.

"You do. But Rich, he's just silly and stupid funny. I like to laugh though, Pike. When I stayed with my grandmother, we always laughed and had fun together. Even when times got hard, my grandmother was always laughing, cracking jokes, and making our lives interesting."

"You miss your grandmother a lot."

"I do."

"I never knew my grandmother. Barely knew my moms either. The only person I loved and cared about was my baby sister. She used to come to all of my games and cheer me on. She was always full of life and laughter," Pike said.

Sharon stopped cooking for a moment and went to be next to him. When he started talking about his baby sister, he would always drift into a different place. She sat on the floor next to Pike and placed her arms around him.

"I wanted to give up on basketball after she was killed, but I knew she wouldn't have wanted that," said Pike.

"You did the right thing. She's in a better place now, Pike," Sharon said to him.

For a moment, it looked like Pike was ready to tear up thinking about his baby sister. But he took a deep breath and snapped out of his daze. Sharon held him in her arms; it was a comfortable and supportive feeling.

The two talked for a while, sharing their past and their dreams with each other.

"I always wanted my own family," Sharon said to him. "I want a nice house. I want kids. I want a husband. I want love."

"I wanted the NBA," Pike said. "I wanted the fame, the fortune, the limelight, the adoration."

"And bitches, right?" Sharon interrupted jokingly.

Pike laughed. "Yeah, the bitches too."

"Y'all men are something else."

"And y'all women can be a handful," he returned.

They continued talking, smiling, and laughing. The moment was so welcoming to Sharon, she just wanted to remain on the floor talking to Pike until the end of time. This was where her life was meant to be, with Pike, changing him for the better. She knew he never had a woman like her before.

Pike smelled something in the air.

"I think ya cake might be burning," said Pike.

"Oh shit!" Sharon shouted. She jumped up and ran into the kitchen to save her cake in the oven.

Pike laughed. Sharon snatched her cake out of the oven just in time. She then pivoted toward Pike and blurted, "What are you laughing at?"

"You tryin' to burn down my apartment?" he replied for a laugh.

"You think you can do better?"

"If you teach me," Pike replied. "I always wanted to learn how to cook."

"Well, you can learn from the master. And there's something so sexy seeing a man in the kitchen and being able to cook."

Pike smiled.

It was the kind of time Sharon yearned to have with him; fun and laughter. When he wasn't thinking about sex or being an asshole, Pike was a pleasure to be around. She was truly enjoying his company this time around.

Sharon had no problem cooking for a man she wanted to love and have love her back. She and Pike set the table and the two sat down to the delicious meal. They talked about everything in the book. Pike was smart. He was educated. He just had some misfortune in his life and made some mistakes. Everyone made mistakes.

After dinner and conversation, Pike removed himself from the table and went back into his closet. He removed a loaded pistol and his illicit product. He looked at Sharon and asked, "Can you make another run for me?"

Sharon sighed heavily. She didn't want to, but she was going to do it anyway. Whatever he needed from her, she was down, even if it meant risking her freedom, and probably her life.

She put on her sneakers, took the bag with the drugs, kissed Pike before she left, and went out the door to become his drug mule once again. In some way, Sharon felt pleased that he trusted her with such great responsibilities.

He was still using her, and she was still loving and so sweet to him.

DAY FORTY-FIVE

Every day in training was grueling and painstaking. There were days where Cristal didn't sleep, barely ate, and was taught about survival. Day forty-five felt like two years in Cristal's mind. She was training heavily, being educated on everything in the book, and she also started a regimen of more intensive training that included etiquette from table manners to speaking well to first-aid survival—how to heal the body when it was broken, injured, bleeding, and in pain. She started to miss home, but she was told there was no home for her anymore. The Commission was her family. Her friends—she didn't know if they were still in training or gone. The outside world didn't exist to her anymore. There was no news, no gossip, no entertainment, TV, or film. The only films she watched were of those the Farm deemed necessary for her training. She felt isolated and hardened.

However, each day at the Farm, she was growing better. She was healthier and smarter than ever, and becoming more educated and more deadly. She was taught how to shoot every caliber of weapon, how to aim and fire center mass, or fire a head shot to kill her targets. Guns became her routine and weapons training was fun for her.

Also, she was becoming better in speaking German and Spanish. Every day she was taught and tested. Every day she was shedding the old layers of herself, her old ways, and becoming someone—or something—different.

Twice a week, doctors gave the remaining candidates a pill called P7C3 to take. The drug was to help induce strength and help the brain grow new cells. The pill was to enhance the users' memory by 60 percent and structure their development.

Cristal and the others started to train in martial arts and hand-to-hand combat. They fought each other in the gym and were trained in several different ways to break limbs and bring their foes down, even if they were twice their size. When it came to knowing how to kill someone, Cristal loved it.

Out of the thirty so applicants in that church on the first day, only seventeen remained. And out of these seventeen, more were to leave. The Commission was handpicking the best of the best.

There was one female in Cristal's group who caught her eyes. She and Cristal were the only females amongst the males training. She was black, a beautiful girl with dark skin and dark eyes. Her face was always stone, cold and unhappy. She had long, jet-black hair down to her butt. She had a slim figure, small boobs and ass, but she had long legs. She was shaped like a fashion runway model, tall. She looked half-black and half-Asian, and she spoke with a Jamaican accent.

Cristal didn't know her, but she didn't like her. For some reason, the girl's presence was very strong.

DAY SIXTY-SIX

Every morning, the candidates did a six-mile run to enhance their cardio and stamina. Afterwards, it was an hour of calisthenics, followed by a light breakfast and another punishing day of training from sunup to sundown. Not a minute was wasted on the Farm. The candidates slept only a total of five to six hours a day.

On day sixty-six, they started to learn about poisons—both traceable and untraceable. Cyanide, arsenic, propylene glycol, and ricin—an extremely toxic protein obtained from the pressed seeds of the castor-oil plant—were some of the many poisons they started to become familiar with. They learned how each poison worked, how to apply it, what damage it did to the body, and how long it took for the poison to affect the victim. It was interesting to Cristal.

A week later, the candidates went on to experience the gas chamber. In the classroom, the recruits were educated on how to use a gas mask—how it could save their lives anywhere if used properly—to help build their confidence about being in an environment with a potentially hazardous substance.

Each recruit spent approximately three to five minutes, and it was perhaps the longest three to five minutes of their lives in the chamber—depending on how well they wanted to cooperate. The recruits entered the gas chamber with their masks donned and clear, but once the doors were sealed, the masks came off. The first task was to break the seal of their mask, which would allow them to breathe in a little of the gas. Just as the tearing eyes and coughing set in, they were instructed to put their masks back on.

Cristal had never before felt anything like the first whiff of that gas in her system. It felt like her lungs wanted to explode and she wanted to pass out from the inhaled fumes.

The next step was to break the seal again, but only this time, they would set the mask on top of their heads. This was the time when everyone felt they had lost control and panic started to set in. The recruits' eyes were now filled with tears and the coughing got worse because the gas was in their lungs.

The gas started to burn their skin a little, similar to sunburn. It was agonizing. Some fell to their knees, crying out for help. Five minutes inside felt like hell to everyone. The Commission wasn't lenient to their recruits. They strongly felt that for one to truly want to survive, they had to almost experience death, and know what it was like to die.

Cristal's face was in complete anguish. It felt like the heavy fumes from the gas were eating her alive. Some were scared to remove their masks and shout out their social security number and name. Everyone quickly realized they wouldn't be able to leave the smoke-filled room until they completed the exercise, and they regained some of their sanity.

When the exercise was completed, everyone filed out of the gas chamber with their arms spread out to their sides. Their eyes were watering as though they had just stepped out of the shower, and they coughed uncontrollably as they prayed that they would never go through anything like that again.

DAY SEVENTY-FIVE

Cristal was highly trained in almost everything. This new chapter in her life was unbelievable. She was a completely different woman. The Commission had molded her into the perfect assassin. She was almost speaking German and Spanish fluently. She was becoming an expert in hand-to-hand combat. She'd learned how to shoot and kill with accuracy. Her etiquette was on point, she spoke eloquently, and her computer skills were more advanced than ever before. Her ninety days of training were coming to an end. It had been a grueling process, but Cristal knew it was going to be worth it.

Fourteen recruits were left standing.

Now she had to pass the test of empathy.

One by one, recruits were tossed into a single room.

Cristal was thrown into the concrete room with no windows, no furniture; it contained only emptiness and two doors on both sides. There were cameras above watching her every move. She was handed a loaded pistol and told to wait. Dressed in her white jumpsuit with her hair pulled into a long ponytail, fashion felt irrelevant to her. The instructors were observing her. She was told this was one of the final tests she needed to pass. So far, Cristal had passed everything with flying colors. Her physique was phenomenal, and her mind was sharper than a samurai blade.

Cristal stood in the center of the room holding a .9mm Beretta. It felt still and dull. She looked around—nowhere to go and nowhere to hide.

Her actions inside the room were recorded and watched closely.

There was a loud buzz, and the door on the opposite end opened up. A man was pushed into the room. The door shut behind him. Cristal looked at him. He was dirty and black, his tattered clothes soiled with stains, and he gave off a heavy foul odor. His beard was unkempt and scruffy. He also appeared to be drugged up and helpless. Probably too high to protest whatever was about to happen to him.

Cristal could smell him. He stank like a garbage dump. She scowled. The man wandered around the room like a leaf blowing in the wind. He stumbled a few times and used the wall for support.

"Kill him!" a voice crackled through the intercom.

It was a direct order. She couldn't show any empathy. This was still her training. He was only another obstacle she had to overcome. A human life didn't matter. Cristal cocked back the hammer to the .9mm and approached with a scowl. She outstretched her arm and aimed at the man's head. He was oblivious to the danger toward him. Cristal couldn't hesitate. They were watching and waiting.

The man turned and looked at Cristal blankly. He seemed like a simpleton—just one less stupid muthafucka on this earth to be concerned about. She fixed his eyes on the man and fired a hot round into his forehead.

Bak!

The homeless simpleton dropped to the hard ground like a sack of potatoes. He lay dead by Cristal's feet, crimson blood pooling underneath him.

"Well done," the voice boomed through the intercom.

She passed.

She was ready to move on to the next phase.

Murder was now in her blood.

DAY EIGHTY-FIVE

Cristal was placed into another dreary concrete room with the .9mm in her hand. She expected it was going to be the same test like before, another killing, but who would it be this time? She looked around the room and the smell of death permeated her nostrils. It was a kill room. Blood stains from previous murders decorated the hard concrete ground.

The Commission had brainwashed her into feeling no remorse for the murder she committed. It was only a job to do—a task, like taking out the trash. In her mind, it was for a good cause. He was a homeless man anyway, a blight on society. No one was going to miss him at all.

Since day one, the Commission had control over her. They sculpted Cristal into a stoic machine, ready to spill blood on their command. She gripped the gun tightly and stared menacingly at the opposite door. She was waiting for the next victim to be pushed out so she could shoot and kill.

The room buzzed loudly, indicating the door was about to be opened. This time, an unknown person was pushed into the room. It was a female, but her identity was concealed with the potato sack over her head. She wasn't homeless like the last victim. This one was well-dressed in a skirt and heels, and she was shapely.

Unlike her last kill, this woman appeared scared this time, highly aware that she was in some kind of danger.

"Please, let me go. I just want to go home," she cried out.

Cristal stared at her, emotionless. She remained silent and observed the woman's movement. Even though she couldn't see who else was in the room with her, the woman moved around the room frantically, feeling some kind of alarming presence and running into the wall and falling down to her knees.

"Kill her!" the same voice from before crackled through the intercom.

Hearing this command, the unknown woman became hysterical and frantically pleaded for her life.

"Please, don't kill me! I have children. I have two daughters," she shouted out.

Cristal raised the gun and aimed it at the frantic woman, but before she could shoot, the voice through the intercom spoke, saying, "What if this person was someone important to you, a parent, a friend, a family member. Would you still pull the trigger for money? If you truly loved this person, would you still murder them for money?"

Cristal hesitated for a moment, thinking about what the voice said to her. She had some assumptions. Who was the face behind the potato sack? Could it be someone she was close to or someone she loved greatly?

"If it was your beloved Grandma Hattie, would you still pull the trigger for the Commission?" the voice asked.

Cristal's heart jumped thinking about her grandmother. She dwelled on the question for a moment. The gun still aimed at the woman.

On her knees, begging for her life, the unknown woman hollered, "Please, I don't want to die! I don't want to die! My kids, I'm all they have."

Fuck it!

Bak!

The bullet ripped through the woman's skull like it was paper thin. She dropped dead, face first against the ground. Cristal stood over the body and fired again.

Bak! Bak! Bak! Bak! Bak!

It was overkill, but the Commission was proud. She had advanced and proven herself. Now she was ready to begin life as a sleeper agent for the Commission.

DAY NINETY

●●

The last day of training wasn't a celebration. There was no ceremony, no congratulations, but merely a transition into a different and darker world than the one they already came from. Out of the thirty recruits in the beginning, only thirteen made it through the program. They were now highly skilled assassins. They were to be given further instructions and assigned to a new location away from their old.

Cristal was ready to leave and start a new life as someone different. She was still Cristal on the outside, but inside, she was deadly. The past ninety days had been pure hell for her, but it had all been worth it to become the threat that she was today.

Cristal became shocked when she saw them again: Tamar and Mona. They made it. They'd survived the rigorous training too. It was a somewhat warm feeling to see familiar faces again. They were relieved, but also knew what they'd all done to get the position they received. The women didn't greet each other with hugs and kisses, but with emotionless gazes and respect. But Lisa was missing. It was announced that a few applicants were dismissed from the program, but there were a small handful that were so advanced, they were relocated to another program because they were going to receive additional, intense training.

Lisa? Cristal was shocked to think that it was Lisa who had advanced. It wasn't possible to know who hadn't made it and who would advance into becoming a lone wolf. Lisa seemed to be weaker and reluctant—how was she able to advance and become a lone wolf, when they all had to work in groups? Or had she not made it through at all?

FOURTEEN

Cristal and the others found themselves twenty-four thousand dollars richer after the ninety days of intense training. It was the most money they'd ever seen at once. The recruits were more than happy, but it certainly wasn't the millions they wanted to make.

Everyone was young, ambitious, and ready to make their bones.

They owned her now.

They warned everyone.

Cristal and everyone else were given an overseas bank account, a new name and identity, and a set of rules to follow during their transition back into society. Cristal was instructed to live her life mostly in the shadows—no excess or extravagant living. You couldn't stand out: no kids, no attached boyfriends, definitely no marriage. A solitary existence. They were told by the Commission that until their twenty-fifth birthday, they wouldn't be allowed to live a normal life.

At twenty-five, everyone aged out from the organization. After their twenty-fifth birthdays, they were free to live their lives however they wanted. They could not have children or get married before they aged out; it was repeated to them continually. If so, then there were repercussions.

There were so many rules to follow, from their way of living to how they spent their money, and Cristal absorbed it all into her memory. She didn't want to fuck this up.

On their last day, the speaker for the Commission this time around was a black woman with a British accent. She held court with the young, trained killers ages eighteen to twenty-three. Her name was Malkina, which came from "Grimalkin," meaning "an evil-looking female cat." And Malkina looked hardened and deadly. She'd made her bones with the Commission long ago, and now was the teacher instead of the killer.

She fixed her cold, menacing look on the thirteen deadly souls that remained, and announced, "The organization will contact each one of you when needed. We come first; everything else is not imperative in your life. We do not accept failure from any of our people. When you are needed, you will be contacted through a message. You will do us this service, and after the job is complete, funds will be deposited into your bank accounts. Everyone works in groups if necessary; the same faction you arrived with. Some of you will be lone wolves…but every one of you will kill for us. One final rule: You will not commit any murders unless they are sanctioned by the Commission."

Cristal stood expressionless with her peers in the room as she heard Malkina speak with assertiveness, and there was no forgiveness for mistakes in her tone. If anyone had any complaints, they didn't dare to voice them. They only listened and understood what was expected from them. Within the twelve weeks they had grown to trust the elaborate organization and believed anything that they were told.

New locations and apartments were given out to everyone, along with vehicles and stipends for daily expenses—all paid for by the Commission. Even though their bank accounts would show large sums of money after they completed a job, their overseas accounts were set up in such a way that they wouldn't be able to access them until they aged out of the Commission and, perhaps, lived a normal life.

Cristal received her folder and it showed that she now had a small 700-square-foot condo in SoHo, Manhattan. She smiled at her new location. She was out of Brooklyn, and was thrilled that she was able to remain in New York. She also was given a new Honda Accord to drive around in. It was something modest and inconspicuous. She was ecstatic to move in right away.

Tamar was placed in a co-op in Harlem, a place she was very familiar with. She was given the same Accord for transportation. Mona was placed in a co-op in the Bronx, and assigned a Civic for her own personal transportation. She wasn't too thrilled about being in the Bronx; she didn't know anything about the borough. But she couldn't argue with the Commission. It wasn't a democracy.

Immediately, Tamar and Mona felt slighted and jealous that Cristal was chosen to live in a better neighborhood while it felt like they were still slumming in the ghetto, especially Mona. It left a bad taste in their mouths. They suspected that Cristal received a better living place because she'd fucked E.P., and that he'd somehow put in a good word for Cristal.

• • •

Cristal walked into her new SoHo condo in disbelief that she actually had her own place and a new life. SoHo felt like the perfect neighborhood for Cristal. Nestled in Lower Manhattan, SoHo was notable for being the location of many artists' lofts and art galleries, and for the wide variety of shopping, ranging from trendy boutiques to upscale stores.

Her spacious condo was located near the cast-iron buildings on Grand Street between Lafayette and Broadway. Cristal adored the hardwood flooring, the floor-to-ceiling windows, and enough space to park her new car. She was eighteen years old and was already on a serious come-up. The only thing she needed to do was furnish and decorate her place, get adjusted, relax, and wait for further instructions from the Commission. From her understanding, a message to do a job could come from anywhere at any time. She had to be ready.

After doing some minor cleaning, she ran around her brand-new condo with a huge smile and did cartwheels in the empty living room. The little girl in her came out—like being home alone. She went to the window and gazed outside. Living in Manhattan was a dream come true. From the eighth-floor window of her condo, she watched people rushing by on the crowded sidewalk, traffic in gridlock on Broadway, numerous shops lining the city block, and more noise echoing into her apartment than Yankee Stadium. She closed her windows to breathe in a little silence.

She had her twenty-four thousand dollar stipend to spend on anything she wanted. The Commission took care of her rent and other minor expenses. It was her petty cash fund for food, clothing, and maybe some entertainment.

Cristal gazed out the window, and her mind became fixed on her training on the Farm. They had completely brainwashed her and desensitized her to violence and bloodshed. It became easy to watch gory videos of hundreds of people getting slaughtered and not feel any sympathy for the victims. Killing had become the norm for her, along with apathy.

She thought about the two lives she had taken at the Farm. Pulling that trigger came so easily to her. Cristal took a deep breath and snapped out of her daydream. She wasn't in any rush to go back to Brooklyn. She didn't miss that life. Like a butterfly breaking away from its cocoon, now she could fly, now she could live. She felt like somebody—a powerful somebody that people didn't want to fuck with. With the skills she'd so quickly attained, she felt like Neo from *The Matrix*. There was this feeling of wanting to go out and do whatever she wanted. She was warned to stay out of trouble; remain humble and low-key.

The rest of the day was spent cleaning and getting to know her new place and the neighborhood. It was late September, and the cool, evening air was a welcoming comfort. Cristal exited her residence and became swallowed up in the city that never sleeps. She went window shopping at a few boutiques, and then she went in and out of some stores, buying a few trinkets for her condo.

She made a stop at a quaint café on the corner where she sat nestled in the back, sipping on a latte, eating a piece of red-velvet cake, and thinking about her family and friends. She thought about her Grandma Hattie heavily. She missed that old, caring woman. Considering the person she was now, it was going to be hard to be around a woman who was a saint when she was trained to be a sinner.

Cristal watched the city from her seat. The people, the crowds, the cars, it was all passing her by. The sun was fading and fall was approaching. She sipped on her latte and just thought about the future. While she sat in the privacy of her mind and in her own world, she suddenly noticed someone watching her from across the room. His noticeable stare disturbed her daydream. Cristal gazed back at this towering and hunk of a man. He was standing next to another attractive male. They were on line waiting to make an order at the counter. Cristal looked at him, and there was a presence to him—an air of power about him. He had dark, deep-set eyes and his skin was milk-chocolate smooth. His goatee was thick and groomed nicely.

He continued to watch Cristal, ignoring what his friend was saying to him. Oddly, she had his undivided attention. He looked like he had seen the ninth wonder of the world when looking at Cristal, captivated by her young beauty. They locked eyes. Who was he? Was this handsome specimen of a man only there to watch and spy on her? Was he too being paid by the Commission to make sure Cristal didn't stray from the instructions given to her?

He was intriguing. His clothes were name-brand, stylish blue jeans that just covered the fresh beige Timberlands on his feet. He sported a little jewelry: diamond piercing in his right ear, and a platinum and diamond watch.

This man screamed either drug dealer or danger. Cristal was able to read people. She quickly sized him up and knew his type—womanizer, bad boy, from the streets, maybe a gun runner. He probably represented trouble. And it was the last thing she needed to come in her direction.

Cristal finished off her food, dropped a twenty on the table for payment, and walked toward the exit. As expected of him, the stranger moved her way with the intentions of trying to strike up a conversation with her.

He followed Cristal out the door and hollered, "You are an extremely beautiful woman, and can I get your name?"

Her back was to the man and her attention wanted to be elsewhere. It was her first day in SoHo, and already she had the men's attention. She wanted to continue walking away from him, but she was captivated by his strong, raspy voice and how fine he was.

"My name is Hugo," he continued politely.

Cristal turned toward him and remained stoic. It had been a long moment since she'd had sex. The Farm taught her how to suppress her sexual urges, but that was on the Farm; this was now. She knew that she couldn't get involved with this man. She had other priorities to take care of. She didn't have time for intimacy with anyone.

"I just want to know your name, that's all," Hugo added.

"My name shouldn't be important to you. I know your type," Cristal responded with a scowl.

"And what is my type?"

"Not mine," she coldly replied.

"Wow, a bullet to the heart. You gonna be that difficult, huh?"

"I'm not someone you should be getting involved with anyway," Cristal warned.

"And why not?" Hugo moved closer to the woman of his dreams.

"Because, I'll break your heart."

"Well, a broken heart can always be fixed. I wanna take you out. I wanna get to know you. You caught my attention inside and believe me, that is something hard to do. Women come at me; it's not the other way around." He was straightforward, no chaser.

"I don't go out," Cristal uttered sharply. "And you are a cocky nigga, aren't you?"

"When I see something that I like, I go after it."

"But you don't chase women, right?"

"I chase nothing but the best."

Cristal remained aloof.

"Damn, you are one hard woman to make laugh or compliment. What are you, bionic?" he joked.

"Sometimes."

"Well, Ms. Bionic, what will it take to get your name and have you go out with me? Just one date, something simple," Hugo said cordially.

"Nothing is ever simple."

"It could be."

"Well, I'm not a simple woman."

"I can already see that," he said. "Damn, you about ready to have a man on his knees asking you out. But I don't beg."

"You never should beg. Unless it's for your life," Cristal responded.

He chuckled. "You're different. I can see that. But I like different."

"And you're wasting my time," Cristal replied coldly.

Hugo chuckled again.

"Is my rejection that amusing?" she asked.

"You're intriguing."

Cristal turned and was about to walk away from him. She had entertained him too long. She had better things to do with her time. Hugo jogged up to her. He gently grabbed her arm and Cristal was ready to put a hurting on him, but she restrained that feeling and scowled as though he'd just tried fondling her.

"Damn, beautiful, you need to lighten up a little. But I do like your style," he said.

"Well, like it from a distance," she shot back.

"Ooh, now that's cold."

"I'm a cold bitch."

"Well, you need a man in your life to melt some of that ice in your heart and eyes," Hugo said.

"And you that man to melt my cold heart, huh?" Cristal returned with sarcasm.

"I am." Hugo smiled. His pearly white teeth and full lips were appealing, but Cristal was unreceptive to his charm and silver tongue.

Cristal started to walk away from him again. Hugo kept his cool and award-winning smile. "So, it's like that, beautiful? The cold shoulder, the sharp tongue, and the attitude? You know I'm a really nice guy when you get to know me."

Cristal kept on walking.

"A'ight, but I promise you this, we gonna see each other again, and when we do, then it's meant to be, and I'm not hearing any excuses from you," Hugo shouted at her.

Cristal walked on.

Hugo kept his eyes trained on the fierce beauty and watched her bend the corner. When she was out of his sight, he still looked that way. He was stuck on stupid for a moment. No woman had ever had the audacity to reject him. Cristal was the first and it turned him on even more. He kept a mental memory of her along with her unfriendly attitude stored somewhere inside of him.

A moment later, his friend exited the café with both their orders in his hand.

"You bagged that, yo?" he asked.

"Nah, she was colder than Aspen during ski season," he joked. "She wasn't trying to hear one word I said," Hugo replied, being honest with his friend. He had no reason to lie on his dick.

"She probably a lesbian then," his friend mentioned.

Hugo shook his head. "Nah, she ain't a lesbian. I can tell."

"Yeah, whatever, bitches today be switching up on a nigga. Don't stress that, though, there are more hoes out there."

But he was stressing it. There was something different about this one, Hugo thought. He knew it. The way she moved, and the ways she spoke, even her sarcasm, it left him awestruck, somehow. Hugo wasn't going to forget about this one. He had a feeling in his bones that they were going to cross paths again. He would bet on it.

●●●

Cristal walked into her condo and immediately began peeling away her clothing. She walked into her bathroom with her bare feet feeling soothed against the white, tiled floor. She started to run some lukewarm bathwater into the porcelain tub and pulled her long hair back into a bushy ponytail. The tranquility inside her new place was calming like drinking a cocktail on a Caribbean beach.

She lit some scented candles she'd just bought from a fragrance store in the area and placed them strategically around her tub. The off white walls and ambient lighting created a radiant glow. Cristal turned the radio to Hot97 and slowly submerged herself into the tub, allowing the lukewarm water to engulf her petite frame and propel her mind into this journey of slackening.

She closed her eyes and moaned.

This was life after the Farm, nothing but bliss—from the bottom to the top. The only thing missing was some alcohol and a joint to smoke. Besides that, it was the perfect scene. Hugo came into her mind briefly. The man was the archetype of fine and sexy. Cristal was proud of herself; before her training on the Farm, she would definitely have given Hugo the time of day, probably even fucked him that same night. Now, she didn't entertain it. The last thing she wanted to do was fuck up a good thing, especially over some dick.

FIFTEEN

Pike stared at Sharon's thick frame as she lay sound asleep on his comfortable bed. It was a sultry night, so she barely had any clothes on: T-shirt and panties, the perfect tease to him, especially since he hadn't fucked her yet. He lit a cigarette and took a few pulls. His mind was fixed on the chocolate woman with long, shoulder-length natural hair and shapely figure, sleeping like a baby. She looked so beautiful asleep. She was even more beautiful when she was awake.

Pike couldn't avert his eyes from her. He wondered what she was dreaming about. The look on her sleeping face seemed so peaceful, like she was in some kind of nirvana.

He hated to admit it to himself, but he was seriously falling for Sharon. There were so many good traits about her. So many things she did to make any man fall easily in love with her. And he was becoming one of those men.

He went to the window, shirtless and clad in his boxer briefs, and gazed outside. He exhaled the cigarette smoke through the open window and then took a seat in the wooden chair. He started to think back to the day of the party when he had first pushed up on her. She was defiant then, and she still was defiant now.

For some strange reason, he now respected that. She didn't rush to open her legs to him like so many other women had done previously. It had been three months and she still wasn't fucking him. The ironic thing was, he kept her around when if it was someone else, he would have been kicked them to the curb. The one thing Pike loved was pussy—slim, tall, dark, light, black or white, he'd had every type of woman in the book. He done sampled every type of candy in the candy store.

Pike had chosen Sharon because she was different, and he knew out of all her friends that she would be more of a giver than a taker. She hadn't proven him wrong yet. Since that first day, she did for him; cooking, cleaning, caring, and helping him move his drugs—risking her own life and freedom.

In his opinion, Cristal, Tamar, Lisa, and Mona were no different from his ex, Mesha. They would say that they loved you, and get you open and believing in something that might be real, something genuine—but instead of being a good woman, a great girlfriend and lover, they would become his dependent—like children. He wasn't looking to take care of any children. If he wanted children, he would make some of his own.

Pike felt women were always begging once they fucked him. He hated when a woman asked him for anything. He had been so spoiled most of his life by eager college scouts, coaches, teachers, neighbors, and cheerleaders. They fed him whatever he needed or asked for: sex; drugs; maybe changing a failing grade into a passing one by his teachers because he was the star of the basketball team; bitches doing homework and assignments for him; money under the table to play for certain teams in summer and spring tournaments; or scouts buying things—jewelry, clothes and most of all, his popularity. Everything was at his beck and call.

He was a spoiled man growing up. His talents on the basketball court were a gift and a curse. Now that he found himself becoming a has-been, he wanted to feel spoiled again. He wanted the overwhelming attention he used to receive. He was still a great baller on the courts, but he was getting older every year and more forgotten. The new bloods coming up were twice as fast and strong.

She was beautiful to him, even though she was the least pretty out of her crew. Pike was used to dating dime pieces. He had been with women so attractive that one look their way was hypnotic. Sharon couldn't physically hold a candle to the majority of the women in Pike's past, and at first, he only wanted to fuck her. What he didn't factor into his plan was that in spending so much time "using" her over the past few weeks, he would actually fall in love with her. She was so loving and nice to him. His own mother didn't treat him as good.

Pike remained seated by the window smoking his Newport. He watched her. He became captivated by her. He didn't want to lose her so he stopped treating her badly. It took a strong woman to stick around something negative and continue on with a positive attitude when it was so easy for her to leave.

Sharon moved in her sleep and suddenly woke up. She turned to her side to see Pike seated in the chair by the window finishing off his cigarette. She propped herself up against the headboard and asked, "Is everything okay?"

Pike nodded. "Yeah, I just couldn't sleep."

"Why not?" she asked with some concern in her voice. "You want me to make you some tea?" She was always concerned about him and doing something for him.

"Nah, I'm good."

"You sure?"

"Yeah, don't stress yourself. You already do too much."

Now Sharon was wide awake. She happened to smile at him and he smiled back. Their chemistry was just there; it wasn't forced or anything, they just seemed to connect like Legos.

"What time is it?" Sharon asked.

"One o'clock," Pike answered.

Sharon removed herself from the bed, scantily clad, placing her feet against his stylish rug. Her body seemed to sparkle like diamonds on the ocean floor in the moonlight coming through the window.

She stood up, and now that she was up, it was going to be hard for her to go back to sleep. Pike took one final pull from the cigarette and tossed it out the window. "I didn't mean to wake you," he said.

"Nah, I'm a light sleeper," she said.

Pike lifted his buttocks out of the chair and walked toward her. The two locked eyes and the tension between them was so strong, it would have been able to support a truck from twenty stories up.

"You sleep like a princess," he said to her.

Sharon smiled. Pike looked like a Greek god in his tight boxer shorts with the outline of his big dick showing. His abs rippled like water crashing onto the beach and his biceps looked strong enough to support her in any position they found themselves in.

Pike wanted her so badly it ached like hot, sharp needles being stuck into his skin. He felt such a salacious feeling inside of him that one look at Sharon's scantily clad body covered in chocolate made him rise to attention.

So many times she'd turned down his subtle advances or harsh approach for sex. So many times he had gone to bed sexually frustrated and horny. So many times he felt the urge to leave the cock-teasing Sharon alone and do him, because it was always easy to do him with any woman he wanted. But what was shocking to him was that since Sharon had come into his life, he hadn't thought about any other woman, and surprisingly, he hadn't had sex in weeks. Pike found himself only wanting Sharon more and more.

Pike stood behind Sharon, pressing his body against hers, and wrapped his arms around her, placing his hands on top of hers. It was a romantic position. She didn't resist him. His strong and alluring touch against her skin was comforting. Her heart felt like it was about to race out of her chest. Sharon closed her eyes. Pike could feel the fullness of her ass against him, his chest against her back. His arms were strong but his hands were gentle.

With her eyes still closed, Sharon lay her head back against Pike's strapping chest for a moment and they just stood in his room, dreaming. Now this was her nirvana. He started to massage her shoulders. She felt like melting in his arms. His chiseled frame rubbing against her started to make her pussy wet, drenching her panties with her womanly juices. She could feel the warmth of his breath on her ear, and at that moment, she felt like his woman. She felt loved and truly wanted by him. She leaned back into him fully, subconsciously rubbing her ass on him and she detected the slightest movement in his boxer shorts. His snake was growing in his boxers and was ready to be released and coiled inside her pulsating pussy.

"I love you," Pike uttered unexpectedly.

It came suddenly to Sharon. She was shocked to hear those words come from Pike. *Has he ever uttered these words to any other woman?* she asked herself. Pike wasn't the one to fall in love with anyone. The next thing she felt were his lips pressed softly against hers, his tongue softly exploring her mouth. Pike pulled her body tightly to his and Sharon cupped his face in her hands. They kissed passionately. Their tongues and breathing entwined. His hands explored her back, and the farther down they went, the more she moaned into his mouth. One kiss turned into deep soul kissing, and there was no turning back.

Sharon folded herself into his arms, feeling her nipples harden against his naked chest. They kissed passionately; the sensations engulfed her. Pike sucked her tongue gently into his mouth and she tasted considerably fresh.

Their lips parted, and Pike uttered huskily, "I want you so bad, baby. I need this. I want to feel you so much."

She felt every bit of his yearning from his heated breath. Pike fondled her body as he started kissing her neck. His technique was sensational. He soothingly sucked her hot spot and nibbled on Sharon's flesh while his hands pulled her closer, rubbing his woman all over.

They both fell on the bed and started making out like two teenage lovers in high school. There was something breathtaking about being in the arms of Pike—a black man. She felt his muscles against her, the power of his grasp as he pressed his full body weight into her. He had put his leg between hers and she started humping on him.

The little clothes that they wore were slowly peeled away from their bodies, and their nakedness became entwined on his bed. Sharon's body was magnificent from head to toe, and Pike's hard flesh was ready to conquer the unfamiliar territory between her legs. She took his hand and placed them on her succulent breasts and he started massaging them. Instinctively, his mouth found her nipples and he started sucking on them like they were ripe pieces of fruit. Sharon moaned from the feeling of his mouth against her skin. She held her tits up for him, feeding him, throwing her head back and enjoying the sensation of Pike's tongue moving from one to the other, licking her hardened nipples.

She also wrapped her hand around his hard dick and stroked him lovingly. His big, thick dick felt like a steel pipe in her manicured grip. Without missing a beat, Pike buried his face between the soft flesh of her breasts and pushed both nipples together and sucked them at the same time.

He pulled his face back and said, "I want you so bad I can't see straight."

She reached between his legs, holding his big dick and rubbed it on the slit of her pussy. She wanted to feel him so badly. She wanted Pike to fuck her. But first, she wanted intimacy with him. He reached into the nightstand near his bed and pulled out some condoms, the Magnum size. He definitely couldn't fit his dick into anything less. Pike opened the package with his teeth and slid it on his big dick. He was ready to take his glory. It had been too long of a wait.

Sharon started grinding on him, and then she straddled his lap and pressed her hands against his chest. Neither of them could wait any longer. Pike pushed the head in, and she moaned and felt her body tighten from the intense sensation inside of her. She was tighter than usual from not having had sex in so long. Pike took his time entering the dripping wet punani. She slowly felt his hard flesh piercing her insides and collapsing her walls as he had to work hard to get it all in. She felt his balls slamming against her as he thrust upwards with the head of his dick deep inside of her.

"Oh shit, oh shit…damn baby, you feel so good. Ooooh, this pussy feels so good," Pike cooed.

Sharon moaned and fucked him with her eyes closed. She felt his throbbing dick rolling in and out of her. Their sweaty bodies collided on the sheets. They locked lips again and Pike squeezed her tits as she unhurriedly and soothingly bounced up and down on him in a romantic lock.

They gripped each other lovingly—twisting, kissing, sexing, and turning, wrapping themselves into each other and in the sheets. It was intimacy at its best. Pike pushed every inch of dick inside of Sharon, rhythmically, methodically, and sensually. She grabbed his ass and tried to get him to fuck her harder. They grunted and groaned, fucking each other senseless until Pike cried out, "Oh shit, I'm gonna fuckin' cum!"

"Cum in this pussy, baby."

With togetherness, they came as one with their damp bodies slipping and sliding in sync. Pike shot so much semen into the condom, it felt like the dam was about to rupture. Sharon held him close to her heart. He soon rolled over on the bed and was exhausted, staring at the ceiling, his chest heaving up and down, and not saying a word.

"That felt so good," he finally said.

"I'm glad you enjoyed it. Was it worth the wait?" she asked.

He smiled.

She had finally given in to him, and when she did, it was much more than sex or fucking; they made heated and passionate love. Sharon was bringing out the better man in Pike, which made him want to do better things in his life.

As they lay snuggled up next to each other, they started talking about so many things, including him returning to school to finish his education. They talked about basketball—Sharon encouraged him to play basketball overseas—and then they talked about their past. And then Pike started talking about saving his drug money so that he could get them a bigger and better place and, maybe, a legit job.

One thing was for sure: Pike and Sharon were officially a couple. She was so happy and relieved. It looked like things were going to move ahead for her. She always had trust and faith, and it had paid off for her. She was confident that she'd truly made the right choice in her life.

She pulled the covers over them and they drifted off to sleep together in happiness.

SIXTEEN

●●●

The block was no different. Brooklyn was always going to be the same; ride or die, rowdy, and cluttered with the same old bullshit. But no matter what, Brooklyn was Cristal's heart and what she knew. She was getting used to her new SoHo apartment with a whole new attitude, but she needed something to do. Being in Manhattan around the uppity white folks all the time was getting depressing. So she made her escape to Brooklyn.

Under the rapidly graying sky in the fall weather, she parked her Accord on the busy two-way street and gazed out at some familiar faces on the block. The hustlers, players, and thugs were crowding the block like clockwork, and the hoochie mamas in their tight and scanty attire were right behind them, flaunting their goodies and flirting with smiles. Just a few short months ago, Cristal and her crew were among those frivolous bitches hugging the block with the bad boys, trying to catch their attention and snatch up a money nigga to spend that paper on them.

But that was back then.

Cristal had already blown through most of the twenty-four thousand dollars on nice furniture, music, clothes, jewelry, electronics, and other expensive items. Being low on funds, it felt like her life was returning back to normal. Cristal didn't want her life to go back to normal. Normal was difficult. Normal wasn't fun. She was ready to prove herself to the Commission, but since her return there hadn't been one murdergram delivered or any assignments to execute, and her life in SoHo was starting to become boring and out of touch.

It had been a month too long of waiting. She started to hang out with old friends again—Tamar, Mona, and Sharon, minus Lisa. Old routines, feelings, and habits started to set in again. The girls started hanging at Pike's apartment once more, smoking weed and joking around. When Sharon would ask about Lisa and why she was the only one that didn't come back, the girl's only explanation to their friend was that she loved being on Long Island so much, and that she met a guy. They tried to sell that she decided to stay and be happy with her new man and her new life. In reality, the girls were clueless about Lisa's absence. They thought she'd become a lone wolf for the Commission, which they'd all thought was impossible. Lisa was never an aggressor like that; mostly she was a follower. She was quiet most times, but they always said "Watch out for the quiet ones."

Whatever had happened to Lisa, lone wolf or not, the Commission kept it a secret. They were the only ones who knew the truth, and the unwitting girls were only pawns moving on a chessboard so big, it was hard to see the end.

"Why don't she ever call?" Sharon would ask.

The girls would be dumbfounded by the question. It would be Tamar who was smart enough to perpetuate the lie. "Yo, fuck that bitch! She went up that way, got strung out over some dick, and now she act like she too fuckin' good to call a bitch. That bitch was fake in the first place."

Cristal cosigned on that. "To forget about your friends over some dick, fuck it and fuck her. If she wanna stay away, then that's her life."

Mona didn't say a word.

"Did y'all have a falling out?" Sharon asked.

"She had the falling out. Her true colors came out," Tamar said.

Truth be told, Tamar, Cristal, and Mona were becoming increasingly worried about Lisa. Their gut told them that Lisa wasn't capable of being a lone wolf assassin. No one wanted to say it out loud in fear that their words would manifest into truth, but what if Lisa never made it out of that camp, alive?

However, in order to protect themselves and Sharon, they had to disparage their best friend's name. They could never allow Sharon, or anyone else, to find out the details of the Commission.

The sudden, harsh attitude toward their friend was boggling for Sharon. Why were they against Lisa and talking badly about her so suddenly? And since they been back, all three of them had been hush-hush about their new lives and their employment, not uttering a single word to Sharon. She found it strange for her friends to leave for three months to train for a job with little to show for it and basically never having to go to work.

Nevertheless, for Sharon, it was good to have friends around again, especially when Mesha made it clear on the streets that she wasn't happy to hear about Pike and Sharon's relationship. She threatened to cause bodily harm to Sharon when they crossed paths.

"So, you and Pike, wow! You actually got the nigga to commit to a relationship with you. Damn, Sharon, you must got that platinum pussy between your legs," Mona joked.

"Yeah, bitch, how that happened?" Cristal asked.

"Easily. He knows a good woman when he sees one," Sharon replied proudly.

"You finally decided to wipe the cobwebs from your pussy, snatched away the 'do not enter sign,' and finally allowed admission, huh," Tamar said. "That's what up, bitch."

Sharon proudly smiled with that smug look aimed at her friends, *I told you so!* It felt good to be wifey. So many bitches tried, but she was the woman who conquered. She had moved in and was already turning his place into a home.

The girls shared a blunt and some drinks and talked shit to each other like nothing had changed. Pike wasn't home; he was on the streets taking care of business with Rich, and they had the apartment to themselves.

Sharon took the blunt to her lips and inhaled the burning Kush a few times. She passed the blunt over to Mona and leaned back into the cushion with her eyes seeded from the high she felt. She smiled, looking reflective, and thought about how Pike had eaten her pussy out the night before. His tongue had traveled so far up her pussy and his lips and mouth had sucked on her clit so fervently that it didn't take long for her to cum like a geyser exploding.

"Bitch, I see you glowing over there," said Tamar. "It must be nice."

"Joyful," Sharon said.

"Damn, Pike got you open like that?"

"He do," she admitted.

"So, when is the wedding and the baby coming? Cuz you know I'm gonna be the godmother of that baby," Tamar proclaimed loudly.

"No bitch, I'm gonna be their baby's godmother," Cristal uttered.

Sharon laughed. It was only two weeks into their relationship, and her friends were already planning her wedding and baby shower and making her barefoot and pregnant in the kitchen.

"So y'all fuckin', huh, you suckin' his dick like a porn star. Shit, wit' ya big lips and his big dick it's like giants colliding," Mona said.

"Anyway, y'all bitches are perverts and need to stay out my business, because y'all damn sure ain't telling me about yours. But I'm so happy to finally have y'all back. I missed all of y'all," Sharon exclaimed affably.

"We happy to be back."

Sharon sighed, though. "I just wish Lisa was here with us. I miss her."

Her friends remained quiet.

The girls left the apartment building with the urge to chomp down on some snacks; they had a serious case of the munchies after smoking for hours. They headed to the nearest corner bodega up the street.

Cristal, Sharon, Tamar, and Mona continued talking and laughing while walking, unaware that Mesha and her wild band of misfits were close by and on the hunt for Sharon. Constantly hearing about Pike and Sharon's relationship was making Mesha crazy. Pike was her boyfriend, and no one was going to tell her any different.

The girls walked into the bodega and started snatching up every kind of junk food off the shelves and racks. Cristal piled up on chocolate bars and cigarettes. Tamar went for the potato chips and cupcakes. Mona raided the fridges for juices, and Sharon needed to take a call on her cell phone. Before she stepped out of the store, she hollered out, "Don't forget my Doritos."

She stepped out to answer the phone call from a friend. The minute she was outside, she found herself in danger. Mesha zeroed in on Sharon, and she and her squad stormed toward her, brimming with rage.

"Bitch, I told you to stay away from my fuckin' man!" Mesha shouted.

Sharon pivoted to confront Mesha. She scowled and didn't even see the attack coming. Mesha was never the one to talk, and her fists went flying toward Sharon. The punch coming from Mesha wasn't powerful, but it stung like a bee sting. And before Sharon knew it, she found herself surrounded by four of Mesha's scowling cohorts. They swarmed in on her crazily; punches and kicks came from every direction.

"Fuck that bitch up!" Mesha shouted.

"Yeah, bitch, what!"

Sharon tried holding her own, wildly swinging back at them and shredding clothing and kicking madly at her attackers, but to no avail; she was swiftly overwhelmed by pure rage and hatred.

"You stupid fuckin' bitch!" someone screamed.

"Get the fuck off me!" screamed Sharon as she felt herself being forcefully dragged to the ground so they could stomp her out.

The melee in front of the bodega started to draw a crowd who circled around the beatdown of a single woman. Sharon felt her hair being pulled out, her shirt tearing, her side caving in like a wall collapsing, and her tits being exposed because Mesha made it her business to embarrass her.

Hearing the melee outside, Tamar was ready to sprint from the bodega and aid her friend. But when Cristal grabbed her by the shirt and held Tamar back from intervening, Tamar looked back at Cristal like she was crazy.

"What the fuck you doin', Cristal?! Get the fuck off me! They jumping Sharon!" Tamar shouted.

Mona looked on helplessly for Cristal and Tamar to jump in, but Cristal shot her a sharp look. It was their friend being beaten badly outside. Why weren't they helping her?

"We can't, you know the rules," Cristal spat.

"What?" Tamar shouted.

"We just fuckin' can't!" Cristal reiterated.

It suddenly dawned on Tamar and Mona that the Commission wouldn't allow it. They couldn't afford to get arrested or mess around and end up killing one of the girls jumping Sharon. They had the skill, but it was a mere street brawl, and despite their friend being involved and torn apart by their rivals, the three of them had to helplessly watch and show apathy toward her.

Mesha wanted to really hurt Sharon. The bottom of her sneakers repeatedly came across the side of Sharon's face, along with several other shoes crushing down on her, spewing blood and mangling her. Her natural hair was in disarray. Mesha's female goons punched, kicked, pulled, tore, and spit on Sharon as she lay vulnerable and unaided against the hard concrete. They were ruthless, like a pack of hyenas in the jungle attacking some prey.

Out of the blue, Rich's car came to a screeching stop at the curb near the bodega and the melee. Pike leaped out from the passenger's side like a bullet discharging from a firing gun and went flying into the crowd watching the fight. He had a gut feeling his girl was involved in a fight and when he saw Mesha and her goons jumping on Sharon, he didn't hesitate to protect her. With his fists clenched, bitches or not, he went in swinging like Floyd Mayweather, going crazy and going hard as a muthafucka on Mesha and her crew. Pike began knocking bitches out.

"Get the fuck off her! Y'all bitches crazy!" he screamed.

Mesha went flying back like the wind lifted her off her feet with one hit from Pike. And when her bitches tried to fight Pike, he let them all know who was boss on the block. He went at each one of them like they were men, not giving a fuck if they were females. Rich aided his friend in the scuffle; they were outnumbered, but not overwhelmed by tits and ass trying to fight them back.

Things quickly got uglier like a fire raging out of control when a male bystander watching the conflict shouted to Pike, "You gonna hit bitches like that, nigga!"

"Fuck you, nigga! I'll fuck you up too, nigga!" Pike retorted.

And in a heartbeat, he charged at Pike, and Rich charged at the man. The chaos on the corner started to spiral out of control while Sharon lay badly injured and bleeding. She felt like she had been run over by a truck. She thought her ribs were broken and could barely move from the pain. But what hurt her more was not having any help from her friends.

Cops came pulling up on the curb like they were ready to do a raid and a half dozen uniformed officers came bursting out of their cars ready to break up the fight and make arrests. Cristal and her crew watched from a distance as disaster unfolded in front of them, and just as she predicted, Mesha, her crew, Pike, Rich, and a few others were quickly arrested, while Sharon was placed on a gurney and rushed to the nearest hospital.

Mona felt like shit. It shouldn't have gone down like that. They were all best friends. But what could they do? While Mona wrestled with her feelings, Tamar and Cristal stood stoically like statues.

It was the right choice to stay out of the fight. And that's that.

SEVENTEEN

Sharon lay badly beaten and bandaged in the emergency room at Harlem Hospital Center. She was fortunate that she hadn't suffered any internal bleeding, but the damage had been done. Her face was almost unrecognizable. She'd injured her hip and had a broken arm, a sprained hand, broken fingers, and more cuts and bruises on her face than a contender in a Mike Tyson fight.

It was an ugly fight, and Pike, like the man he was, came to her rescue like her knight in shining armor. But what had happened to her friends? Why did they abandon her like she was some stranger on the street? It was the million-dollar question everyone wanted to know.

Cristal, Tamar, and Mona walked into the emergency room searching for their friend. When they saw Sharon sprawled out on the gurney near the back of the emergency room looking like she had been run over a few times by some dump trucks, they felt awful. Back in the day, something like that would have never gone down. They would have torn Mesha and her crew apart. But things had changed, and they couldn't give anyone a reasonable explanation why they hadn't all come to Sharon's aid when she truly needed them the most.

The neighborhood started talking. Word had gotten out about the fight, and it reflected badly on Cristal and her peoples. They had to wrestle with feelings of guilt, but Cristal had to put it all back in the right perspective—they had a future to protect and they weren't about to throw it all away on some hood fight. She used Pike as an example: His stupidity in life had cost him his career in the NBA.

Mona went over to Sharon first. Her friend lay still with her eyes closed. Cristal and Tamar followed her over. It was a sad sight. First Lisa was gone and now Sharon was lying in a hospital being badly beaten. It seemed like it all was falling apart for them.

"We should have helped her," Mona said quietly for only her friends to hear.

"And if we had, we would be in the same predicament as Mesha and Pike," Cristal responded coolly.

"This is wrong. She's our friend," Mona countered.

"And we are about our business."

"What business, Cristal?" Mona shouted, startling people in the surrounding area.

"Mona, chill," Cristal warned.

"Nah, fuck that! Who are we? What did we fuckin' train for if we can't even help out our friend when she's getting jumped in the street? Look at her!" Mona pointed at Sharon on the bed.

"I do feel sympathy for Sharon, Mona—"

"Do you, Cristal?" Mona shot a dubious stare at her friend.

"This is not the place and damn sure not the time to talk about this," Cristal warned with a heated stare.

"Fuck this! I need some air." Mona pushed her way past Cristal and Tamar and hurried toward the exit.

Cristal and Tamar followed her toward the exit. They'd already created enough attention with Mona's outburst. Mona pulled out a cigarette and quickly lit it. Cristal and Tamar joined her outside on the steps of Harlem Hospital. It was late, and the fall air was becoming a bit chilly.

Before Cristal could say a word, a livery cab pulled up and came to a stop in front of the hospital and Pike jumped out. The girls were shocked.

They'd thought he was still locked up. The minute he saw Cristal, Tamar, and Mona standing outside the hospital, he went off.

He marched up the stairs in a frenzy, shouting, "Y'all supposed to be her friends, and y'all let her get jumped like that! What the fuck is wrong wit' y'all?"

"Pike, you need to calm down," Cristal replied through clenched teeth.

"Nah, fuck that, my girl is lying fucked up in the emergency room because y'all bitches just stood there and watched. What is y'all, fuckin' stupid? She's your fuckin' friend and you abandon her."

"Your girl now, huh?" Tamar snickered.

"Pike, you need to walk on by and go check on your girl," Cristal spat.

Pike was so upset that he was about to burst into flames. He glared at all three girls. He couldn't understand why they'd done what they did.

"Wit' friends like y'all, who the fuck needs enemies?" he barked, then charged by everyone and went into the hospital.

Pike rushed into the emergency room to Sharon's bedside. She was asleep, but she looked so beaten and battered, it almost brought tears to his eyes. The last time Pike had gotten emotional over any woman was when his little sister was killed. He couldn't lose this one so soon.

The first thing he did was take Sharon's listless hand in his and caress it while gazing at her battered face. The longer he looked at her, the angrier he became with everyone. It was inevitable—the tears started to trickle down his face. He was truly in love with this woman. He wanted to protect her, and it tore him apart inside that he wasn't there for her when she needed him. She did so much for him, more than any other woman in his life.

How could Mesha do this to her? *What kind of animals are they?* he thought. His ex was a monster, and he hoped she rotted in jail for her crimes. And as for Cristal and her friends, they were cowards. *They talked all this gangster shit, but when the time came, they shriveled up like old prunes.*

Pike wanted to carry out revenge, but he had to make sure his girl was taken care of first. He wasn't going to leave Sharon's side until she was 100 percent healed.

Pike pulled up a chair and started talking to Sharon in such a loving tone that his voice was like a serenade. She couldn't respond right away, being heavily sedated and medicated. He sighed heavily, knowing they were going to get through this rough patch in life.

He kissed her bruised face, and while massaging the back of her hand, he uttered, "I love you, baby. I truly do."

He did. It hadn't happened overnight, but it happened. Pike felt he had finally found the woman of his dreams, and he vowed to never let anything happen to her again.

•••

To get her mind off of Sharon, Cristal went for a three-mile run around SoHo in the early morning. Training from the Farm was still in her blood. Her workout included numerous push-ups, an intense cardio routine, sit-ups, and other rigorous exercises in her condo. She had to keep her body physically fit. And she had to keep up her appearance.

Six weeks home, and the girls were still impatiently waiting for their first murdergram to arrive. It was not that they were eager to kill anyone; it was that they were becoming paranoid. The girls fell in love with their new lifestyles, the amenities, and their own places to live with expenses paid. Plus, they wanted to prove themselves.

Cristal had armed herself with a small arsenal of handguns and a few knives. She kept them hidden in her apartment. She wanted to become like Angelina Jolie's character in *Mr. and Mrs. Smith*. Angelina was a bad bitch in that movie, and Cristal wanted to become a bad bitch in real life.

While training on the Farm, she'd fallen in love with two weapons, the .9mm Beretta and knives.

Seated at her kitchen table and getting ready to dine on crab legs and crab cakes, one of her favorite seafood meals, Cristal was ready to enjoy a quiet evening to herself. Before she could dive into some fine cuisine, her cell phone rang. When she answered, it was Mona on the other end.

"Sharon is out of the hospital."

"That's nice to hear," Cristal replied with detachment.

"You think we should go and visit her?" Mona asked.

"Why?"

"Because she's our friend, Cristal, and we did just stand by and watch her get assaulted."

"I don't think she and Pike are going to be in a joyous mood to see us. It's not a good idea, Mona."

"Well, we need to do something."

"Mona, we don't have to do a damn thing. She's a grown woman, and we have our own problems," Cristal stated coldly.

"She's our friend, Cristal, and who made you the boss over us?" Mona spat. "We sit here, living away from each other in different areas, waiting for some instructions from this so-called Commission like idiots, and I get placed in the fuckin' Bronx, while you get to live it up in SoHo, cozying with the white people. And don't think that Tamar and I didn't notice how you're living in a condo with a concierge and we are in co-ops!"

"You talking crazy, Mona. This is for the best."

"Best for who?"

Cristal sighed. Her crew was becoming impatient. Funds were running low and from paranoia it felt like they were being closely watched. It also felt like they were being taken for granted. Did the Commission truly believe in these young girls? Cristal's mind was spinning in every direction.

"We endured training and we took a job—made an oath. Something will come our way," said Cristal.

"Well, oath or not, Sharon is my friend. And with or without you, I'm gonna go visit her and see how she's doing," Mona said.

She hung up.

Cristal didn't know what else to say to Mona. The natives were becoming restless, and truth be told, Mona wasn't the only one becoming impatient and feeling neglected. Why would the Commission go through all of the trouble training and setting everyone up if they weren't going to put them to use? Cristal asked herself.

EIGHTEEN

●●●●●●●●●●●●●●●●●●●●●●●●●●●●●●●●●●●●

Pike carefully helped Sharon into his apartment. She had spent three days in Harlem Hospital recovering before they okayed her release. Doctors told her she was going to be fine and needed to rest. She had a cast on her foot, and her body hurt like it had never hurt before, but Pike was ready to make her recovery comfortable. She wasn't able to walk without a cane or his help, it was going to be challenging for her to bathe herself, and eating solid foods was going to prove to be a little bit difficult.

Pike helped Sharon to the bed and gently laid her down to rest.

"Baby, how you feeling? You okay? You need anything?" Pike asked.

Sharon smiled at his hospitality.

"No, baby, I'm good."

"You sure? I'll cook you something, since you're always cooking for me," he said, eagerly. "What you wanna eat?"

"Pike, I'm okay."

"No, ya not okay, look at what those animals did to you. I'm ready to retaliate, and ya fuckin' friends, how they gonna just stand there and watch it happen? What kind of fuckin' friends are they?"

Sharon was more forgiving about it. "Baby, don't stress yourself. Things happen. Maybe they had their reasons," she said.

"Nah, fuck they reasons! Ain't no fuckin' forgiving this, Sharon. Look at ya face, look at ya cast on your foot, what kind of man am I if I don't react?"

"You would be a good man, Pike, if you just let it go. I'm alive and I still have you, baby. That's all that matters," she said.

Pike couldn't believe his woman was willing to be so forgiving. He was seething and couldn't help but to clench his fists. His heart racing with adrenaline, he was ready to punch a hole in the wall.

"Let it go, baby . . . let it go," Sharon softly advised him.

Pike stood over her, not responding, but thinking. He shook his head, trying to transform his heated scowl into a nice smile for his boo. He wanted to let it go. He wanted to smile, but the callous brutality done to her was embedded in his mind.

"I'll make you a sandwich and chill out, get my mind off of things."

"Please do that, let's just spend the day together, watch a movie and make the best of things. Just you and me, baby," said Sharon with her affable attitude.

Pike exhaled. "You right, just you and me, baby. Things could have been worse. I'm tryin' to be a changed man, and I got you to thank for that."

"Now that's what I like to hear come from my big, strong man." Sharon smiled.

Pike leaned toward her and gave her a loving kiss on the forehead. It was like he'd planted his seal of a promise to her. She was an angel. So how did his angel get mixed in with a bunch of bipolar bitches?

He walked into the kitchen in a lighter mood than before and started making her a turkey and cheese sandwich. He turned on the radio to free his mind from the bullshit. He felt a little better, but that seed of vengeance was still inside of him, like an unearthed bad root. While in the kitchen, he heard knocking at his door. He wasn't expecting company, and he dared it to be Cristal, Tamar, or Mona having the audacity to come by to check on his girl when they damn near left her for dead. Pike didn't know what he would do if he came face to face with any one of them bitches, including Mesha.

He went to answer it, but was relieved to see it was Rich on the other side. He exhaled and allowed his friend inside.

"Rich, what's good?"

"Came by to see how you were holding up," Rich replied. "How she doing?"

"She's doin' fine; could be better . . . but she's alive and smiling, right? And that's all that matters."

"Well, Mesha is still locked up, and everybody is talkin' on the streets, saying Cristal and Sharon must have some beef between them, because how they gonna allow their friend to get jumped like that."

"I've been wracking my brain over the same thing."

"So what you wanna do about it?" Rich asked.

"Nothing right now. My girl wants me to chill out. She ain't stressin' it, and she don't want me to stress it."

Rich looked at his friend with composure. "So you falling back, huh?"

Pike nodded.

Rich saw the change in Pike. Rich walked behind his friend into the kitchen. As Pike continued to make Sharon her sandwich, Rich said, "You really feeling this one, huh?"

Pike temporarily stopped his preparations in the kitchen and gazed at his best friend. He looked like a balloon ready to deflate. "I'm not even gonna lie to you, Rich. I am. I'm really feelin' the fuck outta her."

"We've been friends for a long time, Pike, and I've seen you go through woman like a fat bitch going through a buffet, and this is the first time I ever heard you speak like this."

"Because it's real, Rich, it's fuckin' real. Sharon is so different. She's fuckin' genuine, my dude. This is the first woman I've been wit' who's willing to put me first and cares about me. She ain't selfish at all. And she made me wait damn near three months to fuck. And you know me, Rich, I never wait for pussy," Pike whispered.

"Yeah, I know." Rich chuckled. "So when's the wedding?"

"Not anytime soon."

"Wow, did you just say no time soon? Damn, Sharon must definitely be the one, cuz one mention of marriage or a serious relationship and you usually tense up and ain't tryin' to hear that shit."

"Yeah, I know."

"I'm happy you finally found someone, Pike. Sharon's good peoples. Shit, I think it's time for this jolly old big swinging-dick playboy to settle down too and get it right too," Rich said.

"It's a good feeling, having a woman having your back. I love her, Rich. I really do," Pike said wholeheartedly.

Pike smiled. Despite Sharon's beaten condition, she still was the most beautiful woman in his eyes. With Rich having his back, his life was going in a positive direction. He was ready to give up his whores and become a one-woman man.

NINETEEN

●●●

Cristal lay naked under the white sheets with a .9mm tucked under her fluffy white pillow. She slept like a newborn baby in a quiet place within a noisy city. In her new life, getting peace of mind was a stroke of luck. She still felt no remorse about abandoning Sharon. It was for the best. Mona needed to get that through her thick, naïve fucking head. The last thing they should do was upset the Commission. The Commission was some idolized, invisible entity that appeared to be everywhere yet nowhere.

With dawn rising and the morning light coming through her bedroom window, she was becoming an early bird. The morning was just about fresh when she woke up from a soothing sleep feeling ready to take advantage of a new day.

Cristal was about to get out of her bed, but there was something wrong and she became troubled by something strange in her bedroom. She'd had some unwanted company last night. The proof was the large manila folder on her bed. It creeped her out. With a strong feeling of apprehension rising, Cristal snatched the .9mm from under her pillow and, remaining butt-naked, went searching for intruders with the intent to shoot to kill. She thoroughly went searching room by room with the gun outstretched. Her bare feet pressed gently against the hardwood floor, not to create a sound. She looked everywhere, but no one was in her place.

She looked outside her bedroom window; the city was steadily coming alive at six in the morning. Her front door was still locked—no forced entry—and everything was in place. Nothing taken, nothing broken, but one thing added. She turned and gazed at the unexplained manila folder placed next to her as she slept. Whoever had been inside her home moved with the stealth and silence of a ninja. If they wanted to, they could have taken her life while she slept. This was the Commission's doing, Cristal knew it.

She picked up the folder and breathed out. This had to be it. The murdergram they'd been waiting for. Finally! It was their first target. Her heart beat like drums in a rock concert.

Cristal opened the folder and when she saw the face and name of their first kill, she stood aghast, not believing her eyes. This had to be a mistake. "What the fuck?" she muttered.

This mark, why him? It didn't make any sense.

The name of her target was Parnell Watkins, AKA Pike.

●●●

"What the fuck, Cristal? This has gotta be a fuckin' mistake. This is Pike we're talkin' about," Mona griped.

"It's no mistake, Mona. They want him dead," Cristal said.

"This shit is crazy," Tamar added.

The girls were torn up about the hit. Even though Pike was angry with them and had cursed the girls out the other day, he was still a good dude and Sharon's new boyfriend. They felt despondent about taking a friend's life. They had their meeting on the project rooftop underneath a canopy of a clear fall night. They shared a cigarette and felt hopeless. They were supposed to feel apathy for their targets…but this one was different.

"Look, either we do him, or they gonna do us, but either way Pike is still a dead man. They just gonna get someone else to kill him," Cristal spat harshly.

Mona heaved a depressed sigh. "What could have he done? This is Pike, a has-been star basketball player and low-level drug dealer," Mona exclaimed.

"He knows E.P., and that could be dangerous enough," Tamar uttered. "They might have been in bed together, some secret shit. It probably went bad between them."

Tamar's assumption made sense to them all. But was it true? There were so many speculations. Did he owe someone money? Did he fuck someone's wife? It didn't matter, though; the order was given and it had to be executed by any means necessary.

"It's a job; we don't get paid to ask why. Pike just gotta go. He has to die, and by our hands. This is just business, it's nothing personal," Cristal stated coldly.

Her crew stood around silently. Their silence displayed their agreement. This was the life they had chosen. It was going to get ugly, but this thing with Pike, it felt disastrous.

"Fuck it, let's just get this shit over wit'," Mona said aloofly.

Cristal took the final pull from the passing cigarette and flicked it off the roof. She blew smoke, nodded and said, "We can't fail or go backwards."

TWENTY

●●●●●●●●●●●●●●●●●●●●●●●●●●●●●●●●●●●●●●●

Pike woke up next to Sharon, and the first thing he did was hug her devotedly and give her a good-morning kiss. Sharon was still healing, but with Pike around, her road to recovery was a lot easier. She couldn't help but beam from ear to ear and feel protected by him. It felt like a glorious morning to them both.

"Baby, you want breakfast?" Pike asked.

"I'm not really hungry."

"Tea, coffee?"

"Some tea would be nice," she said.

"Then tea it is."

"Oh, and I think my prescription is ready today. You gonna go pick it up from the drugstore?" she asked him.

"I got you, baby."

Sharon smiled and replied, "I bet you do."

"Whatever you need done today, it's done."

He gave Sharon another loving kiss, donned his shorts, and went into the kitchen. He made some tea, toast, and scrambled eggs; though Sharon wanted just tea, he decided to add a little extra to her diet.

He put everything on a tray and served his woman breakfast in bed. She was delighted.

"Pike, I told you I just wanted some tea."

"Yeah, I know, but you gotta eat something."

She couldn't complain. There weren't too many women getting this kind of treatment at home. She felt special. She took a sip of tea and started eating her eggs. For the next hour he kept company with her, talking, and then he helped her get dressed. The cast on her foot was annoying. She couldn't move without limping, and there were a few body parts aching her. The painkillers she was taking were doing her some good, but having Pike by her side was doing her more good.

Pike donned his jacket. He kissed Sharon, uttered, "Baby, I'll be right back," and left the apartment with a smile on his face. Sharon lay back against the fluffy pillows behind her and beamed. What would she do without him? She knew he was going to be the perfect man for her. For once, life was good.

•••

Cristal and Tamar sat parked in the stolen maroon Chevy on the quiet, narrow Harlem block and observed Pike exiting his building. He zipped up his jacket in the cool, fall air and started to walk down the street alone. The girls—clad in oversized black hoodies, dark, baggy jeans, latex gloves, Timberlands, and ski hats—tried to give off the impression that it was two black males seated in the car. Cristal was behind the wheel with the .9mm loaded and cocked back in her lap. Tamar gripped the same caliber of gun. They both were ready to get it over with. Their forty-eight hours to do the hit were counting down. They had devised a plan to make it look gang-related. It was no secret that Pike was a drug dealer and a womanizer; therefore, his death could have come from anybody—rival dealers or a jealous boyfriend.

Pike would probably be their easiest target, but in way, their hardest, too. It was close to home, and it carried some emotions. They thought about how the aftermath was going to be following his death, especially with Sharon. How was she going to take it? But they didn't have time to dwell on outcomes and emotions. This was business, and these bitches were broke and needed to prove themselves.

Mona had opted out. She just couldn't bring herself to do it. Cristal didn't argue with her. It wasn't going to take the three of them to take out Pike. They already knew his whereabouts, who he was connected with, and his comings and goings. And besides, it wasn't like he walked around with any bodyguards all the time. From where she sat, Cristal could take him out with one shot; her training on the Farm had prepared her for this. But though it was an easy hit, it still had to be calculated and precise.

"When you wanna do this?" Tamar asked.

"When he comes back," said Cristal.

"That could be hours."

"He won't be gone long," she returned.

"How you know?"

"I just know."

Cristal knew it wasn't going to be a long wait. She observed what Pike had on: some sweatpants, sneakers, and a gray hoodie underneath his fall jacket. He was only making a run to the store and a few other places and coming right back. If Pike was going to the park to play ball, he always carried his basketball either under his arm or dribbling down the street while walking. And if he was going out somewhere for a long time, then he would have been dressed to the nines like he always was. It was his character. She knew Pike was making a run to pick up a few things, probably for Sharon. There was no doubt that she was inside his apartment waiting for her newfound lover to return. The girls knew today was going to be the worst day in their friend's life.

"Remember, make it look gang-related. We in and we out," said Cristal.

Tamar nodded.

They sat for thirty-five minutes in the cut, nestled between a commercial van in front and a brown hooptie behind them, and waited patiently. The flow of traffic, both foot and vehicle, was sparse regardless of it being late in the morning. Cristal puffed on her cigarette and shared it with Tamar. There was some edginess between them. Yes, they had killed before, but that was on the Farm and in a controlled environment. Now, this was no longer textbook killing. This was the real thing, and if caught, they were looking at a lengthy imprisonment for premeditated murder.

Cristal observed Pike rounding the corner, returning from his trip up the block from the corner store and local pharmacy. He carried a plastic bag and smoked a Newport. He was content in his own environment and unaware of the threat lurking. He definitely seemed to be a different man—a changed man. It didn't matter, though; his life was about to be cut short in a matter of moments.

Cristal turned the key and started the ignition. They placed the ample hoodies over their heads, pulled out of the parking spot, and headed in Pike's direction. To him, it was just another car leaving the block. He didn't pay the vehicle any attention. His only focus was getting back to Sharon.

The maroon Chevy revved forward and came to a halting stop just a few feet from Pike. He stood startled by the sudden approach and eyed the car with a baffled gaze. The doors flew open, and two hooded assailants quickly exited the car with their arms outstretched and pistols aimed at him unexpectedly.

Pike stood aghast.

He didn't recognize the assailants. Their faces were covered, their body language so threatening, Pike was frozen with fear. His shaky voice uttered, "Yo, yo what is—" but before he could finish his sentence, they opened fire on him.

Cristal and Tamar showed not an ounce of hesitation to kill their longtime friend. The shots rang out loudly like firecrackers on the Fourth of July, and the hot slugs tore into Pike's chiseled physique, knocking him off his feet, and he collapsed face-down on the concrete, smoking hot with burning lead inside of him.

There was no time to linger over the body. Cristal and Tamar jumped back into the idling car and sped away. Witnesses peered at the bloodshed from above, seeing what appeared to be two black males committing the murder.

Pike was dead. The girls had carried out their first murdergram.

●●●

The gunshots screaming from outside abruptly snatched Sharon out of her peaceful catnap. Her heartbeat skipped like hopscotch. It was a scary sound that sent an icy chill throughout her entire body. The room was still, but outside was chaos. She heard screaming and thunderous activity coming from her bedroom window.

How long had she been asleep? She immediately looked around for Pike. He wasn't around.

"Pike?" she called out. "Baby, are you back? Baby?"

There was no answer, only silence and the sudden feeling of uneasiness. She picked herself up from her horizontal position, removed herself from the bed, and limped toward the window. She had a bad feeling. Sharon lifted the window more and tried to gaze between the bars covering it. She looked down and saw people gathering around something and police cars racing down the block. Somebody had gotten shot, but who? She couldn't see what was going on outside clearly from her bedroom window. The victim was unseen.

"Pike, baby, are you back?" Sharon called out once again, this time her voice laden with concern.

No answer.

She donned one of his T-shirts and went limping throughout the apartment. It was obvious that he wasn't back yet. She dialed his cell phone—it rang, but there was no answer and her call went to his voicemail. She dialed again; same results. Her third straight call resulting in the same now brought about panic. He had only gone to the store to get a few things and he wasn't back yet.

By now, the block was flooded with marked cop cars and police officers swarming from corner to corner. It was another murder. The looky-loos were coming out in droves to view the crime scene. They were familiar with the victim and his reputation. It was heartbreaking.

Sharon knew something was wrong. She tried to hurry out of the apartment and downstairs the fastest she could. Clad only in Pike's T-shirt and a tiny jacket, she limped her way down several flights of stairs, desperately holding onto the railing to keep from toppling over. She held back her emotions, praying it wasn't her man who had fallen victim to gun violence right outside their home. A wave of concern spilled all over her, and Sharon hurried outside in an undignified haste. Her expression grew ghastly when she rushed out of the lobby forgetting about the cast on her foot and saw the body sprawled out half a block away.

"No, no, no, no! Please God, no . . . not this," she cried out, seeing the foot of the corpse in the midst of the surrounding crowd.

Cops pushed the crowd of looky-loos back from the crime scene. The homicide detectives arriving needed room to work and investigate the man's murder.

"Oh shit, that's Pike yo," one small teen uttered.

Sharon was behind him trying to push her way through the wave of people. When she heard Pike's name, she figured it had to be a mistake. The young teen didn't know what the fuck he was talking about. He was confused and mistaken that the body lying face-down on the cold, chipped concrete, with several bullets in his body was Pike.

Sharon came to the horrifying realization. It *was* Pike—dead. He was gunned down in the street like some mafia member. When Sharon saw the body, everything went blank for a moment. It felt like a nightmare she couldn't wake up from. She suddenly released a blood-curdling scream so loud it startled everyone nearby and felt like her pain-filled cry was about to shatter car windows.

Sharon no longer felt the pain of the bruises and bones in her body. The pain transferred itself into her soul. She fell to her knees with her face washed with tears. How could this happen? And why?

Sharon was devastated. It took several cops to help her up from the ground. Sharon just wanted to lie next to Pike and die also.

"It was two black males in hoodies, I think," an elderly female neighbor informed the suit and tie detectives investigating the murder. "They were driving, I think, a red car—I'm not sure of the model, though."

TWENTY-ONE

Cristal checked her bank account twenty-four hours after the murder, and she was ten thousand dollars richer. It wasn't the amount the girls expected, considering the emotional connection alone. It was assumed that they would get a hundred thousand each, but they only got thirty thousand dollars for the job, divided between them. Ten grand was chump change for murder, especially for a personal hit like that. They all were baffled, but somewhat okay with it. It was money they weren't used to seeing at all.

To free her mind from the murder, Cristal decided to spend some personal time with her grandmother, Hattie. Cristal missed her dearly loved grandmother, and she needed to feel a peaceful and loving environment. She drove her Accord to Brooklyn on a crisp, fall evening and parked in front of her grandmother's place. She stepped out of her ride looking stylish in her tight-fitting jeans, highlighting her luscious curves and protruding booty, a chic shirt underneath her leather jacket, and new shoes.

Cristal couldn't help but feel guilty that it'd been months since she'd seen her grandmother. Before the Farm, two or three weeks couldn't go by without her checking in to see how the woman was doing. When Cristal stepped into the apartment, she gave Grandma Hattie a loving hug and kiss.

Ms. Hattie stepped back, stared at Cristal looking like a million bucks in her new attire, and said, "Chile, look at you. You looking mighty fancy in them nice clothes."

"You like it, Grandma?"

"I do. That new job of yours must be paying very well for you to look like that."

Cristal felt guilty, but remained impassive. She smiled. "It does, Grandma. I mean, I like it."

"Well, come on in, Cristal. I have a surprise for you," Ms. Hattie said.

When Cristal walked into the apartment she was taken aback to see her cousin Mia seated in the living room looking like a diva herself in her red Valentino heels, sparkling diamonds, and Armani jeans. Mia smiled. Cristal didn't.

"Your cousin Mia just came back from California. Lord, this is a very blessed day, my two favorite granddaughters are here," Ms. Hattie proclaimed with joy. "I'm gonna go into the kitchen and make us a meal."

Ms. Hattie walked into the kitchen ready to cook and bake until her kitchen was inundated with food. When she was out of sight, the cousins finally acknowledged each other.

"Hey, Cristal," Mia greeted halfheartedly.

"Hey, Mia," Cristal returned dryly.

It was clear that the two first cousins who were once like sisters were now at odds with each other. Mia was a money-hungry woman who did whatever to get her way and to get paid. Cristal still couldn't forgive or forget that three years ago, Mia fucked her then-boyfriend Damien. She'd loved Damien and her cousin snatched away that love. They argued, they fought, and when things got too heated for Mia, she had packed her bags and moved to California to pursue an acting career. She always wanted her name in glitz and glamour.

Cristal figured her acting career wasn't turning out too good, since she came back to New York and was staying with Grandma Hattie again. However Mia's wardrobe demonstrated that she had made it, or she'd bagged a rich man to take care of her. When they were younger, it had been their dream to find a fine hustler to trick on them. The girls were always in competition with each other, and for a while, it seemed that Mia was winning.

"It's been a long time, cousin," Mia said. She stood up to display her finest attire and her curvy frame.

Cristal smirked. She knew what her cousin was doing. But this time, she could match the bitch in wealth and wardrobe. While growing up, it was Mia who was always the best dressed one who dated the big-time dope dealers in their hood. But now, Cristal didn't need to depend on any man; she was making her ends meet and becoming independent.

"You look good, Cristal. I see you finally coming up," Mia said.

"I do my thang," Cristal replied dryly.

"I like your earrings."

"Thanks," she replied tersely.

"Look, let's just cut out the bullshit. I know you still pissed about what happened back in the day, and I just wanted to let you know that I'm sorry. I was wrong. I was wrong about so many things, and I shouldn't have fucked your man when I knew how strongly you felt about him," Mia said.

Cristal didn't respond to her apology right away.

"The past is the past, right?" Cristal finally said.

"I'm glad you feel that way," Mia replied.

"You look good, too."

"Thank you."

It was only small talk between them. Cristal wasn't about to get into a full-blown conversation with her. She'd only stopped by to see Grandma Hattie because she missed her and wanted to give her some money. Cristal went into her pocket and pulled out a stack of hundreds while Mia watched. Her twenty-four thousand dollar stipend was dwindling and she couldn't wait for the next one. She peeled off five hundred dollars in twenty-dollar bills.

"Damn, you really came up, huh?" Mia said.

"I did more than come up. I'm running shit," Cristal haughtily replied.

She pivoted on her nine-hundred-dollar shoes and went into the kitchen to see her grandmother. While her grandmother was preparing a few things over the stove, Cristal slipped the five hundred dollars into her apron pocket and kissed Ms. Hattie on the cheek.

"Cristal, I don't need your money. I'm fine," Ms. Hattie protested.

"Grandma, I don't need it. My bills are already taken care of," Cristal replied. "And I already treated myself."

Ms. Hattie sighed. "You're spoiling me, girl."

"I know." Cristal smiled. "But I can't stay for dinner."

"Why not? I'm making some of your favorites tonight."

"I have a few things to take care of and I'm in a rush, Grandma."

Cristal kissed her grandmother on the cheek again and walked away, but before she could leave the kitchen, Ms. Hattie asked, "Cristal, is this money legal? Because I don't want it if it's not."

Cristal hated lying to her, but she felt she had to. She was tired of seeing her grandmother struggle. With a straight face aimed at Ms. Hattie, Cristal replied, "It is, Grandma. I worked hard for it. I promise."

Ms. Hattie smiled. "I believe you, chile. You never had a reason to lie to me before."

Cristal felt like shit on the inside. Her stomach churned like there was a sickness settling in, and she felt like lightning was going to strike her where she stood for telling such a boldfaced lie.

"I gotta go, Grandma," she said again.

Cristal hurried away from her grandmother fast, like the kitchen had caught on fire. Mia was seated on the couch talking on her cell phone. When she noticed Cristal leaving, she curtailed her call and asked Cristal, "Why are you leaving? I thought you were going to stay and let us catch up."

"Well, you thought wrong," Cristal snapped.

"I thought it was all good between us."

"It is. I can forgive, but I damn sure can't forget," Cristal responded.

Cristal walked out the apartment leaving it at that. The blood money she'd given her grandmother weighed heavily on her conscience.

Cristal walked out the lobby with her car keys already in her hand. She was ready to escape back home and be by herself. She only took three steps toward her parked vehicle on the other side of the street when she heard someone shout out, "Hey, Ms. Bionic."

Hearing the nickname, Cristal already knew who was calling her. Was it possible that they had run into each other again? She turned to her left and saw the driver door to a silver Bentley GT opened up. Hugo stepped out the car with his pearly white teeth showing and looking too fine in his brown leather jacket and sparkling jewelry, his low-cut waves shining and his eyes lighting up in Cristal's direction.

"I knew it was meant to be," he hollered with excitement. "I knew I would see you again."

Cristal was literally speechless.

What was he doing in Brooklyn? And why was he on this side of town, parked in front of her grandmother's building out of all places?

"You stalking me?" Cristal asked throwing a hard scowl his way.

"Stalking? Hell no, this is fate, beautiful. But I'm like ubiquitous out this bitch, you gonna see me everywhere."

The way he spoke and the words he used, it made his presence even more unique and him very intriguing.

"But I have peoples in this building. Brooklyn is my first home. I was born and raised here, Brownsville and East New York. I'm surprised you never heard of me . . . not to toot my own horn, but my name do ring out," he continued. "And I already see it in your face, you wondering what was I doing in SoHo…see I'm never the type to be provincial. I like to get around."

"Even with the ladies," Cristal uttered, taking shots at him.

Hugo could only chuckle at the slick comment toward him. "I really like you, Ms. Bionic."

Cristal was becoming annoyed by the nick name. "Please, stop calling me that."

"Well, it would be nice if I knew your real name. You was so cold before, you damn near left me with frostbite in the heat," he joked.

Cristal laughed. He was funny. He had a magnetic personality, and Cristal couldn't help but to be drawn to him.

"See, there go that smile and laughter. I knew you had it somewhere in you. You are beautiful, like, extremely, and you have been on my mind since the day I met you."

"You got game, I give you that," said Cristal.

"Nah, it's no game with you. It's the truth. You look like a woman who doesn't have time for games, and I'm not the Parker Brothers."

"I don't," she agreed.

"So let me start this again. My name is Hugo, in case you forgot, and can I have the pleasure of knowing the angel I'm talking to?" Hugo stretched out his hand to shake hers.

Cristal looked reluctant for a moment, but he was so funny and smooth with his approach, it was hard to deny him a second time. And maybe it was fate. New York was a big city, and the chances of them bumping into each other were almost zero to none.

She finally told him the name the Commission assigned her. "My name is Elizabeth."

"Elizabeth. Now that's a beautiful name for a beautiful woman," Hugo complimented.

"Thank you."

"You know that invitation to take you out to dinner is still open. I'm a patient man."

"I bet you are."

One date with him seemed harmless, but Cristal was still apprehensive about it.

"Who you know in this building? You said your peoples. Who's your peoples?" she asked.

"My mother stays here. She's sick with cancer, so I come by on a regular to make sure she's very well taken care of. I hired a full-time home attendant to look after her. That woman is the only family I have left," Hugo admitted.

"No brothers or sisters?"

He shook his head. "My older brother died from an asthma attack when I was twelve. I never knew my father, and any distant family out there never gave enough of a fuck about me and my moms to come check on us or help us out when shit got bad. So at a young age, I got smart and business-savvy really fast."

It was sad to hear.

Despite going through the third degree with Cristal and having to remember losing his older brother, there was this strength and assurance about him. He stood tall like a general. He had swag and charm.

"Funny thing, I never saw you around before," Cristal said, skeptically.

"I don't hang out. I'm about my business from sunup to sundown. I come see my mother and then I'm ghost."

"Mama's boy, huh?"

"I confess, I am. But you know a few things about me now. Hope it brings you some comfort, but I only know your name," he said.

It was hard to spill out, but Cristal decided to let her guard down a small inch and disclosed to him, "I got family in this building too. My grandmother."

"See, we both have something in common."

"Nice car," she pointed out. "What is it that you do, Hugo?"

"Honestly, I do me. I'm a hustler, I'm not even gonna lie to you," he admitted.

It was a bold thing to do—to expose the truth to a complete stranger—but Cristal gave him strong points for doing so.

"So by the looks of things, you're the man in charge, huh," she replied.

He smiled. "I wasn't born to follow, but to be the commanding general of my own army and run my own empire."

"And how big is this empire?"

"We can talk about this over dinner."

"You're very persistent."

"Because I know you're a good thing worth chasing," he said coolly.

His conversation was interesting. He was an appealing and amiable man. Cristal gazed into his eyes; they spoke out a gangster and a gentleman, just her type of man. His smooth complexion and soft hair, mixed with his strong jawbone and nose was magnetic. He looked like he was a mixed breed with a weird name.

She lingered near his Bentley longer than she expected, conversing with Hugo about everything. He had much talk to him, but it wasn't nonsense. The man was educated: He knew business, politics, and history, and if he had not been a big-time drug dealer, then maybe in a different life he would have been running a Fortune 500 company.

Two hours passed, and Cristal found herself seated in the passenger seat of Hugo's gleaming Bentley and hanging onto every word he was saying. She was sucked into him. Two hours already, and time flew when she was having a good time. They were still parked outside her grandmother's building, and their conversation sparked so lively that it electrocuted them both.

They made arrangements to meet the next evening. Hugo was going to pick her up from the city. He had a nice place he wanted to take her. Cristal was willing now. His voice, his intelligence, and his demanding swag piqued her interest.

Cristal exited his car with him remaining seated in the driver's seat. He smiled at her. She smiled back.

"I'm looking forward for tomorrow," Hugo said.

"You better not be late," she warned him.

"Oh believe me, I do not do CP time, especially when I'm coming to get you. I'll be there on time. You have my word on that."

Cristal nodded.

Hugo drove off, leaving Cristal standing on the sidewalk with a feeling of ambivalence. Was it right to go out with him? Could things transpire into something more serious? Had the Commission planted him to spy on her?

TWENTY-TWO

Sharon was so distraught over Pike's death that it wasn't safe for her to be alone. Sharon contemplated her own suicide. She was in love, and he was in love with her, and now that love was gone without any warning. She couldn't believe he was dead—murdered by two thugs like his life was meaningless. There were savages out there, and Sharon wanted extreme vengeance for his death—an eye for an eye.

The newspapers were calling Pike's murder gang-related: *"A once-talented athlete shot down in gang warfare,"* the paper read. Sharon became furious when she read "gang warfare." Pike wasn't in a gang, but the media steadily attributed every murdered black man to gang violence whether it was true or not. His murder only received a small mention in the paper. It wasn't the headline and no one cared about another young black male being killed. The only reason Pike's murder made the news at all was because he used to be a high-school star athlete, and his talent and past had been profiled in the media prior to his death. Pike was known, and now he was gone.

Sharon was taken to Mona's place to convalesce. She couldn't be alone, especially in Pike's apartment. Mona wanted to be a good friend to her. She wanted to help her. She had to make up to Sharon for everything. First, they had let her get jumped by Mesha and her bitches, and then they'd murdered her boyfriend. Of course she couldn't let Sharon know, but Mona had to do something to make things right.

Sharon cried in Mona's arms. Her tears trickled down her cheek like a downpour, soaking Mona's shirt with her tears. Mona did her best to console her friend with Cristal and Tamar absent.

"I loved him so much, Mona, and he loved me," Sharon cried out.

Mona continued consoling her friend, but her heart was burning with guilt.

"What kind of animals would do this to him? Why? He was changing, Mona. He was becoming a better man for me. Why was he snatched away from me? Why kill him?" Sharon cried out.

"I don't know. Pike did have a past, Sharon. He did sell drugs and was known to fuck anything wit' a pulse. He did have enemies, and his past probably came back on him," said Mona.

"What the fuck, Mona!" Sharon spat, angry. "Are you justifying his fuckin' death? Seriously?"

"No, I wasn't. I was just saying—"

"Just don't say shit," Sharon heatedly interjected. "You know what, fuck you!"

Sharon jumped up, scowling at her friend with her tearstained face.

"Sharon, I'm sorry. I don't want to upset you."

"You already have," she exclaimed.

Sharon quickly grabbed her things and limped with her cast to the front door. She truly felt alone. All of her friends were so distant from her. Since they had all left for "job training," things had changed with them.

"Sharon, I'm sorry. I didn't mean to be so callous toward your feelings."

Sharon turned. "When did you start using words like 'callous,' Mona? You, Cristal, and Tamar, y'all all changed."

"Sharon, I'm still the same person," Mona replied.

"No you're not. Who are you?"

Mona remained silent. She didn't know herself anymore.

TWENTY-THREE

• •

Cristal stood in her sweet-scented and relaxing bathroom in her white, cotton terry bathrobe. The water was rushing out of the faucet like a waterfall, filling the porcelain tub with warm and soothing clear water. She had Sade playing from the Bluetooth speaker on the bathroom countertop, and Cristal was ready to get naked and submerge herself into a watery enjoyment. It was that time to shut her eyes and escape somewhere mystical. She allowed the robe to fall around her feet and sat at the edge of the tub and ran her fingers through the warm water. She couldn't wait to get in.

As she was about to slip her feet into the tub, she heard someone knocking loudly at her door. It was almost 11pm, and she wasn't expecting any company. The knocking interrupted her tranquil mood.

She threw her robe back on, grabbed the .9mm from the bedroom, and went to see who it was. With her robe tied tightly, concealing her goodies underneath, Cristal looked through the peephole with her gun in hand and was shocked to see E.P. The Commission had made it clear that they would never see their recruiters again. But there he was, standing outside her apartment as clear as day.

Cristal hesitated answering the door. She felt some nervousness. Why had he shown up so unexpectedly? And why after they murdered Pike for the Commission? Did they do something wrong? Pike was killed within forty-eight hours as requested. They made sure to do the hit right and not have it linked back to them.

He knocked again. "I know you're home, Cristal."

She sighed and then opened the door carefully. E.P. stood in front of her looking so handsome in his tailor-made suit, his black, dark skin shimmering. He was an intimidating man. His strongly built structure showed in the dark black suit he wore, and he appeared too cool in her sight.

"Hello, Cristal," E.P. greeted with a slight smile.

"Why are you here?" she asked.

"It's obvious. I wanted to see you."

"But the Commission made it clear that we would never meet again," she said.

He laughed quietly. "You have no need to worry about the Commission."

"And why not?"

"Because I say so."

Cristal was slightly taken aback by his bleakness, but she kept her cool with her emotionless gaze.

"Can I come in?" he asked.

Even if she didn't want him to, she couldn't tell him no. "Yeah, sure."

Cristal stepped aside from the doorway and allowed E.P. to walk inside her new home. He looked around her small apartment and said, "You have a nice place here."

"Not as nice as yours."

"We all need to start somewhere."

E.P. unbuttoned his suit jacket and removed it. His black slacks and collared shirt hugged his physically fit body. He looked too good in Cristal's eyes. He appeared to be unarmed. He looked at her. He didn't appear to be a threat to her, but Cristal could never be too sure. She kept her grip on the pistol.

E.P. glanced at the gun in her hand. "You got a problem with me now?"

"No, I don't."

"Then why the gun?"

"The Farm—it changed me."

"It was supposed to do that. And I'm glad you made it through. I knew you had it in you," he said. "But I'm no threat to you, Cristal. If I wanted you dead, you wouldn't even see me coming."

Cristal knew he was right. It had to be a social visit. Maybe he missed her. She did miss him somewhat. E.P. hung his suit jacket over the back of one of her chairs. He simply made himself comfortable in her apartment like he was her lover.

"Were you the one that left that folder on my bed while I was asleep?" she asked.

"No."

"Then who did?"

"You don't need to concern yourself with worries about who the messenger was. They were given a job to do, and you were given a job to do. The inner workings of the organization should never be your concern. The less you know, the better."

She had to ask him. "But why Pike? What did he ever do to you or the Commission?"

"The murder of your friend was only a test. The Commission had to be sure about you and the others. Once you murder a close friend, the other kills are easy to do," he said.

"And what about the money, E.P.? Ten thousand apiece. We expected more than that, especially since it was someone close to us."

"You should be happy the three of y'all saw that much for someone who wasn't significant," he returned. "You have passed training on the Farm, but you are not considered a professional yet."

Pike was just a test, and it showed how heartless this organization really was. Taking a human life was only business to them. It was a cold world with the organization, and Cristal wondered how much colder it was going to get. However, she had more questions for E.P. She never thought he would be seen again, but there he was, in the flesh and looking magnificent.

He took a seat on her sofa and crossed his legs like a gentleman. "You have anything to drink?"

"Just water," she replied.

"That'll do."

Cristal turned and went into her kitchen and poured some tap water into a glass. E.P. sat evenly on her sofa. She brought him his cold glass of water, he gulped it down, and then she bombarded him with more questions.

"Why did it take so long for the Commission to give us our first job? We sit here twiddling our thumbs like idiots while trying to adjust to our new lives," she complained.

"The Commission reaches out when they feel the crew is ready. They have hubs all around the world, domestic and international. Some hubs stand out more than others, and so do assassins."

"Assassins, like who?"

"Aren't you Twenty-One Questions tonight?"

"I'm just curious, E.P., that's all. I want to be the best. I want jobs, me and my crew. I want to prove myself."

"Prove yourself, huh? Is it just you? What about Tamar and Mona? And haven't you heard the proverb 'Curiosity killed the cat?'"

"I'm a hard cat to kill."

"You think you are."

"But who's the assassin that's progressing?" she asked, dying to know.

E.P. gazed at her for a moment, taking in her dynamic figure covered up in the robe she wore and licked his lips thinking about how great her body looked underneath the soft fabric. He had his reasons for coming to see Cristal. She had been on his mind since the day she'd left his place. He had a strong urge to plunge his dick in her tight, warm pussy. But for now, he would play questions and answers.

"This one particular female was in your class, and it wasn't one week after graduation when the Commission reached out to her to do a job. And she did it fast and subtle. The Commission has had an eye on this girl for a while. They brought her in, sharpened her skill, and made her into a killing machine," he revealed.

"Who is she?"

"She's half Jamaican and half Japanese, tall, beautiful, with dark skin and dark eyes and quiet," he described.

The way he continued to describe the girl, like he was infatuated by her, made Cristal extremely jealous. She thought, *Why this bitch?* But Cristal exactly knew who E.P. was talking about. She always stood out. Cristal had noticed her in training. It was the same girl she'd been fascinated with on the low. There definitely was something cunning about her.

"I'm not supposed to be giving out this information to you, but I like you, Cristal. There's something special about you."

She was flattered.

And he was drawn to her. "This assassin calls her crew 'Killer Dolls,' and her specialty weapon is a dagger. They've already made two major headlines with their kills: one in Europe and the second in D.C."

Cristal screwed up her face. "They're traveling around the world like that? While we sit on our asses and wait, and then we kill a friend, get paid peanuts for it? And this bitch is international?"

"It's not me, Cristal. It's the Commission. They run things, and I shouldn't be telling you this shit," he said.

"Then why are you?"

"Because I really like you," he admitted.

E.P. stood up, towering over the young beauty in his expensive attire. The two locked eyes with a moment of silence between them. The attraction was mutual. E.P. stepped toward her and took her hand into his. He was ready to disrobe her and witness her goodies. Her touch alone made him lust for her.

"What is it that you want from me?" Cristal asked.

"I came to see you. I missed you, Cristal. I want you, and I want you now," he confessed with his attention fixed on her.

Cristal didn't know what to say. She was flattered, and the attraction was there, but Cristal felt her heart might be elsewhere—like with Hugo. Although they'd just met, there was something magnetic about him that appealed to her more.

E.P. leaned forward and pressed his lips against hers. They kissed, while his hands tugged at the knot on her robe, trying to loosen it. She didn't resist or fight. She allowed him to reveal her glory underneath.

"You are truly beautiful," E.P. said.

"Thank you."

"I missed you," he stated wholeheartedly with a strong grin.

She really hadn't missed him like that, but she was too afraid to admit it to him. He had power and influence, and being the smart, savvy woman she was, she felt it was wise to use him to get what she wanted, and if that meant giving him some pussy once in a while to come-up, then she was ready to do so.

They kissed fervently again. E.P. locked her in his arms, holding her dearly. It was hard to believe that she had a man like E.P. open like the freeway at three in the morning. He was falling for her. As they kissed, E.P. unfastened his pants hurriedly and pulled out his throbbing black tool. He couldn't wait to be inside of her again. He dropped his slacks and his big dick was so hard, it probably could break stone.

He pushed the butt-naked Cristal toward the couch and had her curved over with her ass in the air and her legs spread. E.P. couldn't wait to feel her wetness. He grabbed her naked hips and situated himself behind her. Cristal gripped the cushion and waited for his entry.

"You got a condom?" she asked.

E.P. removed a Magnum condom from his pants pocket on the floor. He swiftly tore it open and rolled the latex back on his big, black and hard dick. Once it was fitted snugly, he slammed his firm erection so deep into Cristal, she moaned loudly and her eyes widened. It had been a while since she'd had sex.

"Ooooh shit!" she cried out.

"I missed you, baby," he uttered, feeling her glorious insides overwhelm him with unadulterated bliss. Her juices started to leak and her walls contracted around his girth. E.P. fucked her from the back like a porn star. Her tits flapped back and forth, and her grip on the sofa intensified as she felt his dick tunneling in and out of her. She felt every inch of him. He gripped the back of her slim neck and pounded and pounded into her so hard, he almost flipped her over the couch.

Her pussy was so good, E.P. looked like he was about to have a seizure. He positioned Cristal on the carpeted floor and buried himself deep between her thighs in the missionary position, and as his dick dove in and out of her, he sucked on her sugary nipples and cupped her breasts. Cristal had her legs cocked back and closed her eyes, moaning from the great fuck she was receiving.

They used her entire condo as a sex haven, fucking on the couch, on the table, the kitchen, up against the wall with her legs straddled around him, and then taking their action into the bedroom. E.P.'s stamina was phenomenal. It was going on over an hour and still he fucked her like a young teenage lover. His erection kept on going, and going, and going. With her hair in disarray and sweat glistening on both their bodies, Cristal rode his big dick like a jockey leading a thoroughbred race horse to the finish line. She felt her orgasm brewing like a pipe ready to burst open.

"I'm gonna cum!" she cried out.

Up and down, back and forth on his energetic dick, her pussy throbbing profoundly with her hands pressed against his strapping chest and rippling abs as he smacked and grasped her phat ass with his strong hands. They both were driving themselves into utter delight, and after an hour of fucking, Cristal couldn't hold it in anymore and she exploded like an eruption all over that big dick. E.P. came right after, shooting so much sperm into the condom that it felt like it had broken through the shield and slipped some of his babies into her.

Cristal collapsed against his chiseled physique, still blowing hard from the forceful fuck. E.P. held her in his arms and he didn't want to let her go.

What was that? Cristal asked herself. Was he back in her life for good, or was this a one-time thing? With E.P., everything was a risk. But Cristal was ready to take that risk in order to secure a future for herself with the Commission. She wanted to become a killing machine also. She wanted to become number one in the organization, and that was going to mean taking risks.

Fuck it; if E.P. wanted some pussy, it was his. She would use her sexuality to benefit her. But there was one problem—as she was in the arms of E.P., she was thinking about Hugo.

TWENTY-FOUR

●●

Cristal walked into the four-star restaurant Le Bernardin on 51st Street clad in a sexy black J. Mendel dress and a pair of Gianvito Rossi silver pumps that made heads turn.

When they walked into the restaurant, men and women gazed at such a stunning beauty as if she were a celebrity entering the four-star restaurant. With Hugo by her side, dressed handsomely in a gray Dolce & Gabbana three-piece suit, his pricey Rolex showing, he was the quintessence of suave. They looked like a high-profile celebrity couple.

Hugo pulled out Cristal's chair and allowed her to be seated first. When the two were situated at the decorated table, their waitress came by to take their orders with a warm smile.

Le Bernardin had the freshest seafood in the city. It was prepared using simple techniques to highlight the fish's best qualities. Broken down into "Almost Raw," "Barely Touched," and "Lightly Cooked," the menu reflected the preparations of the fish, and a plate ranged anywhere from ninety-three to three hundred dollars with wine pairings.

The place was lovely. Cristal remembered her etiquette and table-manners classes on the Farm and put what she had learned to use in the restaurant. Hugo was impressed. He smiled and said, "I see your mother taught you well."

"My mother didn't teach me anything," she shot back.

"Damn, didn't mean to offend you," Hugo apologized.

"I'm not offended. But it was my grandmother who taught me, and pretty much raised me, and who always looked out for me," she said.

"I respect her for that."

"I do too," she said.

The waitress walked over with the wine menu that Hugo requested. He was a big wine drinker and loved the best, even if it cost. He picked out the Altesino Brunello Di Montalcino. It was expensive, six hundred for the bottle. He told the waitress to place it on the table. She did. Money wasn't an issue.

Cristal was impressed.

The waitress poured some of the red wine into his goblet and he took a sip, savoring the taste of it in his mouth, like he was some sort of wine connoisseur. Cristal smiled. What was he doing? It smelled floral, cherry, and woodsy aromas and flavors. He swallowed and smiled.

"Now this is good wine," Hugo uttered. "You need to try some."

The waitress poured Cristal half a glass and she downed it straightforwardly. It was good. She poured her another half glass. Cristal took her time drinking this one.

"You like it?" he asked.

"I do."

"Sweet and silky. Distinctive and delicious, my kind of wine."

Once again, Hugo had her intrigued by another one of his many qualities.

"Where did you learn to love wine so much?" she asked.

"My mother, she has a love of wine. She used to drink it when she was able to afford it. And when I briefly lived in Atlanta, I took a wine-tasting class."

"They have a class for that?"

"They do, and it was interesting."

"So did you ever go to college?"

"Briefly. I dropped out my sophomore year," he said.

"Why?"

"Things got complicated. My mother became ill, I needed to make money, and when I came back to Brooklyn, I hit the block hustling for a friend. He said he was doing me a favor, but I felt like it was the other way around. He was the brute while I was the brains in his crew," Hugo said.

"And let me guess, you worked hard and took over the operation from him."

"Something like that. Me and a friend of mines just blew his brains out when he didn't see it coming," he admitted.

"You serious?"

He smiled.

"Hey, it was either me or him. The one thing I've learned about this business is there's no such thing as friends, only business partners and who they fear the most. See, they thought I was weak because I was smart, grew up different, and went to college. They underestimated me and it cost them dearly," Hugo said in a low tone, for Cristal's ears only.

"You are a very impressive and intriguing man," said Cristal.

"I've heard that about me a few times."

"And this empire you run, how much is it worth?"

"You know, you ask a lot of questions to be someone that I just met. I mean, this question-and-answer session should be a two-way thing. I would like to know some things about you."

"What is there to know? I'm not as interesting as you. I grew up poor and rough, ran with a crew that didn't take shit from anyone. I learned how to survive, and my grandmother took care of me. I sold drugs, fought bitches, stole things, and had my share of run-ins with the law. My mother was hardly in my life. I'm not a virgin."

Hugo laughed. "I kind of figured that."

"Oh really, and why's that?" Cristal asked him with a raised brow.

"Because, no offense, but you do look experienced."

"Experienced?"

"I'm not calling you a ho."

"Then what are you calling me?"

"A beautiful and lovely woman that I really want to be with."

"Uh-huh, climb your way out of the fire to keep from getting burned, that's how you do, huh?"

"I don't expect to get burned. Ever," Hugo replied.

Cristal smiled. "You have an answer for everything, don't you?"

"My mother always told me, the sharper your knife, the less you cry."

"What?"

"It was my mother's saying. She's a smart woman."

"And the apple doesn't fall too far from the tree," Cristal said.

"I take that as a compliment."

"You should."

"You like me, don't you? I know you do," Hugo said out of the blue.

"And why would you say that?"

"Because I know women, and I can see it in your eyes. You find me attractive, don't you?"

"Well, aren't you cocky and narcissistic?"

"I always say that you can tell how a person is feeling about you through their eyes, and right now, your eyes are smiling at me. But I remember when we first met, and they were so cold and reserved."

Cristal took a sip of wine.

"Things can change."

"And what changed them?" he asked.

"You ask too many questions."

"I just don't like to be in the dark," Hugo replied.

"Me neither."

He was telling the truth about her. She really liked him. Their chemistry was mind-blowing. She was actually enjoying Hugo's company and conversation. Hugo exposed his dark side as a drug dealer, but he also said that he didn't want to sell drugs forever. He had dreams of running his own legitimate company and having a family of his own. He wanted kids. He wanted a future and he didn't want to see twenty-five to life behind prison walls. He had goals for himself, and Cristal couldn't help but respect and admire his ambitions.

Cristal went on to tell him more about her life, but she left out the critical details about being a hired assassin for a secret organization. They talked while feasting on the lightly cooked fish and wine. It was turning out to be such a wonderful evening that Cristal wanted to freeze time.

The two spent over two hours in Le Bernardin. They had dessert, drank more wine, and talked about everything under the sun, from music to the streets. They had so much in common it was scary.

Cristal walked out of the restaurant with a smile on her face. The date went so well she didn't want to leave Hugo's side. There was a tune of contentment enveloping her, and a breath of fresh air fulfilling her. Not even E.P. made her smile and laugh as much as Hugo had in one night. Hugo dazzled her, captivated her, and had her undivided attention—she felt like she had known him forever. Cristal couldn't help but imagine what other pleasantries and surprises he might be about to pull out of his sleeve.

Hugo opened the passenger door of his Bentley for Cristal to slide inside and plant her firm ass against his expensive leather seats. They drove around the city for a long while, talking and taking in Times Square then parking on the West Side of Manhattan gazing at the Hudson and New Jersey shoreline. Cristal felt attached to him. It was a crisp fall night, but inside Hugo's heated Bentley, things were just about to get started.

Cristal couldn't resist the attraction and urge anymore. She leaned toward him and kissed him, pressing her full lips against his and slipping her tongue into his mouth, as he did the same. They excitedly locked onto each other in the front seat of the silver Bentley like teenagers. Cristal all of a sudden found herself pulling up her black dress and getting a little too comfortable with Hugo so unexpectedly.

Hugo hurriedly removed his suit jacket, tossing it into the backseat along with the matching vest as Cristal snatched open his trousers and mounted him in the driver's seat, feeling his throbbing, hard erection between her legs. Things went from zero to sixty as they explored each other's bodies, capitalizing off of each second of sensual pleasure. They kissed for what seemed like hours in the driver's seat.

Hugo kissed and licked her neck, finding her hot spot and making her moan in pleasure. He then cupped her breasts in front of him, licked her ears, and whispered the sorts of naughty things he wanted to do to her. Cristal liked what he was saying to her. He was a freak. She was ready to do whatever. She responded by spreading her legs across his lap, his manhood exposed and rising like a flagpole as she ground her body in his. Her hands roamed freely over his chest, caressing him and unbuttoning his shirt.

Hugo's body matched E.P.'s; they both had strapping smooth chests and washboard abs. Hugo's defined, muscular arms wrapped around her like tight clothing. "You're beautiful," he said to her once again.

"And you are fine," she returned.

Cristal was more perfect than he ever imagined. Her beautiful breasts were round and full and capped off by the most delicious, dark and suckable nipples he'd ever seen in his entire life. Her curved figured seemed to sparkle in the moonlight. And her big, round ass was what made women envious and men weak with lust.

While they kissed passionately, Hugo reached beneath her soft, brown thighs and inserted his finger into her hole. He could feel her slippery, wet juices flowing freely. Cristal responded with more moaning in his ear, grinding her pussy against his penetrating finger inside of her. Hugo gently rubbed the tip of his finger over her exposed and hardened clit and saw her body respond to his touch. He toyed with her moist inside and tender clit.

"I wanna fuck you so badly," he passionately revealed to her.

"You do, huh?"

"Hells yeah."

Hugo was so hard it felt like he was going to detonate like a grenade between her legs. But they both delayed the sexual intercourse. The foreplay ensuing in the hundred-and-seventy-thousand-dollar car was much more exhilarating. Cristal liked him so much that she was ready to do him a favor and please him to the fullest. Her pussy throbbed as he pinched her nipples gently.

"I wanna fuck you," he growled with lust dripping from his tone.

Cristal smiled. She wanted the same thing. Her pussy pulsed like electricity was flowing through it.

"You got condoms on you?" she asked, always ready to practice safe sex, but when Hugo shook his head no, Cristal was stuck between a rock and a hard place. She wanted to feel every inch of his big, hard and sexy black dick buried deep inside of her, but without any protection, it seemed like her sexual bubble had burst and she was going to be left high and dry and horny as hell.

"Let me just put it in you real quick and feel that pussy raw. I'm good, baby," Hugo tried to persuade. "I want you so bad."

He wanted to fuck either way.

Cristal looked in his eyes, and for some reason, she trusted him. Why, she didn't have a decisive answer. She was just in the mood to feel some mind-blowing sex right now. She bit down on her bottom lip and said to herself, *Fuck it!*

Hugo grabbed his dick and lined it up with her sweet hole. He slowly thrust himself inside of her. He could feel the muscles of her pussy walls grabbing him before the head was even inside. Hugo held her hips and pushed upwards into her, hearing Cristal cry out from the thick penetration between her soft and delicate lips. Once he was completely inside of her, he pumped his engorged cock in and out of her wet, hot pussy. Cristal straddled him and rode his dick slowly in his pricey car. He stroked and thrust every sole inch of his hard meat inside her.

He fucked her harder.

She moaned louder.

Cristal's full ass wiggled and bounced up and down on him. He palmed her ass and sucked on her nipples. He could feel the cum in his nuts brewing, and as much as he wanted to cum inside of her, he couldn't, not too soon anyway.

"I'm coming!" Hugo cried out, feeling the intensity brewing inside the hot and steamy Bentley as the sounds of wet sex filled the car.

She was going wild, chanting and moaning and begging for more. And when he couldn't hold back any longer, Hugo pulled out of her and shot his cum all over her and himself, rubbing his rock hard penis against her shaved pubic hairs and feeling complete bliss. His dick glistened with her juices and Cristal kissed him all over.

It was good and she wanted more of him.

The two collected themselves afterwards and continued conversing in the night. Cristal saw something in him that she definitely wanted to continue.

He came, he saw, and he conquered.

TWENTY-FIVE

●●●●●●●●●●●●●●●●●●●●●●●●●●●●●●●●●●●●●●

Once again Cristal and her crew met on the project rooftop in the middle of the night to discuss a few critical things. They talked about their future with the Commission. She updated them about E.P. coming to see her and the things he said. She didn't want to keep her girls in the dark. But Tamar seemed to have a minor problem with it. She twisted the corners of her mouth into a frown.

"So he just came to see you in the night like that, and y'all just had a good ol' social gathering, huh?" Tamar remarked with some sarcasm.

"Why is that an issue with you, Tamar?" Cristal shot back.

"It's not."

"Then don't let it be," Cristal warned lightly. Her eyes displayed authority among her crew.

Tamar continued to frown, her and Cristal exchanging unpleasant stares.

"Who left you in charge?"

"Do I really need to answer that?" Cristal retorted.

Mona was left standing in the middle and feeling the tension between her two friends. Mona thought about what Sharon had said to her. They had all changed. And with Lisa being absent, they were all jealous of her being the lone wolf, because she hadn't returned to Brooklyn.

"Since E.P. came to see you, did he give you a reason why we had to kill Pike?" Mona asked.

"*We* didn't kill Pike. Tamar and I did, so cut the bullshit guilt trip."

"Ain't nobody tryna to put you on a fuckin' guilt trip. I just wanted to know why is all."

"He was only a test, to see if we could pull it off."

"A test?!" Mona cried.

"Yes, a test, Mona. This is how these people get down. Taking a human life means nothing to them, it's murder for hire, and that's the damn life we chose," Cristal exclaimed. "Now we either can deal with it or not, but we can't get emotional over every fuckin' hit, because if we fuck up, then we gonna be the ones with the contract out on us. Do y'all fuckin' understand?"

Cristal's outburst was heard clearly, leaving Tamar and Mona speechless.

"Now, we need a name to call ourselves and a signature calling card."

"Why? What the fuck good is that?" Tamar argued.

"Why," Cristal said, rolling her eyes. "Because I said that's what we need to do, and it will be good for business. There's already this bitch in our camp, and she's competition. She's already moving up quickly in the organization."

"Who is she?" Tamar asked.

"We need to be worried about who *we* are—*our* damn reputation! If y'all wanna keep going unnoticed while there's no telling what this bitch and her crew are making, then we ain't gonna make real paper."

"What kind of name?" Mona asked.

"I don't know, something like the Cristal Clique," said Cristal.

"The Cristal Clique? Are you fuckin' serious?" Tamar protested.

"Y'all have any better suggestions?"

"What are we, killers or a bunch of R&B bitches on a fuckin' pop tour?" Tamar griped.

"What do this other bitch go by?" Mona asked.

"Something called the 'Killer Dolls.'"

"Sounds like a bad B-rated horror movie to me," Tamar said.

"We could be the Gucci Girls," Mona mentioned.

"What the fuck, we the Kardashians all of a sudden? What kind of fear will that put in our enemies?" Cristal said.

"And the Cristal Clique is a better name?" Tamar exclaimed. "Hell no, that ain't right. How we gonna be named after only you?!"

"Not me, you ass!" Cristal retorted. "After the champagne."

"And who's gonna think that? No one, because you spell it the same way."

"And how is that my fault? The name is classy and it represents what we do, get money. Cristal Champagne is the best, as are we," Cristal proclaimed.

Tamar and Mona were still against it, no matter how much Cristal justified the meaning. But Cristal was adamant about keeping the group's name the Cristal Clique. Without her, they wouldn't be where they were today. And they owed her a lot. She was the Head Bitch in Charge, and no one was going to tell her any different.

The girls continued with their meeting on the rooftop and it was made clear what they had to do next: become the best at their job! There was a feeling that there was nothing else for them to do—having regular jobs was out of question because they were now under the Commission's thumb. They were willing to make a name for themselves and become rich women. Cristal was a big influence on them, and with E.P. in her corner, she felt they would become unstoppable. She wanted to rival the Killer Dolls and match them kill for kill, national or international.

She yearned to be internationally known.

The first thing Cristal did when she was back in her apartment was Google daggers and murder to get a better understanding of their work done so far. She found some international murders of high-ranking officials that were brutally killed with a dagger, and she knew it was her—the nameless girl, the killer doll.

The next several days, Cristal took to conditioning her body and her mind, honing her skills in killing techniques she'd learned on the Farm, especially with a chrome-plated razor blade that she wanted to become exceptional with. She mastered concealing the razor inside of her mouth, hiding it under her tongue while still being able to carry on a conversation without someone noticing it. It was a dangerous thing to do, but Cristal mastered the skill.

It was important for her to stand out. She also needed a calling card after each of her victims was killed. It had to be something that suited her perfectly. It came to her one day while she was shuffling a deck of cards and came across the Queen of Spades. She researched the meaning behind the card and saw that it was a short story by Alexander Pushkin about human avarice. The Queen of Spades also represented that she was at the top of her game, right underneath the King—the head of her clique—and the Spades represented her black heart.

Cristal was ready to display her bloodthirsty skill, cause serious fear among her victims and get paid handsomely for her services. Now the only thing she needed was another murdergram from the Commission.

●●●

The second murdergram came a week after their rooftop meeting. It arrived the same way as before, in a manila folder placed strategically on her bed when she arrived home one late night. The messenger was once again undetected, and the target this time was Daniel Davidson, a thirty-eight-year-old Caucasian male from the city who was soon to marry his fiancé of five years, Leslie. The wedding was in forty-eight hours, and the Commission wanted him dead within forty-eight hours.

Why the Commission wanted him dead wasn't any of her concern. She had a job to do, and she was ready to carry it out.

Cristal was well prepared this time. She wasn't about to fail the organization. Forty-eight hours wasn't a long time. She didn't have ample time to stake out the target. She figured the best way to strike was at his wedding. It was risky, but it was the only way.

●●●

The Midtown Loft and Terrace was an elegant place for a huge wedding for the CEO of MRC cooperation—Miller, Reye & Comer—a vast hedge-fund firm in downtown Manhattan that had made 11.5 billion for its investors last year. Daniel Davidson was becoming the world's most successful hedge-fund manager. His wedding was nothing less than extraordinary. The lavish location by the water accommodated over two hundred for a seated dinner. There was little need for decoration with the natural ambience and brand-new SoHo lounge-style décor. The venue brought the most unique vendors of flowers, music, and décor, as well as photographers and AV equipment. An exclusive red carpet made guests feel like celebrities when they arrived at the wedding.

Their target, Daniel, was handsomely clad in a three-button notch-lapel tuxedo; his groomsmen were drinking and laughing by his side. He was now a happily married man. His bride, Leslie, looked marvelous in her flowing wedding dress—a gorgeous sweetheart neckline gown. She danced with her bridesmaids on the dance floor. The smile plastered across her face indicated that she was the happiest woman on earth. She was now Mrs. Davidson, the wife of a fine-looking millionaire and the perfect guy with his tan skin, lean stature, and blond hair. It was her day, the perfect day, and there was nothing that could ruin it for her, or them. They seemed blissful together—their holy matrimony sealed forever.

The bride didn't count on Cristal observing the happily married couple from a distance. It was going to be a shame that she had to transform this blissful day into their worst nightmare. There was no emotion coming from Cristal; it was nothing personal, only business.

Cristal disguised herself as one of the well-dressed staff serving the wedding crowd. She blended in perfectly with the employees, moving about the jovial Jewish crowd in a white buttoned shirt, white gloves, black bowtie, and black slacks. Her dark hair was in a long ponytail, and the fraudulent smile she wore while serving a silver platter of hors d'oeuvres gave her a low profile. No one noticed that she was a threat to the groom.

The hired band playing was lively. Their guitars, drums, piano and the lead singer moved the revelers like in a nightclub. The 1994 hit "Hold My Hand" by Hootie & The Blowfish blared throughout the venue. The guests were so caught up in having such a good time and celebrating Daniel and Leslie's new marriage that the food and drinks being served and eaten were unwatched.

Cristal saw her opportunity to strike. She carried a fatal dose of cyanide, 300 milligrams concealed on her person. She planned on blending the fatal dose in the groom's drink. His glass of champagne was left unattended as he danced with his lovely bride on the floor. All eyes were on the bride and the groom as the couple found they were out of step with the music, but they didn't care. It was their day. Their love.

Cristal watched and waited patiently like a snake lurking in the high grass for its prey to devour. She had to be aware of her surroundings and be precise when she made her move. This wasn't like gunning down Pike on the Harlem Street and making it look gang-related. This target was a completely different ballgame, and one slip could cost her dearly.

Tamar and Mona weren't truly needed for this hit. They couldn't look too obvious in a sea of mostly white faces at a high-end event in midtown

Manhattan. So they waited for Cristal to execute the contract from afar. They would be her backup and her getaway.

Tamar felt a twinge of jealousy when Cristal volunteered herself to pull off the job. They were a team, but it felt like Cristal wanted to get all the recognition and accolades for the job. Tamar didn't like how it played itself out. Cristal took charge because she was connected with E.P., but Tamar felt she was just as highly skilled and deadly as anyone. And she wanted to prove herself too. Why should Cristal have all the fun, including fucking E.P. and having better perks?

When the moment presented itself, with most of the wedding guests dancing to "It's Electric," Cristal removed the fatal dose of cyanide from her person with the tray of food still in her hand and maneuvered toward the bride and groom's table. She craftily poured the 300 milligrams into the groom's drink, mixing the untraceable, deadly toxins into his glass. She went unseen. Now it was show time.

She slipped away into the crowd to continue with her serving job. She smiled at the groom's mother in her long gown and offered the bright-faced woman a drink. The mother happily accepted.

To spite the bitch, Cristal went out of her way to say, "Your son looks happy with his new bride. I'm sure they're going to have a long life together."

"Thank you," the mother replied.

Cristal floated away from her, smirking. She yearned to see the nightmare begin. A true assassin didn't leave until they were confident their target was dead. And it was going to be a pleasure to see her work carried out in front of everyone.

After the song, the father of the bride walked onto the elevated platform with the band to make his special announcement. He quickly drew everyone's attention as the music stopped playing and with him having everyone's undivided attention. Cristal stood off to the side with the other servants in the back and watched.

"Hello, everyone," the father of the bride started with his jovial smile and holding champagne in his hand. "I want to thank everyone for coming out on this celebrated day. And I also want to thank you, Daniel, for taking my daughter off my hands. My credit cards needed the rest."

Everyone laughed at the joke.

"Daddy," the bride uttered with a smile.

"Hey, sweet cake, I know you're in good hands now," he said.

"She is, Mr. Abrahamson," the groom said, holding the tainted glass of champagne in his hand.

The man continued his hearty speech while Cristal kept her eyes on the groom. The minor distractions kept him from downing the drink. The bride's father was holding court on the stage talking about love and longevity and how he was happy to gain a son-in-law like Daniel. He praised the man and was extremely happy for his daughter's happiness.

When the speech was over, Mr. Abrahamson raised his glass in the air and said with glee in his voice, "I wish you all the best and excessive happiness and many, many grandkids, maybe not the Brady Bunch, but maybe something close. To the bride and groom."

"To the bride and groom," the wedding crowd repeated with their glasses of bubbly raised in the air, and then everyone downed their drink.

Cristal watched the groom down the champagne, inhaling the lethal concoction while standing next to his beautiful bride. He kissed her deeply and smiled. "I love you, Leslie," he announced wholeheartedly.

The chemical was commonly produced in a salt form and tasted and smelled like bitter almonds. The groom had no idea he had just digested the poison into his system. Everything was fine so far. It wasn't going to take long before the cyanide took aggressive action in his system. It didn't take long for it to be immediately present in the blood going to the brain and everywhere else in the body. Cyanide reaching the brain causes it to cease functioning virtually, instantaneously.

Once ingested, the cyanide could kill someone in five minutes.

One minute had passed.

Cristal noticed the sudden change of expression in the groom's face. His good-humored appearance quickly transformed into panic as the chemical, once absorbed, slowed down his respiration system. His breathing seemed sparse. He started to sweat profusely. He quickly undid his bowtie to breathe better. He clutched his throat, triggering a worried reaction from his bride.

"Baby, are you okay?" she asked with grave concern.

Suddenly, the groom couldn't speak. His sudden illness caught the attention of the best-man and a few others. Daniel wobbled toward the table, trying to keep his balance. All of a sudden it was hard for him to stand on his own two feet as nausea set in. He used the table to support himself. His mother came rushing over.

"Daniel, are you okay? Sweetie, talk to your mother. What is wrong with you? Tell us something, please," she exclaimed with frightened uneasiness.

He started to vomit; this was followed by a seizure, confusion, and lack of consciousness. The celebrated wedding moment turned into pure panic. Daniel passed out and collapsed in front of his bride, and there was a collective screaming and concern. Everyone rushed to the groom's aid.

"Somebody call 911!" the bride screamed.

A doctor tried to perform CPR, but the attempt to help him would be futile, because Daniel was already dead.

Cristal remained unemotional. With the satisfaction of fulfilling the contract given to her, while the place was erupting into chaos, she placed the tray of hors d'oeuvres onto the table next to her and tossed her signature card, the Queen of Spades, onto the floor next to the dead groom.

She made her way toward the freight elevator and quietly slipped out of the venue. She casually walked out of the building and in the direction where Tamar and Mona were waiting in a parked Dodge. Cristal climbed into the backseat smiling like the Cheshire cat.

"We good?" Tamar asked.

"Mission accomplished," she revealed. "Now let's get the fuck outta here."

Mona started the ignition and drove out the parking spot. Cristal felt relieved. This was only the beginning of their new life to come. If she could keep pulling off subtle kills like this, the organization had to respect her and pay her what she was worth—a fortune.

TWENTY-SIX

Cristal was falling in love with Hugo after several weeks of dating. Whenever he came around it was like a breath of fresh air. He was fun to be around, he educated her about different things, and the sex was amazing. He took her mind away from the recent killings she and her crew executed for the Commission. The Cristal Clique had carried out two other murdergrams for the organization. Their third hit was on Antonio Hernandez, a self-made and compassionless millionaire who fled to rural upstate of New York with ten million dollars from his Ponzi scheme. He'd swindled dozens of people out of their money, draining several savings accounts and bankrupting numerous others into depression.

Cristal, Tamar, and Mona drove the hour-long trip into Troy, New York in a rent-a-car. They bypassed his top-notch security system and sneaked into his luxurious home nestled in the backwoods on a large hill. They hid in the shadows of the four-bedroom home and waited nearly three hours for their mark to arrive. The problem was he didn't show up alone. He was accompanied by two beautiful prostitutes, and he was ready to have a threesome with them in his master bedroom. The two bitches weren't on their contract to kill, so they had to wait until he was alone, and Cristal cut Antonio's throat from ear to ear with her chromed razorblade, and left her calling card on his bloody frame in the master bedroom.

It was a clean hit and a profitable one, too. The girls received five hundred thousand apiece for it. Antonio Hernandez was a despised man, and because so many people wanted him dead, it benefited the girls financially.

The fourth hit was Junior Dante, a mafia member and captain in the dwindling Lucchese family, which used to be one of New York's dominating five families. The organization wanted him done immediately. He was a snitch, a big-mouth rat, but hard to kill, and some powerful people needed to see his demise. The crew hit him while he was being chauffeured in his limousine coming from Kennedy Airport. Cristal disguised as a limo driver and picked him up outside the arriving terminal. Once they were away from the bustling area, Cristal lowered the partition between them and shot Junior Dante multiple times in the head and chest. She tossed her card at him and exited the limo, leaving no prints or anything that could connect her to the murder.

The fifth kill, A.J. Reckon, was a degenerate gambler who owed some dangerous people too much money and wasn't able to pay off his debts for going on six months. This time, Tamar did the honors, and he was gunned down exiting a hole-in-the-wall casino in Brooklyn. The Queen of Spades was shoved into his mouth.

The sixth hit was their hardest, a Washington, D.C. drug kingpin named Sammy Locks. He stayed with bodyguards, was flamboyant and at all times, was heavily armed. The Commission wanted him dead ASAP. The girls didn't have ample time to clock their target and get a good read on him, so it was going to be risky. Cristal noticed Sammy Locks loved the club life. He was always out all night drinking, smoking, and having sex with multiple women. They decided the club he attended frequently was the only way to get at him.

Cristal keenly observed the man partying like it was New Year's Eve 1999 in the VIP area. He stood six-one; a stout, intimidating man. He downed Moët like it was water. Sammy Locks was guarded by several armed goons who took their job seriously. Tamar was the bait. She was able to slide into VIP with Sammy in her black, sexy dress that revealed all her curves and cleavage. And while he was sidetracked, she slipped liquid laxative into his drink without incident and waited for the outcome.

Half an hour later, Sammy Locks felt the unsettling and churning feeling in his stomach. He started to get gassy and farted.

"Oh shit!" he had uttered, knowing what was about to break out from his asshole next.

He jumped up holding his stomach and retreated toward the bathroom, hurriedly leaving behind his goons. Sammy couldn't afford to have any embarrassing incidents in the club. His reputation meant everything to him. And therefore, it was embarrassing for anyone in his crew to see him take such an intense shit from the diarrhea bubbling in his stomach.

When Sammy Locks was in the bathroom, Cristal was already there, waiting to confront him alone. Once the door shut, before Sammy Locks could take comfort in one of the stalls to squat and take his shit, he noticed Cristal glaring at him from behind. He smirked at the pretty young thing and uttered, "Bitch, ain't you in the wrong bathroom?"

"No, I'm in the right bathroom," she replied coolly.

"You are, huh? What you want, a piece of me?"

Cristal looked fiercely at him. He was her payday and there was no way she was leaving out the bathroom with him alive. Their eyes locked, and Sammy knew she wasn't there to jerk him off. His stomach still churned like a royal rumble happening inside of him, his belly cramping up.

"Tell me who fuckin' sent you?" he demanded.

She remained silent.

Sammy Locks wanted to charge at her and snap her neck like a twig. She was a petite, harmless-looking girl, but her eyes revealed a cold-blooded and deadly killer. When he tried to attack her, he doubled over from the pain in his stomach. The laxative was taking a strong effect on him. He let loose an echoing fart like an engine motor revving in a high speed race, and it gave Cristal the advantage to strike.

She confronted him and a violent hand-to-hand battle ensued. She struck him multiple times in areas that mattered—the knee, his chest, his rib cage, and his throat, kicking and punching him fiercely. He fought back, assaulting Cristal with hair pulling and then grabbing her petite frame and hurling her across the bathroom like she was a Frisbee. Cristal went sliding into the wall, but she didn't stay down. Sammy Locks stood to his full height, towering over Cristal with a menacing scowl. He wasn't going to die easy tonight.

"I'm gonna fuck you up, bitch!" he exclaimed, blood dripping from his lips.

Cristal dared him to try. She used the combat training she learned on the Farm to fight him. He outweighed her by 150 pounds. Sammy farted loudly again, which was followed up by a foul smell, indicating he'd shat on himself. He no longer cared about the discomforting feeling inside his pants; his life was on the line. He had underestimated the pretty young thing. She was a fighter. He swiftly lunged at her to grab her, yearning to break the bitch in half, but Cristal was ready for him, and Sammy Locks was met powerfully by a roundhouse kick to his face that dazed him. Her high heels went crashing into his cheekbone like a 787 smashing into land.

Sammy Locks stumbled. The blow came unexpectedly—Cristal finished off the attack with a crushing low kick outside the back of his knee, and Sammy fell to his knees in defeat. He was hurt badly. She didn't have much time. She removed the razor blade from under her tongue, positioned herself behind him, took his head into her hands, and while Sammy Locks was stunned and on his knees, placed the razor to his throat and cut it open with no hesitation, spraying his blood all over the floor.

Sammy Locks frantically slammed his hands against his slashed throat, his eyes bulging with panic and his mouth gurgling from choking on his own blood. Cristal stepped back and watched him die a painful death. He turned around with his bloody hands still clasping around his neck, fighting to live and breathe. He gazed at Cristal in horror as she stood stoically, watching him expire. He collapsed face-down on the tiled floor, sprawled out in a pool of his own blood.

It was sloppy. But mission accomplished.

Cristal flushed the bloody razor down the toilet, and washed her hands. Without touching the contents inside the small Ziploc plastic bag, she unzipped it, dropped her Queen of Spades signature card on the floor next to the body, and bounced. It was time to retreat. She checked her condition in the mirror, took a deep breath, and exited the bathroom coolly, but surprisingly, she was met by one of Sammy's goons approaching to check on his boss. They exchanged a hard stare; seeing a woman come out of the men's bathroom was odd.

She took off running, fleeing down the hallway toward the back exit of the club. He gave chase with a gun in his hand. She slipped out of her high heels, carrying them in her hands, and made her escape from the goon. She pushed her way through the crowd like a maniac, screaming out, "He got a gun!" creating disorder in the nightclub as she rushed through the place and hurried into a back alley. It was dark. It was cold, but she wasn't going down without a fight. Fortunately for Cristal, Sammy Locks' goon was confronted by security, and a shootout ensued inside the place. Hordes of partygoers came running out of everywhere, shielding her with cover and the perfect escape.

She met with her crew, exasperated. The girls rushed back to New York, having completed the job. It was their most challenging kill, but they knew there would be more challenging kills to come their way.

TWENTY-SEVEN

Cristal needed the massage Hugo was giving her. The tranquil setting with scented candles burning, rose petals displayed everywhere, R&B playing, and baby oil being applied to her skin was so soothing. She laid face-down on his king-size bed, butt-naked, with his magic touch relaxing her in so many ways. He massaged her shoulders, sides, and back like he was a licensed masseur and gently worked his way down to her soft buttocks. Cristal closed her eyes and enjoyed his pleasurable touch.

When Hugo asked about the few bruises on her skin, she lied and said she'd gotten into an altercation on the streets with some bitches that tried to jump her. Hugo asked who. He was ready to have her back and protect her, but she declined to give any names, and said it was nothing. Hugo wasn't a fool, though. They'd been dating for several months and he knew she was hiding something from him. He wasn't sure what it was, but he was determined to find out.

The D.C. hit almost turned into a disaster for Cristal. It wasn't subtle and too bloody. She was lucky to have made it back home in one piece and unnoticed, except for the goon who saw her exit the restroom. But the Commission didn't have any complaints—another bad man dead. Sammy Locks' murder made the front-page news. He was a heavy hitter in the area, plaguing the neighborhoods with drugs, murder, and guns, and he had a strong influence in his community. They wanted him dead.

Despite the risk, Cristal wanted more jobs—maybe international hits, like the nameless killer from the Farm was doing. She wanted to become a heavy player—a well-known killer for the Commission. The money she and her girls were making was intoxicating, but she wanted to become a lone wolf, like Lisa maybe. It bothered her that Lisa was out there on her own doing her own thing, probably internationally. It was boggling though, Lisa was never about that life like that. So how was it possible?

However, when Cristal brought numerous questions to E.P., wanting information about Lisa, he warned her to let it go and ignore it. It was for her own good.

Cristal began feeling that she was better working alone than with others. She *really* wanted to be the best. The best was fearless and motivated; there was no job too risky and complicated for her. If they told her to assassinate the president of the United States, Cristal would die trying to fulfill her contract.

Also, Cristal's overseas bank account was growing rapidly. The last time she'd been able to check, it had close to a million dollars in it— seven hundred seventy-five thousand, with interest, exactly. Although they weren't allowed to make any withdrawals, and lived modestly on the stipends the Commission gave them, to know that much money was stacking made her feel gainfully employed. She was proud of this life. She felt important. She felt significant in something for once. And finding love with Hugo was a bonus. Finally, she was no longer some hoochie mama hugging the block trying to attach herself to a baller looking for a come-up. She was making her own money and leaving her mark on this planet, though it may have been a bloody mark.

With Hugo, she lived a different life—a somewhat normal life. Outside of fulfilling the murdergrams, she rarely saw her friends. Cristal didn't have time for them like back in the days. Their lives were moving on, and besides business, friendships were drifting apart. When there was no contract to execute, Mona busied herself with growing marijuana discreetly and reading. She became somewhat reclusive in her Bronx apartment, adjusting to life after Pike's murder and Sharon's absence. She missed Sharon, but understood her friend stayed away because, rightfully so, she was in mourning.

Tamar, during her free time from killing muthafuckas, hit the nightclubs in the city, partied like a rock star, and had sex like a porn star. She had freedom and nothing else to do with her spare time. She didn't have a steady man in her life, and she wasn't the shot caller like Cristal. When it came to killing, Cristal primarily did the hits and got the recognition. Tamar felt like the backup singer in a pop group. Everything always went through Cristal—the murdergrams, the money, E.P.'s time and attention. Her best friend had it all.

Tamar had nothing but her grimy reputation and a drive to take Cristal's place. Cristal was the queen bee of it all, and Tamar was envious and wanted to see a change. She wanted more. She was annoyed that Cristal was fucking E.P., and she saw little amenities that Cristal got that the rest of them didn't. Tamar felt all the girls were equal, yet Cristal was getting all the shine. The signature, The Queen of Spades—it wasn't theirs, but Cristal's own personal signature. Tamar thought it was childish and thought their name, the Cristal Clique, was ridiculous. Tamar wanted to become a lone wolf, like Lisa. She didn't want to play well with others anymore. There had to be some way to rock the boat.

● ● ●

Hugo massaged every square inch of Cristal's exquisite body while he was shirtless. His masculine hands were massaging her stress away. He was the man she wanted to be with, and she couldn't see her life without him. But that guilty feeling of being with E.P. the other day was spinning in her head—playing out like a bad 3-D movie. He came to her apartment dressed sharply, looking for her company and needing her intimacy. They talked momentarily and then fucked their brains out for over two hours. Afterwards, he left like a thief in the night, leaving Cristal drained with some regret. The affair had been going on for too long now, and Cristal didn't see it coming to an end anytime soon. E.P. said he was in love with Cristal, but she wasn't in love with him. Her heart was with Hugo while carrying on her affair with E.P. for business reasons. E.P. thought they had a thing, but she was only using him to get more jobs, and she wanted to be respected and admired as he admired the nameless killer doll.

Cristal was playing both sides of the fence.

After the massage, she and Hugo made love. It was at times like these that she wanted to stay in his arms forever.

Together, they were becoming a powerful couple and their wealth was expanding like Jay Z and Beyoncé. Hugo was a shrewd businessman, trying to transition from the streets to the boardroom. He owned a strip club in Brooklyn, a barbershop, a restaurant, a couple Laundromats, real estate, and a recording studio. It all came from drug money, and all of his profitable businesses made it easier for him to launder his drug money. Hugo wanted to become legit with Cristal by his side. But the rift between them came when Cristal had to execute a murdergram and would disappear suddenly, sometimes for days, and sometimes not having a reasonable explanation for her sudden absence. She refused to reveal her business to Hugo, though they supposedly had love and trust between them. It was for his safety. Cristal feared the Commission and she didn't want anything to happen to her boyfriend.

Hugo's organization was expanding, and he had everything he could ask for, but what he wanted truly was a baby, a son or daughter to call his own. He'd never had a family of his own. And in Hugo's mind, it was a way to tie her down to something. But Cristal was against having a family at the moment. She knew the restrictions given to her by the Commission. She wanted to tell her man the truth, but it too was dangerous. They owned her life until she was twenty-five years old, and at twenty, she didn't want to rock the boat. Her life was good, and she planned on keeping it that way.

How long could she keep the truth from Hugo? He already had his suspicions that something was going on, that she was cheating when she went MIA. He loved her, but he hated secrets. And Cristal was running out of reasons to explain her unexpected trips to different areas of the country.

•••

The next murdergram Cristal received was for two brothers named Rawls and Fred "Baby" Dinkins. They were heavy drug runners for a cartel, and were also two ruthless killers out on the west coast—Los Angeles to be specific. The hit had to be executed within the week. The brothers were living on borrowed time, and the Commission wanted them executed together. It was going to be another risky job, but the pay was going to be worth it. Each girl would receive a quarter of a million dollars, to be placed in her overseas account. With the interest already growing from money earned from their previous kills, the girls were on their way to becoming multi-millionaires within the next two years. And when it came time for Cristal to retire at the age of twenty-five, she was going to be set for life.

The hard part for Cristal was telling Hugo she had to leave for California within twenty-four hours. It was pressure put on her and Hugo wasn't going to like her leaving him once again. He was going to raise hell, like he did when she flew out to Miami a month ago to kill Rufus Gibbs, a major gorilla pimp in the city who had a stranglehold over two dozen exotic-looking women. Gibbs was known for drugging and raping his women and treating them harshly. Tamar and Cristal got at him through poison, stabbing him with a syringe lethal dosage of ricin as the two created a façade of beautiful, high-class working girls looking for a pimp's protection. Gibbs took the bait and lost his life. The Queen of Spades was taped to his forehead as the ricin devastated his insides.

California. It would be their farthest trip from home. Cristal had never been to California. She'd heard so much about it and longed to see what the other side of the country looked and felt like. Unfortunately, it was going to be about business instead of pleasure, and she wasn't going to L.A. to sightsee. She and Hugo could travel the world together with the fortune they attained, and live their lives without looking over their shoulders.

Cristal stood gazing at herself in the large bathroom mirror in Hugo's bathroom. She was clad in a white, two-piece sheer pajama set. Her body looked remarkable in it. She was ready to give her man a night of unadulterated and steamy romance—pretty much fuck his brains out before she told him about her leaving for L.A. It was sudden news for them both, but she had taken a vow for the people she worked for. It was going to be hard. Hugo was already impatient with her way of living. He wanted a partner who was going to be there for him twenty-four-seven, not coming and going like a politician running for election. He could take care of Cristal and she would never have to want for anything in her life.

As Cristal gazed at her mirror image, she thought how she was going to tell Hugo about California. She sighed heavily. There was only one way to tell him: bluntly.

When she was about to walk into the bedroom, Hugo entered the bathroom with his eyes fixed on his young beauty. She looked stunning in her skimpy lingerie. Hugo walked toward her and placed a ring box on the marble countertop in front of her. Cristal was taken aback. It was obvious what it was. Next Hugo placed a chromed .9mm in front of her. Cristal was confused.

Hugo wrapped his arms around her, held her tightly, and stared at her mirror image as he gazed also at his own in the bathroom mirror.

"What's the gun for?" Cristal asked.

"I love you so much, baby, and I want you in my life forever," Hugo proclaimed with all his heart. "But I don't want you fuckin' lying to me. I don't want to be played for a fuckin' fool," he then said through clenched teeth.

Cristal stood with an emotionless expression while being held in his muscular arms.

"What are you asking me?" Cristal replied.

"I just want the truth from you."

"What?!" Cristal was slightly annoyed, and his gun wasn't hardly fazing her. However, she pretended to be a little spooked that her life could actually be in danger.

"Are you fuckin' somebody else?" Hugo demanded to know.

She was, but she couldn't tell him the truth. She loved him too much and didn't want to hurt him. However, her life was too complicated to explain it to Hugo. And if she did, where would she start?

"What?" Cristal acted befuddled by his question.

"Don't play stupid with me, Elizabeth. I want to know what is going on with you. I'm no fool. You leaving and coming, in and out of town, sometimes you're gone for days at a time. I never get to stay the night at your place, and you won't move in with me. I want an explanation from you. No lies, the truth!" Hugo exclaimed. "I want you to become my wife. I want a baby. I want us to live happily. I'm ready to retire from the game, baby. I want us to live normal, but that can't happen if you keep fuckin' with me. I want to know what you are hiding."

Cristal turned around in his arms to face him. They locked eyes,

Hugo's was glaring, and hers were defeated.

"I'm leaving for California in forty-eight hours," she said out of the blue.

"What? California? For what?" Hugo growled.

Cristal looked at him for a moment. There was no escaping the truth. If Hugo knew about her affair with E.P., he would try to kill her. He wasn't a man to mess around with. And no matter how she would explain fucking E.P., it would never be a logical enough explanation to the man who would die for her and most likely kill her if he caught her cheating.

Cristal wasn't going to leave the bathroom intact until Hugo got a reasonable explanation from her. It was obvious in his eyes. She had to tell him something he was going to believe.

"Hugo, I don't know how well you're going to take this," Cristal started.

Hugo scowled and kept close to Cristal. He was ready to hear the truth.

She locked eyes with him and whispered, "I . . . I . . . kill people for a living."

"What? You fuckin' expect me to believe some shit like that!" he retorted. "What am I, a fuckin' idiot, Elizabeth?!"

Hugo snatched the gun from off the countertop and cocked it back.

"It's the truth, Hugo!" Cristal screamed. "And my name's not Elizabeth, it's Cristal."

"You fuckin' can't be honest with me, can you!" he shouted.

"How do you want me to prove it? It's what I do! It's what I'm good at and get paid well for," Cristal exclaimed heatedly.

Hugo took a deep breath. It was a farfetched story coming from such a petite and beautiful woman. No one could believe her. But Cristal was adamant in getting her man to believe her. She'd already spilled the beans; she went on to say, "I work for a secret organization called the Commission.

I've been killing for them for almost two years now. We were trained on a Farm somewhere unknown. They taught me everything—different languages to speak, shooting and disarming guns, poisons, explosive, computers—everything I need to know to kill."

She still wasn't believable to Hugo. He gripped the .9mm tightly. Cristal knew it was time to prove to him what she was talking about. She didn't want to harm him. However, like lightning striking, she disarmed him, snatching the gun out of his hand and catching him off guard. She swiftly struck the side of his knee, crippling him somewhat, and kicked him down to the floor onto his back, leaving him stunned by the swift maneuver she carried out on him. Then she picked up the .9mm off the floor and took it apart like it was a Lego set crumbling in her hands.

Then Cristal spoke in German, "*Glaubst du mir jetzt?*"

Hugo was shocked. First, he outweighed her by over 100 pounds, and she'd dropped him to the ground like he was a feather. Then she spoke German and dismantled his firearm like it was some toy.

"What the fuck?" he uttered.

"I say to you, do you believe me now?"

Hugo didn't know what to believe. The woman he loved was *Columbiana* and *Kill Bill* all put into one. Hugo slowly picked himself up from off the floor and was ready to listen to Cristal. She had his full attention. Cristal was ready to finally tell him everything about her life. She looked at him and said, "Where do I start?"

"Just talk to me," Hugo replied coolly.

And Cristal did just that, she talked to him and told him about everything, from E.P.'s party, to the three months of intense and rigorous training on the Farm, to coming home to a different lifestyle, and the people she killed over the years. She told Hugo about the strict rules of the Commission, how much money she had made, the overseas account growing with interest, and the money she would have in the future. The only detail she kept from him was her continuing affair with E.P.

Hugo was stunned by everything she told him. He had to wrap his mind around it and think. She was the same person but different. Different name, different occupation—just different.

"Why at twenty-five?" he asked her about the Commission's age of their killers retiring.

"I don't know," she responded.

"Don't you find that kind of odd, Eliz—I, mean, Cristal?"

Cristal never knew why at twenty-five, they could go back to their normal lives and carry on with their money. She never truly questioned it. But it was odd. They talked for hours in the bathroom. Cristal told him her trip to California was to kill the Dinkins brothers who worked for a cartel. Hugo didn't like it. It was too risky. Cristal told him she and her crew didn't have a choice. If they didn't carry out the hit then the Commission would come looking for them.

Hugo kissed her deeply, finally believing her story. They were learning each other every day, and keeping truthful. But he let it be known to Cristal that he didn't fear the Commission like she did.

The night ended with them both promising to retire when she turned twenty-five. He was going to continue investing his blood money into legitimate businesses and separating himself from the streets. They both knew it would be the wise thing to do. But what Hugo wanted the most was a baby—a family, despite what the Commission said about its operatives having kids or families. Cristal was still adamant about not breaking the rules, which caused some tension between them. It was clear Hugo's yearning for wanting a family was about to become a serious issue between them.

TWENTY-EIGHT

●●●

Cristal took a sip of her Long Island Iced Tea while waiting for Tamar to show up. The Blue Chip bar-and-lounge in downtown Manhattan was a quaint after-work spot for white-collar employees looking to unwind and socialize after a hard day of work and business trading. In the evening, it was teeming with men in their long-sleeved, collared shirts and long ties, and women dressed in formal office attire. The chatter, laughing, and casual drinking were a daily routine. The Blue Chip bar really wasn't Cristal's setting, but it was a comfortable, neutral place where she was able to get away from everything and meet with Tamar in private.

While the men in the place were checking her out, Cristal sat alone at the table with a standoffish demeanor. Juggling two powerful men in her life was stressful enough, and becoming a top assassin added the icing to the cake. She felt relieved that Hugo knew the truth about her. She didn't have to hide it anymore. They still had a lot of work to do if she wanted to continue with their relationship, but in her mind, it seemed like everything was going to be okay.

The girls had an early-morning flight to California in a few hours, but before they left, Cristal needed to have a serious talk with Tamar about her promiscuous and wild lifestyle.

Tamar pulled up to the Blue Chip bar in her new white SL Benz and stepped outside in the warm weather in True Religion skinny jeans and a tight shirt, her Jimmy Choos touching the pavement. She walked into the bar looking around for Cristal and spotted her seated at a corner table, alone.

Tamar strutted over with all the boys heavily eyeing her milkshake moving in the tight jeans. Tamar smiled at Cristal. Cristal stood up and the two hugged and greeted each other with love, but there was a steady air of resentment building between them.

"I'm glad you came," Cristal sat back down and motioned for Tamar to sit.

"What's so important that you had to talk about right before we fly out to L.A. to do a job?" Tamar asked, sitting down and leaning in.

"It's you, and your lifestyle, Tamar."

"My lifestyle?" Tamar spat with a raised eyebrow.

"Yes, you're creating too much attention on yourself—the partying, the whoring around with these men every night. It's not good for us or our business," said Cristal.

Tamar snickered and leaned back in the chair. "Are you serious?"

"Yes."

"Bitch, who are you to tell me what I can and cannot do?" Tamar snapped. "You the last one to talk about whoring when you been slinging your pussy like it's a ping pong ball 'tween two niggas." It was said loud enough for people in their surrounding area to hear.

Cristal was taken aback. Which two niggas? How could Tamar know about Hugo? And if she knew, did that mean E.P. knew as well? Before she panicked, she realized that fucking Hugo wasn't breaking any Commission rules.

"Tamar, this isn't about me—"

"Yes it is. You think cuz you fuckin' E.P. that you got the authority to tell me how to live my life? Bitch, please!"

"Tamar, I'm just trying to help you."

"Help me?" Tamar chuckled. "Help yourself, Cristal, and tell both those niggas you fucking the truth."

Once again Tamar spoke authoritatively as if she knew exactly who Cristal was fucking, yet she evasively didn't mention Hugo's name. Cristal knew Tamar wanted her to ask how she knew about Hugo, but she was too smart to go there.

She exhaled noisily. "Tamar did you forget? If it weren't for me, you wouldn't be here today. I'm the one that made you and got you started. I'm the one E.P. had an eye for, and the one that brought you into this business. We made lots of money this year because of me, and don't you dare fuckin' forget that! And I'm not trying to have you fuck this up for us!" Cristal said through clenched teeth.

"Yes, boss, I didn't forget. But riddle me this . . . how is *my* pussy gonna fuck things up?" Tamar asked. "You must be drinking that Commission flavored Kool-Aid."

"All I'm saying is that we gotta keep a low profile, so you can't be bringing too many niggas around and having them in our business. If we want to move up—"

Tamar rose from the table. "I think something went real wrong with ya mind back at that Farm." She leaned in really close to Cristal's face, her eyes filled with rage, and whispered in a raspy, strained voice, "Don't . . . fuck . . . with . . . me!"

"Tamar."

"Fuck you, bitch!"

She pivoted on her high heels and stormed toward the exit. Everyone in the bar was shocked at Tamar's heated outburst. Cristal was left sitting there like she had egg on her face. Tomorrow they had to fly out to California; they had a major hit to do in L.A. and things were looking sour in her crew. It was about teamwork, but the team seemed to be falling apart.

•••

Sharon stared at her image in the bathroom mirror and felt like a new woman. She smiled and rubbed her head. Her natural afro was gone and her head was shaven low like Sinead O' Connor's. She looked good. The impulsive transformation of cutting off the natural locks that she'd been growing out for years gave her the courage to proceed with her next step. She missed Pike greatly. He was still in her heart, but it had been almost two years since his death, and Sharon was tired of grieving. The men responsible for murdering the man she loved still hadn't been caught. She was infuriated by the insufficient homicide investigation by the local precinct. In Sharon's eyes, they didn't care. To them, Pike was just another black man dead. They considered him a drug dealer and a menace to society.

So she was ready to take the initiative and take matters into her own hands, and make right what she felt was wrong. She was ready to take the necessary actions to change things, and the only way she saw that happening was leaving Brooklyn to join the police academy. She wanted to become a cop. She wanted to become something that her neighborhood needed, law and order—justice to be served. She was smart and ready to climb the ranks, and maybe in a few years become a homicide detective and solve Pike's cold case.

Sharon continued to look at her mirror image. The new her stared back, proud and strong. On the bathroom countertop was the completed application to join the police force. She was ready to become an NYPD recruit. It would surprise her friends, because becoming a cop was just as low as becoming a snitch in her hood. But she didn't care what people thought. In her mind, it was the right thing to do.

In six months, she would be Officer Sharon Green. There was a nice ring to that.

●●●

Hugo sat in the office to his strip club with the door closed and the music blaring outside. He smoked a cigar while seated in his high-backed leather chair and exhaled smoke. He had a lot on his mind. What Cristal told him was probably more than he bargained for. A hired female assassin—it was shit he saw in the movies and it was the last thing he expected Cristal to tell him. It was something farfetched and dangerous, but then again, his life was dangerous too.

They constantly argued about having children. He was ready to have a Hugo Jr. or a young princess of his own. A baby was like a new toy to him, but the reason he stressed having kids immediately was because he wanted to give his mother grandchildren before she died. It was one of her wishes to see grandchildren she could love and play with. His mother, who was in remission, was getting old and weaker every year.

Hugo leaned back in his chair while smoking his cigar and thinking about his girl's safety. She was out in L.A., and there was no way he could protect her from three thousand miles away. It seemed like Cristal knew how to handle herself. Hugo sighed and stared at the security monitors on the wall overseeing various activities going on inside his strip club. He saw one beautiful club stripper approaching his office carrying a tray of vodka. She knocked twice.

"Come in," he said.

The office door opened and in stepped Mesha, scantily clad in a pink thong consumed by her plump booty and a matching bikini top and six inch stilettos. She smiled at Hugo while bringing the vodka-and-Sprite he asked for. She set the drink on his desk in front of him and said, "You look like a man with a lot on his mind."

"I am," Hugo returned.

"Well you always know that I'm good listener," she said with a warm smile.

He smiled too. He took a strong pull from his cigar and stared at Mesha's scantily clad figure. The woman had more curves than the letter S and tits like a video vixen. She was eye candy, a man's wet dream.

After catching her assault case, which was subsequently thrown out by the judge, she took to stripping. It was easy money and an escape after Pike's murder.

Unbeknownst to Cristal, Hugo and Mesha had some history back in the days, pretty much fucking their brains out before she got with Pike. Now she worked for him in his club making good money, and she still felt attracted to him.

"What happened between us?" Mesha asked.

"It was a fling," replied Hugo nonchalantly.

"It was more than a fling to me. I was really feeling you, Hugo," she said.

"Yeah, you liked me so much that you got with that ball player and cut me off."

"I didn't love him like I loved you," she lied. "I thought about you every day, Hugo. I missed you so much that it was hard to live without you."

"Well, things have changed."

"I didn't want it to change," she admitted.

Hugo smirked.

"You ever think about me? About us? What we could have been together?" she asked.

"You know I'm in a relationship, Mesha."

"And? You're a handsome and fine-lookin' man, Hugo, and you're allowed to have some fun. I won't tell if you don't tell," she said seductively.

Mesha moved closer to him and continued her brazen flirting, knowing he had been dealing with Cristal. She wasn't afraid of Cristal or anyone in her crew. They had jumped Sharon, and Cristal didn't do shit.

Mesha positioned herself on his desk. She looked at him with desire, and enticed the man by pushing aside her thong and ramming three fingers into her loose, sloppy twat. She started fucking herself while seated on his desk with her legs spread. Hugo watched. He didn't attempt to stop her. Mesha shoved those same fingers in her mouth and sucked them, tasting her juices.

Hugo found himself unbuttoning his pants with Cristal out of his mind. He was horny and wanted a taste of Mesha's brown sugar. She wasted no time kneeling between his legs and giving him head. She grabbed his erection and started stroking it, making it leak pre-cum. Hugo moaned from her pleasing touch. Her small hands felt so good around his thick, black cock. She licked the salty treat and told him how good he tasted. Mesha took the mushroom head in her mouth and swirled her tongue around it. Hugo closed his eyes and threw his head back against the high-backed leather chair and could barely control himself. She went down on him slowly, licking and sucking with painstaking precision. Mesha made sure to get every big black inch wet with her mouth and tongue, sucking it expertly with her lips.

She moaned and slobbered all over his dick and fingered her pussy at the same time. Hugo moaned loudly. He looked down at Mesha sucking his dick, her full lips wrapped around his dark meat, her head bobbing up and down. He grabbed her dark hair and twisted it in his hand and shoved her mouth down on his dick, making her choke and gag on it. He held her head down into his lap for a moment, seeing how good she was at deep-throating, and Mesha was able to hold her own. She cupped his balls and massaged them in her soft hands.

As her pussy leaked, Hugo continued to fuck her throat hard and deep. Mesha loved the roughness with her mouth, as he slapped her face and called her a stupid bitch. She wanted more and it turned him on. She wanted to taste his cum.

"You like that?" Hugo asked.

Mesha nodded and moaned on his dick. She looked up into his eyes and saw the pleasure in his face. Seeing him succumb to her oral pleasures made her pussy tweak. She started humming on his dick, sending vibrations up his spine and talking dirty. Hugo loved it. He missed the way Mesha got freaky with him.

Hugo grabbed her head one last time and started moving it up and down on his dick, fucking her throat, treating his dancer like she was a cheap prostitute. She sucked and hummed on his balls, jerked him off, spit on the tip of his dick, and swallowed, deep throating him and stroking him like a porn star would. It drove Hugo insane until he couldn't hold it anymore and erupted inside of her mouth. Mesha held his dick steady between her lips, jerking him off as his white, creamy fluids slid down her throat and she took in every last drop.

Hugo sat deflated in his chair.

Mesha smiled and got up from her knees and wiped her mouth. "Just imagine, you fuck wit' me and you can get that every night, baby."

Hugo didn't respond. He had to collect himself for a moment and let Mesha's sexual offer simmer in his mind. It was a tempting proposal. When it came to head, Mesha was the best. Cristal was the woman he loved, but they were having their differences, especially with her constantly leaving to handle business out of town. With her being in L.A., Hugo didn't know what to think of the situation. It was conflicting, and this was the moment where he felt he could have his cake and eat it too.

He looked at Mesha and smiled. Staring at her curvy, brown figure made him grow an erection again. Her bald pussy was eye-catching. He licked his lips. "You ready for round two?"

"What you think?" she responded with a sly smile.

Mesha got butt-naked in his office, still standing erect in her spike stilettos, and bent herself over on his desk, her legs wildly spread, ass in the air and ready for his hard entry. Hugo stepped out of his jeans and positioned himself behind her to fuck her in the doggy-style position. Hugo grabbed a condom and briefly considered doubling up.

He wanted to forget about Cristal for a moment, and he did that by sliding his big dick into the next bitch.

TWENTY-NINE

The Cristal Clique crew arrived at LAX international airport early that afternoon, and they were ready to get down to business. There was still tension between Cristal and Tamar, and Mona picked up on it. She held herself reserved from her best friends and decided not to get into the drama between them. Mona had acquired a peaceful and monkish life outside of her killing career, and reading and growing her plants gave her a peace of mind from the bloodshed.

The Commission wanted this hit to send out a gruesome message. They wanted it to be bloody and gory. The Dinkins brothers had to die a violent death. The cartel wanted the brothers dead within a twenty-four hour window.

The girls were met with a connector who greeted them outside of the terminal. They piled into a dark minivan and cruised west on the 405 Highway. It was their first time in L.A., and the West Coast culture was totally different from their home in the East. Sunny California was a beautiful place with towering palm trees and year-round warm weather, but now wasn't the time to sightsee and act like tourists. The driver of the minivan was of Mexican descent. He had dark hair and a dark goatee, cold eyes, and a strong Spanish accent. He welcomed the girls to L.A. and immediately got down to business.

"I hear good things about y'all. They say youse girls are good at killing," the driver said.

The girls didn't respond. They weren't ones to socialize with anyone, but it felt good to hear that their reputation was out there. It was what Cristal wanted, the fierce brand of being deadly contract killers. She wanted notoriety in the business, and it was happening. She was desperate to add another notch to her belt.

The minivan headed toward East Los Angeles, and in the back of the van was a classic Army heavy machine gun M249 MK II AEG M60, with a full metal magazine. It was a nasty weapon, able to shred men in half. It fired at a dazzling speed of over four hundred feet per second, and delivered eight hundred rounds per minute.

The girls got themselves situated at a local motel in East Los Angeles, off the 405 Expressway. Their trip to L.A. was to be short—kill these brothers and be back on a plane to New York by the next day. The cartel wanted outside killers because the brothers were cautious and were always heavily armed. They wouldn't expect females to be gunning for them.

Cristal advised a plan for the hit while they lounged in the seedy motel room. Since the brothers were cautious and drove around in bulletproof vehicles, she suggested that they strike head on. Everyone thought it was a crazy plan, but she figured out a way to strike when their guard would be down. She told them what she wanted to do, and there was a slim possibility of it working out.

As Cristal suggested, they hijacked a police vehicle, disarmed and stripped the officers, one male and one female, of their clothing, shields and guns. They didn't kill the cops, but kept them captive at an isolated warehouse on the outskirts of L.A. Their marked car and uniforms would become useful. The clock was winding down, every minute was critical.

Mona and Tamar were sent out to tail the brothers at their stash house in East L.A. The dilapidated one-story stash house on the gang-infested block was surrounded by gang members and armed goons. Mona and Tamar sat parked inconspicuously on the block, watching the heavy activity out front. Once the brothers were on the go, Mona and Tamar were to call Cristal and their Mexican liaison.

Two massive men swathed with gang tattoos and battle scars exited the stash house carrying a large duffel bag. Rawls and Fred "Baby" Dinkins looked like heavy hitters and stone-cold killers. The two got into an idling armored black-on-black Escalade and drove off. Tamar made the phone call to inform Cristal that the targets were in motion and they were in pursuit.

It was time to put their plan into action.

The two gang members and their goon were pulled over by the marked police car with its flashing lights on a busy L.A. boulevard late in the evening. As predicted, the men pulled to the side on the instruction of Cristal and the Mexican pretending to be police officers. Rawls was behind the wheel, his brother was riding shotgun in the passenger seat, and one of their henchman was riding in the backseat. They scowled at the police stop. Rawls removed his pistol from his waistband and was ready to blast on police, but his brother warned him to play it cool. He thought it was just a routine stop.

Cristal and her Mexican counterpart exited the police car looking legit in the uniforms. Fortunately for Cristal, she and the female cop she'd stolen the uniform from were somewhat the same size. They approached the Escalade with their hands on their holstered weapons. Cristal went toward the passenger while her accomplice went to approach the driver.

"License and registration," he asked Rawls.

"What the fuck ya pulled us over for?" Rawls hissed.

"You ran that stop sign a few blocks back," the Mexican explained, keeping his cool and playing the role of a police officer to the fullest.

"What?"

"License and registration please," he asked again in a more stern tone.

Cristal keenly examined inside the vehicle with her peripheral vision while remaining emotionless and keeping cool. She could smell weed lingering. The men inside were edgy. They looked like they were ready to pull out and kill two cops. But her Mexican friend played his part well and was on point. He brought the foul-smelling weed to their attention and instructed all the passengers to step out of the car. When the men didn't want to play ball, he lifted his police radio from off his shoulder and was ready to call in backup. Reluctantly, all three passengers followed his command.

The parked minivan three cars down observed everything and were waiting on the right moment to attack. Tamar assembled the lethal machine gun and waited for the signal. Mona was behind the wheel of the idling vehicle.

Cristal and the Mexican were able to get them out of the armored SUV and had them lined up by the back of the truck with minor traffic going by observing it all. Rawls and his brother cursed and disapproved of their vehicle being searched, but he was sure the officers wouldn't find anything. He had placed all handguns and any illegal contraband into a stash box that only he knew how to open. He stood with a smirk across his face, mocking the cops.

"Man, fuck ya mark-ass police, this some fuckin' bullshit. Pig-ass muthafuckas!" Fred "Baby" exclaimed loudly.

Cristal warned them, but they continued their disrespect. Cristal decided it was time to give the signal. She looked Tamar and Mona's way and touched her badge. The minivan sped forward while she and the Mexican made sure to be out of the way of gunfire. The minivan came to a screeching stop where the brothers and their goon were lined up; the side door of the minivan slid back and the heavy machine gun protruded. Tamar quickly opened fire on all three men.

The men didn't even know what hit them. Loud machine gunfire roughly pierced the air on the bustling boulevard, and eight hundred rounds per minute went tearing into the victims, violently shredding them apart. They were cruelly executed—blood, and flesh and brain matter spewing everywhere from the SUV to the ground. The men collapsed to street, their bodies torn in half and contorted by the vicious assault, while several witnesses nearby hurried for cover and safety in an undignified way.

Cristal and the Mexican hurriedly jumped into the minivan and sped away. Another mission completed. The bloody statement was sent out. The Dinkins brothers were dead. Now it was time for Cristal and her crew to return back to New York. She couldn't wait to see Hugo again and have a heart-to-heart talk with him. She missed him. She just hoped he missed her just as much.

Her relationship with Tamar was becoming shakier. On their way back to New York several hours later, they argued and beefed with each other. It was obvious egos and jealousy were getting in the way, and Mona felt helpless trying to rekindle the good old times between them. Cristal and Tamar were on the verge of hating each other.

• • •

When Cristal exited the JFK terminal; she was shocked to see E.P. waiting outside next to his pearl-colored Bentley for her and the girls. He was dressed sharply—as always—in a black suit. He greeted Cristal with a kiss and ignored the other girls. He hadn't come there for them, only for Cristal. Tamar scowled at Cristal receiving the VIP treatment from him.

"You did good, baby," E.P. said to Cristal in front of the others.

Cristal smiled. "You already heard?"

"The Commission is pleased with everything. Message well sent."

Tamar wanted to interject. She disliked that Cristal was getting all the praise from him. Cristal hadn't done it all alone; she had been the one who fired the shots. But E.P. didn't care. They were starting to feel invisible. It was all about Cristal, not anyone else.

"I have a surprise for you," E.P. said.

"You do?" Cristal replied, pretending to be thrilled that he'd come for her. She really wanted to rush home and see Hugo. E.P. walked over to his Bentley and opened the passenger door for Cristal. She looked over at her crew and shrugged. It was selfish of her, but E.P. was the boss. She slid into the seat of the Bentley and she shut the door.

Tamar and Mona were left waiting for a taxi to take them home. They felt like outcasts—all the dangerous work they'd put in, only to be treated as second-rate by Cristal and E.P.

"Fuckin' asshole!" Tamar uttered.

•••

The Bentley pulled away from the curb. They weren't even out of JFK airport yet when E.P. placed his hand between Cristal's exposed thighs and moved it upward. He continued to praise her on the job out in California. The gruesome murder had already made national headlines, and the police out there were baffled as to how it all went down.

"You on your way, Cristal," he said proudly. "The job you performed out there, fuckin' brilliant. It took balls to pull it off that way."

"Thanks."

E.P. looked at her with admiration, but while he complimented her, Cristal's mind was on Hugo. She yearned to feel his touch against her skin and feel his entry inside of her. But her love for her man would have to be delayed. E.P. was driving Cristal back to his place in the city and he wasn't hearing no for an answer. He missed her dearly and wanted her to spend the night.

•••

Once again, Cristal found herself staring at her naked mirror image in the bathroom. She clutched her cell phone, sighed deeply, and stared at the eight missed calls from Hugo. She'd had to ignore them all while her time was spent fucking E.P. in his penthouse suite.

Guilt overwhelmed her. The nasty shit they had done in the past several hours had her pussy sore. E.P. was the ultimate freak, being able to fuck for hours. He wasted no time with her once they stepped into his place. He tore Cristal's clothes from her body, pushed her onto the bed, and started licking and kissing and sucking her brown hole. She ground her ass on his face, pulling her cheeks apart while his tongue buried deep inside of her. The action was making her pussy wet with E.P. being such a dirty muthafucka. He put her in sexual nirvana. Cristal held her legs spread wider as she enjoyed the sensation of her sexy black muthafucka making a feast of her ass.

Despite not being in love with E.P., she was a woman who needed to get fucked and fucked hard. She was desperate to feel every inch of his hard meat rammed into her walls. E.P. had grabbed her hair and pulled it like reigns on a horse and took her pussy from the back.

"Fuck me! Ooooh, fuck me! Fuck me now!" she had cried out.

He had lined up the fat head of his dick with her pussy hole and aggressively penetrated her. Cristal gripped the sheets, feeling her pussy opening wide like a good book. E.P. grabbed her hips and with one fluid, fast motion, he rammed the entire size of his dick deep into her. Cristal had screamed out in pain, but that didn't stop her from begging for more.

Cristal stood staring at her disheveled image after the intense sexual episode she'd experienced and it made her want to cry. E.P. ravaged her body throughout the night. He would smack her phat ass while pulling her long hair and reach around to her swinging tits. E.P. was too aggressive in the bedroom, treating her tits roughly, pinching her nipples and causing her to moan loudly.

How could she go home to Hugo after what E.P. had done to her body?

E.P. walked into the bathroom naked with his dick swinging from side to side. His chiseled body glistened with sweat and his muscles flexed as he walked behind her. He pulled Cristal into his arms and nestled against her backside, kissing the side of her neck. Once again, he proclaimed his love for her, sending Cristal's guilt into a whirlwind of emotions.

"You okay?" he asked her.

"I'm okay," she replied.

"You sure, because you seem distanced from me since you got back from California."

"I just have a lot on my mind."

"Like what?"

"It's nothing."

"The look in your eyes says it's probably more than nothing. You can talk to me about anything, baby," he said.

She couldn't tell him the truth; she was in love with another man and wanted to discontinue their affair.

Cristal felt reluctant to end things between them, no matter how heavy her heart got. She was on her way to the top, and she didn't want to be a fool and rock the boat. She felt she had things under control; as long as she kept E.P. happy, he would never find out about Hugo.

Cristal turned around in his arms and looked him eye to eye. She smiled. "It's nothing, just some drama between Tamar and me," she told him.

"Well as long as it doesn't interfere with the business, then everything's copacetic," E.P. replied coolly.

"It won't. Just girl bullshit."

The two kissed. E.P. lifted her into his arms and planted her naked ass on the granite countertop and placed himself between her soft thighs. He once again lined up the fat head of his dick with her warm hole and thrust himself inside. He couldn't get enough of Cristal. She was his addiction—

his new love. They fucked passionately in the bathroom, and while E.P. was inside of her, the only thing Cristal could think about was how upset Hugo was going to be because he had called her numerous times and she hadn't been able to speak to him since she arrived in New York. E.P. took up all of her time, and there was no escaping the lust he had for her. He'd fucked her six ways from Sunday and wasn't done with her yet.

She moaned and groaned, feeling her pussy stretching out like a rubber band from the pounding dick. As E.P. thrust into her, Cristal silently shed a few tears knowing she was wrong for this. But it felt so good.

●●●

Fourteen hours after her arrival into JFK airport, she finally broke away free from E.P.'s strong lust and was able to go to Hugo's place. When she arrived he wasn't home. She called his cell phone but he wasn't picking up. Cristal sat in his bedroom for over an hour and wondered where he could be. He always answered her phone calls but now her calls were going straight to voicemail. Hugo could be anywhere: at the strip club, maybe out of town, or out on business with his peoples. She could only be upset with herself for allowing E.P. to take up too much of her time when she had a doting man waiting for her to come home.

Cristal felt Hugo not being around was a good thing anyway. After E.P.'s sexual onslaught on her body and pussy, she needed to recuperate and chill for a moment. Hugo was going to want some pussy too once he saw her, and Cristal knew she wasn't up for it. She was drained. She had to wash and scrub herself free of E.P.'s smell and relax and get her body right again. And she did just that, spending over an hour soaking and scrubbing herself in the bathtub and resting up. It had been a long two days and jet lag started to set in. She didn't get much sleep being with E.P., but the minute she closed her eyes, she slept for hours, close to twenty-four hours straight.

THIRTY

●●●●●●●●●●●●●●●●●●●●●●●●●●●●●●●●●●●●●●●

It had been seven weeks since the California hit, and things had been quiet all over, except for home. Her relationship with Hugo had been up and down, rocky, but still loving. They constantly argued about having kids. Hugo continually pressured her for a baby, but when Cristal brought up the rules given to her by the Commission, Hugo would shout out, "Fuck the Commission! They don't fuckin' put fear in me, Cristal. I want a family. I want children. I want us to be normal."

She wanted the same thing, but her life was much more complicated, and she hated that Hugo didn't see things her way. And with her affair with E.P. carrying on, the pressure was building. She felt Hugo pulling away from her. It wasn't the same as it had been a year ago. She felt there was something else pulling Hugo away from her. She didn't know exactly what it was, but she was determined to find out.

Cristal found out what—or who—had Hugo distracted from her when she went to visit him at the strip club he owned. She heard rumors that he was fucking with one of his strippers down at the club, but she didn't want to believe it. She walked into the dimly lit club and immediately stormed toward Hugo's back office. Seeing Mesha exit the office with a smile on her face before she could enter herself made Cristal see red.

The two confronted each other in the hallway. Cristal was ready to fuck her up. Mesha didn't back down, and the quarrel ensuing brought Hugo out of his office and security coming to break things up.

Hugo denied that he was fucking with Mesha and explained to Cristal that the only reason she was seen coming out of his office was to bring the bottle of vodka he requested. Cristal knew he was lying. Cristal wanted to fight everyone in the club, even Hugo, and she became so out of control that security had to drag her away. She loved Hugo, and the thought of him fucking the enemy made her blood boil.

She felt like a hypocrite for becoming so angry at Hugo for his indiscretions and wanting to kill Mesha when she'd been secretly fucking E.P. for so long. She'd tried hard to cover her infidelities, but the more she tried, the more things seemed to fall apart. And when she went to talk or complain about her dilemma to her only friend left, Mona, Mona called Cristal a fraud too, and went into one of her rhetorical speeches about other strange things.

"We're all playing with fire, Cristal, and eventually we gonna all burn in purgatory, trapped between earth and hell for our sins," Mona proclaimed oddly.

Cristal had been dumbfounded by Mona's words.

Unbeknownst to Tamar and Cristal, Mona had been having a change of heart about her career path of murder for hire. She started to see the souls of their victims in her dreams almost every night. She began going to a voodoo priest who told her to burn black candles for the murdered and white candles to release their souls. Mona was chanting, praying, smoking, and drinking all while she was being haunted. She predicted their demise was coming soon. She'd been having premonitions of betrayal and death coming her way, so she continued to live a monastic lifestyle and remained eccentric in her Bronx apartment. She missed Lisa greatly and continued to have doubts about her friend being the lone wolf.

While locked away in her apartment reading and tending to her plants, Mona had time to think. She had time to put the pieces to the puzzle together.

"They killed her," Mona had uttered out of the blue.

"What? What are you talking about, Mona? Who was killed?" Cristal felt her friend was losing her mind.

"Lisa. She's dead. I know it. I have dreams about her almost every night. She's no lone wolf, Cristal. They killed her. I don't know why, but they did," Mona had bizarrely declared.

Cristal didn't believe it. Mona was speaking nonsense.

"Mona, that bitch is dead to us, because she abandoned us and went out to do her own thing. She ain't really dead, psycho!"

"Do you truly believe that, Cristal? Do you think Lisa would ever abandon her best friends?"

Cristal didn't know what to think anymore. It had been over two years since they joined the organization and had their training on the Farm. Together, the girls had performed over a dozen murders and made so much money that they felt not rich but wealthy.

After Cristal left Mona's place, she didn't know what to do with herself. Friendship was becoming a memory, and her love life was in shambles. Hugo wasn't going to give up until she was pregnant and having his baby. Cristal felt their issue was driving her man away to be with other women, slut bitches like Mesha, and she needed to fix her relationship by any means necessary.

And by any means necessary, Cristal came up with a cunning plan that might satisfy them both in the long run, and keep her from breaking the Commission's rule and losing her life—and this plan involved her cousin Mia.

Cristal had gotten Hugo to agree to her cousin, Mia, carrying their baby. They were to find a doctor on the down low to do the in vitro fertilization, combining Cristal's eggs and Hugo's sperm to impregnate Mia. Of course Mia wanted a substantial amount of money if she was going to do this for them, so Hugo offered her fifty thousand dollars to carry the baby, and he also bought her a house on a lake in upstate New York. Their plan was to keep everyone on the low and keep the organization from ever knowing any of this.

When the baby was born, Cristal would have a live-in nanny, but she and Hugo would keep hustling until their retirement age. Cristal planned on keeping the New York condo in SoHo, but would spend most of her time raising their child in an undisclosed location. The two of them figured it was a mastermind idea, and that their child would be under four years old when Cristal could retire from the Commission. And with her twenty-first birthday approaching, the countdown began. She couldn't wait to get out of the murder for hire business.

THE FARM

●●●

UPSTATE NEW YORK

The desolate area that sat on several acres of land nestled in the backwoods of upstate New York continued to be the breeding place for training young assassins to do the Commission's dirty work. Another herd of young-faced applicants were going through the same vigorous and grueling program that dozen before them endured. It was the final stages of the training—the last week when the recruits were pushed into a barren room to kill for the organization for the first time.

Lisa could hardly get her bearings in the cold and foul-smelling room. She lay across the wintry and hard concrete ground like a wet mat in her tattered clothing. She had been continually shot up with heroin and drugged to the point where she no longer knew her name or her history. She didn't even know what year it was. For more than two years, she had been living under extreme and deplorable conditions. While her friends were under the assumption that she was a lone wolf living extremely well, she had actually been yanked out of the course the first week of her training. The harrowing staff noticed she and the others continually failed the tests, and they were weeded out for destruction. She didn't have what she needed to survive undetected as a hired gun.

Lisa was thrown into a barnlike dwelling with several other men and women the Farm felt were disposable. She was hardly fed and was a couple of ounces shy of being anorexic. She barely had enough meat on her to cover her rib cage or hipbones.

She was treated like a test subject. She wasn't groomed or treated for any sickness, and she had been living like a dog. Her hair was nappy, and she was emaciated. She was unrecognizable and looked like she had aged two decades.

She barely knew who she was anymore, and she mumbled to herself and was caked with dirt and stench. Flashes of her past would come and go like lightning striking. Her family would never have any idea what happened to their little girl. Lisa felt death was her only escape from the torture and brutality she'd endured since arriving at the Farm.

The next training group started to pour into the room, and one by one, they were tested on their will to kill easily. Gunshots echoed from a distance, and one by one, the homeless-looking men and women Lisa was grouped with in the inhospitable concrete area were taken from the room to be killed by the trainees.

Today was finally the day of death for some of them. Lisa was picked to become one of the homeless-looking people that potential assassins would have to murder in order for them to leave the Farm to pursue their deadly careers.

The steel door opened to the room the unfortunate victims were hostage in and Lisa was roughly pulled out by two men and dragged into another similar room and thrown to the ground. She thought she was alone, but she wasn't. She was met by a young, stoic-looking woman in a white jumpsuit, holding a .9mm in her hand.

The voice crackled over the intercom, saying to the lean and fit Spanish-looking woman, "Kill her."

The woman trainee raised the gun to Lisa's head and didn't hesitate to shoot.

THIRTY-ONE

●●●●●●●●●●●●●●●●●●●●●●●●●●●●●●●●●●●●●●

E.P. had always been a disconnected and cold character, as well as a shrewd and calculating man when it came to business and murder. His aloofness toward everything in his life had always been his survival. But the twelve-by-eight glossy pictures E.P. gazed at, of Cristal and Hugo together in several passionate ways, kissing, sexing and loving each other, sent him into an emotional freefall. He had been careless and too trusting with Cristal because he was in love with her, but now he saw that she was playing him for a fool. He had risked his life to be with her and he alarmingly found out that she was in love with another man.

He had been feeling the distance between him and Cristal. She hadn't been spending much of her time in her SoHo condo and she was acting strange around him. It sent red flags flying E.P.'s way, so he hired a private investigator for twenty-five thousand dollars—the best at his job. E.P. had Cristal followed and investigated for three weeks without anyone knowing. And what the private investigator came back with made E.P. furious.

Unbeknownst to Cristal, E.P. wanted to marry her, and he was ready to take a chance by asking the Commission to allow her out of her contract. He was aware of the fate that awaited the killers once they reached their twenty-fifth birthday, and he didn't want Cristal to fall into that harsh outcome. The Commission lied to their recruits and their young, lethal killers that spanned the world. There was no retiring from the organization at the age of twenty-five. The only way out was death. They kept track of everyone, and a deadly and meticulous cleaner was sent around the world to wipe out those young killers who were about to age out. The Commission couldn't afford to have any evidence linking back to them or to take chances on someone going rogue, maybe talking to the government about their shadowy business. It was easier to replace and train new assassins every year than to keep around any old ones. Many were wiped out and their bodies never found—victims to their own trade. And the overseas bank accounts, filled with millions that kept the young killers motivated—it was more like Monopoly money because it was never to be paid out.

Her love was a lie, and E.P. felt betrayed. She had gone behind the Commission's back to start a family with Hugo. He found out about her cousin Mia carrying the baby for them via in vitro fertilization, and about the hush-hush location they planned to live at in upstate New York. She had broken the rules; therefore, Cristal was a dead bitch.

●●●

Tamar moaned from his dick being pounded inside her throbbing pussy from the back. Her ebony lover had shoved his eight-inches into her with intense heat and she felt the muscles of her pussy walls grabbing him. He held her hips and pushed forward, listening to Tamar cry out. She looked back at him and said, "Fuck me, nigga! Fuck me!" And that's what he did.

Her tall and brawny ebony lover stroked and thrust and drove every single inch of his hard meat inside her. Tamar was going wild, chanting and moaning and begging for more. Tamar's full ass was wiggling and bouncing up and down, and the wet sounds of sex filled her bedroom as he kept pounding her.

They both were horny muthafuckas on a mission to cum. He fucked her harder and Tamar moaned louder. She was on the brink of exploding her white juices on his penetrating cock inside of her. He could feel the cum in his balls simmering to discharge. And just like that, jointly, they both came intensely and exhaled. Tamar's young ebony lover looked down to see his big dick glistening with her juices.

Tamar removed herself from the bed and donned a long robe. She had the need for a cool drink from her kitchen. Her sweaty male company collapsed on his back on the bed, uttering, "Get me something to drink too, babe," as he tried to collect himself from their dynamic fuck.

The second Tamar turned on the lights to her kitchen she saw it and was puzzled. The large manila folder placed on her kitchen counter was odd. Was it a murdergram? Why was it there, and who placed it there, and why was she receiving it unexpectedly instead of Cristal? She carefully walked toward the folder and opened it to see the target. Tamar was taken aback to see that the target was Cristal.

"The Commission wants her dead," a voice abruptly spoke from out of nowhere.

Tamar reached for a sharp knife out of her drawer and posed in attack mode, pointing the knife in the man's direction. E.P. emerged from the shadows of her kitchen. She was shocked to see him of all people in her kitchen. They glared at each other.

"What the fuck?" Tamar spat.

E.P. was unruffled by Tamar with the knife in her hand. He stepped closer to Tamar and said, "She broke the rule, and she needs to go."

At first, Tamar was ambivalent about the hit on Cristal, but when she learned Cristal was keeping secrets from everyone, especially about her cousin Mia having her baby, Tamar became irritated and angry. It didn't take much persuasion for Tamar to accept the hit. The way E.P. looked at her; she knew she didn't have a choice.

"If I do this, I want to be on my own, no crew...a lone wolf," she said.

E.P. nodded.

Tamar smiled.

THIRTY-TWO

• •

Marvin Gaye's "What's Going On" blared throughout Grandma Hattie's apartment. The smell of Thanksgiving dinner cooking in the kitchen seeped into the lively living room. Everyone could smell the turkey cooking, yams in the oven roasting, catfish frying on the stove, and various cakes and pies being baked by capable hands, while the men watched football on the tube.

Three generations convened in Brooklyn only on holidays. Sixteen relatives came from all over to gather around two lightweight folding tables that were usually used to host card games and eat the best soul food cooked within the Tri-State area.

Everyone was ready to eat except for Cristal. She stood by the window repeatedly pulling the blinds back and gazing outside. She was waiting for her man to arrive. Cristal asked Hugo to stop at the store to pick up a case of Grey Goose and some oysters for her pregnant cousin, Mia, who was craving them.

"Cristal, baby, he's coming, so there's no need for you to keep staring out that window, chile," said her aunt Ruth.

Cristal sighed. "It's getting late, though, and we about to eat and I don't want him to miss out on anything."

"Hugo's a grown man, and he'll be here when he gets here."

Cristal smiled and nodded. She went to join her family in the room.

Fifteen minutes later, there was knocking at the door. Cristal rushed up from the couch and hurried toward the door with a huge smile. This would be the first time most of her family members were going to meet the love of her life.

Cristal unlocked the apartment door, but before she could completely open it, Hugo was roughly pushed into her and the door burst open, allowing three masked assailants to charge inside with their guns drawn. Immediately, they pistol-whipped Hugo and besieged the apartment. Screaming and panic ensued. Cristal's family was wide-eyed with horror and fear. Their celebratory mood had transformed into a nightmare.

"Ohmygod, please! No! No!" a cousin shouted.

"What is this?" another family member screamed.

"Please, this is my family!" Grandma Hattie begged.

One of the masked assailants rushed toward Grandma Hattie with his gun raised at her and shouted, "Shut the fuck up, bitch, before I blow your fuckin' brains out!"

Hugo lay on the floor in Cristal's arms, dazed, bleeding from his head. He glared up at his attackers defiantly, but inwardly he was trembling. Without a gun in his hand, he was helpless.

While one gunman kept his gun trained on everyone in the room, one by one, each family member's hands was duct-taped and they were placed facedown on the living room floor. Everyone except Hugo and Cristal had duct-tape placed over their mouths. Then the masked gunmen searched through the apartment for anyone hiding in the bedrooms or bathrooms.

Why are they here? Who did they come for? Are they going to kill us? It ran through everyone's minds. The panic and fear manifested on the captives' faces didn't do anything to their assailants. It was obvious that the three were heartless and cold-blooded. And, it was also clear that they were experienced. Cristal noticed the black gloves—they were not leaving behind any fingerprints—and the silencers at the tips of their guns—noise control.

One stepped toward Hugo with a .9mm with the silencer trained on his head and exclaimed, "Where the fuck is the money at?"

Hugo glared up at the gunman and boldly replied, "Fuck you!"

The butt of the .9mm came crashing down on Hugo's forehead. He cried out as more blood spewed from his open wound. Cristal wept. Her family looked distraught. The masked gunmen were persistent in getting what they came for.

"The money, where is it?" the masked gunman repeated.

With hurt and agony written across his face, Hugo gazed up again and feebly replied, "I don't have any money."

He was hit again with the butt of the pistol, and again, and again, and again. His face turned red with blood, starting to look like hamburger meat.

"You're killing him!" Cristal screamed. With all of her training, all of her kills, she would have never guessed that she would have got caught, slipping. Her guard was down when they burst in, and they'd subdued her before she could react.

Now Hugo lay listless in her arms. Her tears fell against him. Her hurt and pain penetrated the room. Hugo offered his pocket money to the assailants, but that was an insult. They came for a large lump sum, nothing less.

"Why are you here?" Cristal screamed.

"Okay, I see that we're going to have to do this the hard way," said the alpha gunman in the group.

He was tall, pushing six-two, and looked completely fit. Each gunman was clad in black jeans and a hoodie, with ski-masks concealing their identity. Frustrated, one of the gunmen walked up to Grandma Hattie. He stood over her like the Grim Reaper with his pistol trained on her head and with finality, asked, "Where is the money at?"

Hugo once again refused to reveal any information. Cristal cried out that he should just tell them, but Hugo didn't budge. The gunman fired—*Poot! Poot!*—and two bullets ripped through the side of Grandma Hattie's head, killing her instantly. As blood pooled beneath her, muffled crying was heard through the duct tape as her family gazed on in absolute anguish.

"That's one down. And I swear to you, I'll execute every last muthafucka in this room, one every fuckin' minute, if we don't get what we want," the gunman assured, his cold eyes black like space.

Hugo still didn't budge. He refused to give up his cash knowing they were going to execute him anyway. The look in the assailants' eyes showed they had already made up their minds to kill everyone in the apartment once they'd rushed inside and duct-taped women, men, and kids. Hugo knew the game and how it was played. He had killed many men before in the same fashion; having once been a ruthless and violent stick-up kid coming up on the streets. He unwillingly found himself on the losing end of the pistol this time around. He would rather die as a man who didn't flinch or beg for his life like some coward under the pressure. Hugo would rather die knowing these muthafuckas didn't get their grubby hands on his hard-earned cash. And nobody was going to make a come-up off the blood that ran through his veins.

The men focused their attention on Cristal.

"Where the money at?" they asked.

She didn't know. She stared at Hugo with her eyes pleading to him to fix the problem, to make it right. They'd already murdered her beloved grandmother.

Hugo shook his head slowly, remaining stoic. He wasn't budging. If it was his day to die, then so be it. Cristal and her family were scared to death, but Cristal was also furious knowing time was running out. She knew her grandmother's place didn't have any money, but she helplessly hoped that Hugo could negotiate with their assailants—perhaps take the stick-up kids to his stash, and in return, they might let everyone live.

"Hugo, just tell them where everything is! Please, baby, for my family!" Cristal exclaimed hysterically.

The gunmen once again threatened to execute one victim per minute if their demands weren't met. One of them stormed toward her Aunt Ruth and shoved the gun to the back of her head. He was ready to pull the trigger, but Cristal shouted out, "I have money! Lots of it!"

Everyone turned to look at her. "I have money, and it's not stashed under some mattress or put away somewhere secretly. It's in a bank account. It's yours, every penny. It's more money than you can spend. But it's going to take some time to get it all out—at least twenty-four hours."

They gazed at her but said nothing.

Her family thought she was talking gibberish, only trying to save them before the inevitable. They felt it was only rants coming from a woman who was about to die.

"Shut up!" one perpetrator demanded.

"Why? It's the fuckin' truth!" she screamed.

"We don't want your money," the shorter stocky goon stated coldly.

"Then what the fuck you want?! What is it?! This is my fuckin' family! Please, have some mercy! You know who the fuck I am! Who I'm connected to!" she screamed out, ranting crazily.

The shorter stocky goon stood over Cristal and dryly returned, "I know who you are, and I'm still about to rock you to sleep."

The television and radio was turned up to drown out their victims whimpering and muffled cries through the duct tape. And then one by one, Cristal helplessly watched the shortest and slimmest one of the crew start executing her family members, just innocent victims, by shooting them in the backs of their heads. Each one squirmed powerlessly on the floor trying to avoid being shot to death by the hot bullets slamming into the back of their brains. Mothers poorly tried to lie on top of their children to protect them from the hit, but to no avail. The killers were heartless.

They didn't speak much, especially the shortest one, who hadn't spoken at all. They all stood over a potential victim and aimed, enjoying the moments their captives writhed and squirmed, only to fire two rounds into the back of each skull. The deadly process was repeated until many in the room dramatically dropped down to a handful still alive.

A six-year-old girl, dead. A nine-year-old cousin, dead. Her forty-year-old aunt, dead. Her uncle and first cousins, dead. Cristal began to give up. No longer did she have thoughts of overpowering the room and killing the three assailants, slowly. Her tear-stained face was in absolute misery. Her mind was clouded with grief and anger. Her emotions overwhelmed her and death surrounded her. Hugo remained emotionless. Numb. The pain of her family being violently murdered was too heavy to bear on her heart. She gasped and uncontrollably cried out with every life—young and old—being taken away.

Cristal fixed her teary eyes on the shortest goon, and all of a sudden, something about him stood out. The way he moved, along with his physique. She knew him, or should she say, *her*. The realization of the obvious—that *she* was the target, broke her heart into a million pieces. How could she have been so naïve to think she could outsmart the Commission?

Cristal glared at the shortest assailant and cried out with venom in her tone, "Tamar, I know that's you! How could you? How could you do me and my family like this?"

Movement paused in the room and gunshots from the silencers came to an end, temporarily. Tamar pulled the ski-mask from off her face so her former best friend could see her clearly. Her long hair was pulled back into a tight braid and her hourglass figure was camouflaged with baggy jeans and an oversized black hoodie. Tamar tried her best to look like one of the murderous goons and blend in with the two male hoodlums. However, there wasn't a disguise out there that Cristal couldn't pick her out in.

Tamar walked over to Renee, Cristal's mother, who was face down, duct tape around her mouth and hands bound. Her eyes showed fear. She looked at her daughter for comfort. She didn't want to die.

"Ms. Renee, blame your daughter for this. Everything that happened today is her fault. She fucked up," Tamar uttered coldly before putting two rounds into the back of her skull. The muffling and squirming came to an abrupt stop.

"Mommy!!! Nooo . . . not her! Noo!!!" Cristal sobbed profoundly. "Why, Tamar! Why?" her chest heaved convulsively and her eyes brimmed with anger. Mechanically, everyone in the room was shot down, including Hugo. They decided to save Mia, Cristal's cousin, for last. They wanted her to witness. Tamar stood over Mia's pregnant frame and smiled wickedly. She turned Mia face-up and stared into the woman's eyes. Mia was distraught and plagued with tears as she gazed up at the smoking gun aimed at her. There was a moment of silence until Tamar fired six hot slugs into her pregnant belly.

"Why are you doing this, Tamar?" Cristal cried out heatedly. "At least give me that. I deserve an answer!"

Tamar gazed at her with a cold stare. The realization came front and center for Cristal. She knew the answer to her own question. It was never about money. Tamar crouched low toward Cristal and looked at her intently. "You know what this is about," Tamar countered.

"I could have never done you so dirty," Cristal felt betrayed, defeated. "Who's behind this?!"

Tamar laughed wickedly. "It's only business, Cristal. You know that. It was always about business—what we did, what we got ourselves into—business. But unfortunately for you, your name came up on the murdergram."

"You're a liar!" Cristal screamed. "Since when does the Commission execute a whole family, Tamar? We only take out our targets! You know you could have come at *only* me but you didn't? Why would you do this?!"

"I want this to make the front page news..."

Tamar pointed her pistol at Cristal. Her murderous cohorts stood around to witness. Cristal braced herself for impact. Tamar fired; the first bullet pierced Cristal's left ear. The second bullet grazed her head, splattering her blood all over. Two more body shots were fired, and then, silence.

They all were dead. But there was still more to do. The three murderers tore open a ki of white horse and started to sprinkle premium, high-quality, uncut cocaine around the apartment to make it look drug-related. And then before their exit, the Queen of Spades card, a symbol from their clique, was tossed on top of Cristal.

Murdergram delivered.

The two men were eager to leave the bloody apartment and receive their large pay that Tamar had promised them. But there would be no payday for her homies. Tamar turned her weapon on the masked men, getting the jump on them first, and fired a bullet into both of their heads. She left them among the dead with Cristal's family. It would be the bloodiest scene the neighborhood would ever see.

Tamar exited the scene feeling like a weight had been lifted from her shoulders. There was no remorse for the crimes she'd committed. In her twisted mind, what she had done had propelled her onto a new level, and it was like taking out the trash. She was officially alone. Everyone from her past was dead, even Mona. Tamar killed Mona because she refused to do the hit on Cristal, so Mona became a liability and Tamar strangled her in her Bronx apartment.

What Tamar didn't know was that the murdergram on Cristal didn't come from the Commission. The unsanctioned murdergram given to Tamar came directly from E.P.

Tamar left through the back door of the building, head low, and then she disappeared into the night. New York was about to become a memory for her. She had her sights set on going international.

EPILOGUE

●●●●●●●●●●●●●●●●●●●●●●●●●●●●●●●●●●●●●●

WASHINGTON, D.C.

Two years later...

Tamar sat sunbathing on her twenty-third birthday, outside on the wrap-around terrace of her magnificent penthouse apartment in Georgetown.

Things were good as long as she made other people die, and by her hands alone, she'd executed dozens of murdergrams on the East Coast. She'd become a marksman with guns and canny with knives and explosives. E.P. didn't come around often, but when he did he would always mention the half-bred Killer Doll. Just like Cristal, Tamar was infatuated and jealous of the assassin that executed her victims with a dagger. In Tamar's delusional mind, they were in a competition.

Since dismantling the Cristal Clique, Tamar's new name was Tee-Tzu, and with her deadly skills and a thirst to be at the top of her game, Tamar was ready to teach bitches the Art of War. She was now the one receiving the murdergrams from the Commission, and her most recent murdergram was to kill a woman named Melissa Chin.

Melissa Chin? Now why on the earth does the Commission want to get at her?

HUSTLE HARDER

FEBRUARY 2015